GAME SET MURDER

CHRIS MERRILL

GAME SET MURDER A Stan Powell Thriller

Copyright © 2022 by Chris Merrill

ISBN: 979-8-9872175-0-4   Paperback

ISBN: 979-8-9872175-1-1   Ebook

Acknowledgments

I would like to thank everyone who supported me and encouraged me to write *Game, Set, Murder*. Without you, I would not have had the courage to complete the daunting task of writing my first novel.

To my incredible wife Angie, thank you for giving me feedback along the way as I occasionally dropped new chapters on the coffee table for you to read. You inspired a lot of this story, including one of the characters. There will be more stories and adventures to come for us and maybe another novel or two!

To my great friends Kelly and David Orr, who helped whip my initial manuscript into shape and believed in the story enough to give me the push I needed to complete this journey. Kelly, you truly are amazing!

A final shout out goes to my tennis book club. You guys are the reason this adventure started in the first place.

The characters, companies and events depicted in this novel are purely fictional and cultivated within the depths of my active imagination. But my love for tennis and the racquet sports industry are one hundred percent real, as is my passion for an excellent suspense thriller novel. Thank you to all who I have crossed paths with who inspired the characters on the pages that follow.

Chris Merrill

Prologue

CHRIS PECK'S EYES were playing tricks on him as he drove through the heavy rain on Highway 84 along the Columbia River, east of Portland. Sheets of rain crashed into his windshield, making a blinding mess of the headlights of the oncoming traffic. Rarely used during his time in Southern California, the wiper blades left broad streaks across his windshield, and were badly in need of replacement.

He knew he had to get off the road before he fell asleep at the wheel. It had been a long day of driving.

Peck guided his Toyota 4Runner onto the exit ramp that led to the town of Hood River. He could just make out the sign, directing him to a hotel a short drive off the interstate. Absolutely starved, he was looking forward to some food and a good night's sleep.

He pulled the Toyota SUV into the parking lot of the Riverfront Inn. During his many nights on the road as a tennis equipment sales rep, he had always enjoyed his stays at small, family-run hotels whenever he had the chance. While he paid a bit more for the boutique hotel experience, he was living the good life and enjoyed its perks. But that all seemed so far away now.

It had only been forty-eight hours since Peck had met with Bill Cashman at the LAX Airport Hilton. Cashman, the Vice President of Sales, at the Black Label Sporting Goods Company, was not a pleasant man. A meeting with the overweight, red-faced Chicago native was never one to look forward to. So when Cashman called to set up the meeting, Peck worried that his future with the company was in jeopardy.

It had been less than a year since they had hired Peck to fill the Southern California regional sales position. Now, Peck was at an Oregon hotel: two days' unemployed, forced into a troubling severance package by Cashman, and trying to piece together his thoughts.

Cashman had answered none of his questions and gave no reason to support his termination; only that it was in Peck's best interest to accept the severance package and move on with his life.

Part of the deal involved Peck's immediate departure from Los Angeles, which he thought was odd. They obviously wanted him out of the way and would pay him a considerable amount to make sure that happened.

Movers hired by Black Label were at his Marina del Rey, California apartment the following morning to pack up his belongings, which they would send to his parents' home in Winthrop, Washington.

He was on the road just thirty-six hours after meeting with Cashman on his way back to his family home in Washington. The money Cashman had dangled in front of him was significant enough to make him agree to the questionable terms of the package. The faster he left Los Angeles the sooner they would deposit the money into his bank account.

∽

Hood River is a sleepy town about an hour east of Portland. Known as an outdoor enthusiast's paradise, standing in the shadow of mighty Mount Hood, the winds that whip through

Hood River in the Columbia River Gorge produce some of the best windsurfing and kite-sailing conditions on the planet. With too many brew pubs to count, there was a relaxed vibe to the town. At the same time, it felt like a scene from an Alfred Hitchcock movie. The too perfect sidewalk displays, the absence of pedestrians during the work week, and the fog that could swallow the town at a moment's notice gave Hood River an eerie atmosphere. Did dark secrets lurk beneath the surface of the white-capped Columbia River?

Peck dropped his bag in his room and then headed out the door towards the nearby waterfront restaurants. The desk clerk at the Riverfront Inn had strongly recommended the Solstice Cafe & Bar, just a short walk from the hotel.

The rain had thinned to a heavy mist, helping Peck realize he was really back home in the wet Pacific Northwest. It had taken him a while to get used to the sunny weather in Los Angeles, but for the first time since his meeting with Cashman, a slight smile appeared on his face. Going home would not be all that bad.

While waiting for his Solstice pizza, a wood-fired delicacy of Canadian bacon, pineapple chutney, shredded mozzarella, and jalapeño cream sauce, he made quick work of his first Pfreim IPA. Then he called over the athletically built waitress. Tattoos covered both of her arms, and a small diamond nose-ring and purple hair gave away her Pacific Northwest roots. *She must spend a lot of time on the mountain*, he thought, snowboarding in the winter and mountain biking in the summer.

"Looks like you could use another beer. Another Pfiem?" the waitress asked.

"Yes, please. It's been a long day," Peck said while he wiped the sleep from his tired eyes.

"Coming right up. Hopefully another beer and a pizza will provide a great end to your day." Then she was off to the bar to place his order.

After a long day on the road his second locally crafted IPA was working its magic. But that was short-lived, as his thoughts returned to his strange meeting with Cashman. He never liked him, and considered him a pompous ass, a numbers guy, and someone who quickly made enemies of the entire sales team by openly planning to cut the pay of the racquet sports reps. His reason being that their pay should be more in line with the team sports reps. But the team sports reps lasted about a year or two on the job before they burned out on the extreme hours and the minimal pay. The racquet sports group was a seasoned, well paid team and better connected. They used their considerable networks and relationships with their accounts to help maintain Black Label Racquet Sports as the number one brand. But Cashman wanted to dismantle the way the racquet sports team operated.

It was just two days ago that Chris Peck was enjoying his life in Southern California, making more money than he ever dreamed of, and in the beginning stages of what he thought was a promising relationship. Life was good, then it wasn't. Now he was sitting in a small cafe in rainy Hood River, trying to drown out the world on local craft beer.

But Peck wasn't paid to worry about racquet sports any longer. In fact, Cashman had paid him to not think about Black Label Racquet Sports, so he tried to stay positive. He could do a lot worse than Winthrop. And while it stunned his parents, and they worried for their son when they got the call that he was coming home, they were excited that he could help them at their sports shop, which specialized in snow sports in the winter and bicycles in the summer. Much like Hood River, there was a lot of natural beauty and ample outdoor recreation in Winthrop.

After a couple more beers and the delicious pizza, Peck suddenly felt the weight of the long day. He needed to sleep.

He left a generous twenty-dollar tip for his waitress and pulled a hood over his head as he slipped out the door for the walk back to the hotel. A few steps from the restaurant's front door, he ducked under the cover of a nearby shop's protective awning. It was getting late, and he wanted to make a quick phone call to his girlfriend, who was still back in Los Angeles. After a few rings, his call was sent to voicemail. He left a quick message, ending with "I love you," with the promise of connecting in the morning.

The parking lot at the hotel was nearly empty, so he looked forward to a quiet evening and a good night's sleep. He hoped to be up early and on the road before first light.

Peck fumbled in his pocket for his room key as he reached the door to his room. Just then, a shadow passed over him from the hallway light. Someone was behind him! As he spun to face a hooded figure, he felt a sharp jab in his neck.

His vision blurred and his legs buckled, causing him to collapse to the carpeted floor. It took all of his strength to draw a breath as his assailant dragged him inside his hotel room.

He tried to call out to the man. He recognized him! But before the man's name rose in Peck's throat, his final thoughts ground to a halt, and he felt himself fade slowly into the gloom of the misty Hood River night.

Chapter One

"HEY ROOK! YOU'RE on the phones this week." Deputy Zandy Roberts heard her lieutenant say as she began her third week as a rookie cop for the Hood River Police Department.

At least this would be better than her first couple of weeks, she thought. Just the idea of getting to speak with real people thrilled her, after spending long, mind-numbing days staring at a computer screen, cleaning out old case files and performing general office work. She told herself to stay patient, but she was determined to show her value to her superiors and not become the department's secretary. She had her eyes set on becoming a lieutenant as soon as possible and dreamed of being a detective one day.

Alexandra "Zandy" Roberts was not one to shy away from a challenge. Growing up in the central Oregon town of Bend, she was the youngest of four. Her three brothers were constantly in trouble with local authorities when they weren't climbing the nearby mountains, skiing and snowboarding down double black diamond runs or piloting their mountain bikes down the steepest, rockiest trails in the area. Zandy tried and usually succeeded in outdoing her brothers in every outdoor athletic pursuit and was the only one to bring home straight A's on her report cards.

Zandy saw herself solving the most difficult cases for the Hood River Police Department, not shuffling papers and answering the phone. But if that's where she needed to start, she was willing to pay her dues, she thought, as she pressed the flashing light on the phone that signaled another incoming call.

Most of the calls that morning were fairly mundane. Someone had their bicycle stolen from their garage. An elderly woman had called to report that her neighbor was peeping through her bathroom window while she was showering. Each call offered Zandy an opportunity to connect with Hood River residents and begin making a name for herself as a problem solver with a delicate touch.

Again, Zandy pressed the blinking light on her phone. "Hello, this is deputy Roberts. How can I help you?" She said calmly into her headset microphone.

"Yes, hello deputy Roberts. I am hoping you can help me locate my missing brother," the man's voice said on the opposite end of the line.

"How long has your brother been missing?" Zandy asked.

"It has been a couple of weeks since we last heard from him. He was driving from Los Angeles to Winthrop, Washington. He seems to have disappeared somewhere along the way."

"Are you certain that he came through Hood River?" Zandy asked.

"My brother always paid for everything in cash, so he didn't leave a credit card receipt trail, but the local Sheriff here in Winthrop was able to subpoena his cell phone records, and they show that he did come through Hood River. His phone eventually shut off in Central Washington, near the town of Leavenworth," the man said.

"Sir, I'm not sure what I can do for you. It sounds like it might be best if you contacted the authorities in Leavenworth. They might be more helpful." Zandy said.

"I have spoken with the police in Leavenworth, and they have started a case file on my brother, but I don't get the feeling they are looking very hard for him. I have a military background. My specialty was tracking down some pretty evil men during the Gulf War. Sometimes the obvious location wasn't where we would find our target. I hope that you can at least start a file on my brother and compare it to any John Does you have on file."

"I can do that," Zandy replied. She didn't want to sound too hopeful. She knew that the man on the phone had most likely already assumed the worst, but was just looking for answers.

Zandy continued, "Can I get your name and your brother's?"

"My name is Quinn Peck. My brother is Chris Peck," the man's replied.

Chapter Two

THE WINDS WERE already whipping up on this sunny fall morning, on what looked to be another Red Flag day in Southern California. It was Santa Ana wind conditions in the southland, where dry desert winds blew towards the coast. These winds were reason for worry, as the bone-dry landscape, following a summer with no rain, was ripe for another deadly wildfire season.

"Over My Head" by The Fray filled the inside of Alan Mercer's Ford Escape SUV, as he sped along an uncrowded section of Interstate 5, approaching downtown Los Angeles. "Everyone knows, I'm in over my head… over my head" echoed through Mercer's thoughts. It seemed fitting that just then a gust of wind pushed his small SUV into the next lane. The forty-two-year-old tennis sales rep quickly course corrected without consequence. Usually a parking lot, Saturday mornings found most Angelinos avoiding the downtown area, unless, of course, the Dodgers were playing at nearby Chavez Ravine, or one of the other professional or college sports teams were in town for a game.

As a young boy Mercer spent many weekends riding in the family's Ford Pinto station wagon, as his mother navigated these same Los Angeles freeways on their way to another junior tennis tournament. He had memorized the names of the freeway exits along the way, often associating them with a landmark located just off the exit. Today, as he passed each landmark, it brought him back to his childhood and the memories of playing junior tennis in Southern California.

Mercer was looking forward to a busy day, working the annual fall sale at The Racket King. The Racket King was the largest tennis retailer in Southern California, and perhaps the largest single location tennis retailer in the world. As the Southern California sales rep for Black Label Racquet Sports, Mercer knew this was an important event, one that was critical for reaching his annual sales targets. Since he had come to Los Angeles over four years ago, replacing the previous sales rep, Chris Peck, not a week had passed where he hadn't spoken with the store's owner.

Jackson "Sarge" Turner, owner of the Racket King, was one of a kind. Turner was ex-military and ran the business his way. Because of the size of his business, all the tennis brands looked the other way, as Turner continued to violate each company's MAP pricing policy.

MAP is Manufacturers Advertising Policy, which was an attempt by tennis companies to maintain a level playing field regarding advertised prices. Turner clearly didn't give a shit about MAP, and had threatened legal action several times. To appease other local retailers, some brands had "cut off" direct sales to The Racket King.

"I don't care!" Mercer had heard Turner shout. "I will get their stuff from someone else and sell it for what I want."

With his own network of "bootleggers," Turner had done just that. Over the years, Turner had befriended several tennis shop owners across the country, who gladly supplied him with products that he couldn't purchase directly. It was a win-win for the bootlegger who could get better pricing by reaching higher volume discounts, and a steady flow of cash sales to Turner kept their businesses open in some cases. Pretty much everyone knew what was going on, but when pressed by competitors of The Racket King, the local sales reps could claim that they sold nothing directly to him.

Because he did so much volume, most brands sold directly to Turner. Tennis companies felt that it was better to have a cooperative relationship with the store. This, of course, was a constant battle for the local sales reps, who got pummeled with complaints from the other stores in the area. But in the end, all the local reps were making a very good living off The Racket King account. For all his bluster aimed at racquet companies, Sarge Turner was a gentle giant. He treated all of his local reps with the utmost respect, even if he tried to screw their employers at every turn. Business was booming and tennis players from near and far appreciated the excellent service, the variety of products and the lowest prices anywhere.

As Mercer searched for a parking spot near the store, he noticed a line of customers already snaking around the block from The Racket King.

It was going to be another crazy day at the sale, Mercer thought.

Chapter Three

ACROSS TOWN, JACK Sharp sat at a table on the patio of Patrick's Roadhouse, just off Pacific Coast Highway, in the affluent enclave of Pacific Palisades. The Palisades, nearby Malibu, and Brentwood were home to film and music A-listers, and generally enjoyed cool ocean breezes. However, under Santa Ana conditions, those cool breezes turned to hot, dry winds, which blew out the surfing conditions and kept surfers home for the day. As a result, tables were quite easy to come by at the normally busy restaurant.

After a brief wait, Mark Stephens, who opened with a quick apology about his tardiness, joined Sharp.

"I'm really sorry, Jack, but there was an accident on PCH in Santa Monica. Some idiot on his cell phone crashed his Bentley into a local surf school van. There were foam surfboards scattered all over the road!"

Stephens operated two nearby tennis centers, both of which until recently, had been in dire straits financially. With real estate being so expensive in the area, many wondered how one could justify operating a tennis complex on a property they could easily develop into multi-million-dollar homes. Stephens dreaded each lease renewal, when they presented the new monthly rate. There was no negotiating. It was a take it or leave it situation. But thanks to his dining partner, Stephens had just valet parked his brand-new Toyota Prius in the lot, and his financial worries seemed far behind him. Life was looking up.

Jack Sharp, short with a roundish frame, often described as plump, had ridden his oversized ambition and ego to the top spot at Black Label Racquet Sports, the number one brand in tennis. Once upon a time, Sharp was the sales rep for Black Label in Southern California, where he and Stephens formed their friendship and business relationship. Sharp considered Stephens to be one of his closest allies.

"How was your trip from Chicago?" Mark asked, while he took a seat.

Before he had time to answer, the waiter stepped up to the table. "Would you like something to drink?"

The handsome young waiter was over the top in his enthusiasm, just another kid who moved out to Los Angeles to make it big in the movies, hoping for his big break, Mark thought, as he considered his drink options.

"What are you drinking, Jack?"

"Iced coffee," Sharp responded coldly.

It annoyed Jack to have to wait for Stephens to arrive.

"Okay, I will have one of those too," replied Stephens. He recognized the lack of alcoholic beverage meant it was going to be one of those breakfast meetings. Jack Sharp wanted something from him.

The waiter was off with a dramatic turn to go fetch another iced coffee. Stephens, hoped to lighten the mood, asked, "So your flight was good?"

"Other than the oversized rap artist, who reeked of pot

smoke sitting next to me in first class, it was all right," replied Sharp.

Gone were the days of flying coach. Sharp was too powerful and important to sit with the common folks. But even first class had its issues, especially on flights to Los Angeles, with a constant stream of elites and wanna-bes, who were not always on their best behavior, and often consumed too much alcohol on the flight.

Before Stephens could offer his sympathies, Sharp cut him off.

"Mark, the reason I'm here is that we need to make some big numbers happen. We are coming up against some large shipments from last year, and I want to make sure we don't have a drop in our sales index."

For a company with annual sales of roughly $100 million, the most important barometer used by Black Label management was the weekly sales index report. The report included a lot of information, but the eyes quickly targeted the lower right-hand figure, which showed the company's sales index percentage. Above that figure, they reported each of the thirty sales territories.

The sales index figure measured the sales for the week against the same time period one year earlier. A sales index of 100% meant you did the same sales in the week compared with the previous year. Since the company expected at least 5% growth from the previous year, a 105% or higher sales index was what you were hoping to see every week. Anything below 100% was unacceptable and cause for some missed sleep, and a sense of dread that someone was going to call you out... or worse.

Every Monday morning, they emailed the sales index

report to each rep and company official. For the thirty sales reps, opening the report was the best or worst moment of their week. But even with the good weeks, the dread of producing an even bigger number next year was looming over their temporary euphoria. Thus was the life of a sales rep for the top tennis brand.

"Okay, so how much are we looking at?" Stephens asked sheepishly.

"I need you to get in an order for $50,000 shipped this week. Get with Mercer today, so that the order gets entered first thing Monday morning."

The sales reps emailed orders to their Customer Service Rep for entry, so larger orders could often take a few days to process.

"Do we have the usual arrangement?" asked Stephens.

"Yes, of course," replied Sharp.

"You will make out nicely on this one. I will need you to step up again next month."

"OK, got it," Stephens answered, as he made some quick calculations in his head. On new products, Stephens hoped to make at least forty-two percent gross margin, but through his special arrangement with Jack Sharp, he could expect to double that number.

He felt better knowing that Jack Sharp still needed him.

"I'll give Mercer a call this afternoon with an order," Stephens said.

After a quick breakfast of a chili and cheese omelet, Sharp excused himself. He had another appointment to get to.

Chapter Four

BEFORE THE DOORS opened to the enormous crowd assembled outside, Sarge Turner huddled with his staff, along with a dozen tennis sales reps, who were there to sell as much of their brand's product as possible. The sale was an annual affair that tennis players from around the state looked forward to. The sale also invited undesirables who were looking to grab some of the cash that came through the store that day.

"I've got a loaded twelve-gauge under the front register," barked Turner.

Along with the shotgun, Turner had an assortment of lethal devices hidden around the store to stop anyone trying to rob them.

"If you see trouble, call out the code word *McEnroe*," Turner explained.

"That will alert the doorman to lock the front door, and for all employees to help customers in the store to a safe place."

The rumor was that during the sale a dozen years ago, a gunman came out of a dressing room, ordering everyone in the store to get down on the floor. To his surprise, the last words the gunman heard were, "THANK YOU," then his head exploded from the impact of the buckshot from Jack Turner's trusty twelve-gauge.

As the gunman fell to the ground, with fragments of his skull and brain now covering the surrounding customers and the soon to be discounted tennis apparel, Turner repeated, "Thank you for telling everyone to lie on the floor. It gave me a clear shot at you!"

At nine o'clock, the doors opened, and the first group of customers entered the store.

Alan Mercer took his place alongside his fellow tennis reps in the back of the store. This was where the gigantic racquet wall that spanned the entire length of the store was located. Each wooden peg on the wall held around fifteen tennis racquets. There was at least one peg for each model.

Racquets are divided by brand, with the most popular brands getting a larger presence in the store. Black Label had the largest representation. The wall held a few thousand racquets, all priced well below MAP pricing. The back stock in the warehouse side of the store held twice that amount. Throughout the day, store employees would repeatedly replenish racquets as the pegs emptied.

The customers advanced on the racquet wall and began pulling racquets from the pegs. Some knew exactly what they wanted.

"I want the new Federer stick," several customers called out, while others needed help to choose the right racquet for their style of play. That is where each brand's sales rep used their knowledge and experience to help the customer select the proper racquet.

Mercer knew that the other sales reps would try to persuade customers to change their minds when they walked by on their way to the register. So he walked the selected racquets over to the racquet stringer while the customer moved on to other areas of the store.

Behind the main counter sat ten Prince racquet stringing machines. During the sale, each racquet stringer would not have time to rest, as each racquet took about twenty minutes to string to the customers' specifications.

With only a quick break for greasy pizza and chocolate chip cookies, the day was non-stop for all in the store. By the time the last customer exited the store and the doors locked, the store had been a flurry of activity and the cash registers were still hot to the touch from all the transactions.

Mercer felt relief, along with the other sales reps and store personnel, that the shotgun and other lethal devices were still in their hiding spots.

Chapter Five

THE LINE TO get into Lemongrass was short, as Mercer and fellow sales rep Ted Riley sat down at a table at the popular Vietnamese restaurant in the Silver Lake neighborhood, near downtown Los Angeles. Riley was the local sales rep for Head/Penn Racquet Sports, and one of Mercer's closest friends. A couple of Tsingtao beers and spring rolls arrived at the table as the two exhausted reps toasted another successful Racket King sale.

Mercer knew he was the top dog in the territory, and he worked hard to never act like it. It just wasn't in his nature to boast or reveal how successful he was working with the number one brand. He felt it was better not to show his competitors or customers how much money he was making. Some sales reps pulled up to sales calls in their shiny new Lexus or Mercedes SUV, but Mercer still drove his understated Ford Escape.

Prior to coming to Southern California, Mercer was the sales rep for Black Label in the Southeast, making his home in Atlanta. Born and raised in Southern California, Mercer had moved to Atlanta nine years before joining Wilson to work for the Japanese sports giant Mizuno. Mizuno's USA headquarters was located in Norcross, a suburb on the northeast side of Atlanta. Mercer had been in charge of product development for Mizuno's tennis and golf equipment categories. But after nine years of going into an office every day, Mercer jumped at the opportunity to get out on the road as a sales rep for Black Label Racquet Sports.

During his first four years with Black Label in the Southeast, Mercer grew the business significantly, posting remarkable sales index numbers each year.

Atlanta was one of the hottest tennis markets in the country, with the nation's largest organized tennis league, ALTA.

The Atlanta Lawn Tennis Association had a membership of over 60,000 tennis players, ranging from beginners up to the AA1 division, which was full of current and former professional and top college players. While tennis retail was struggling around the country, ALTA made for a vibrant tennis retail scene in Atlanta.

Over the four years of exploding sales in his territory, the Black Label Regional Manager and management team left Mercer alone to do his thing. But things were changing at the company. The long-time president had been replaced, and the former Southern California sales rep, Jack Sharp, was installed as the General Manager of Racquet Sports.

Sharp had quickly made some moves in the company to surround himself with allies in key roles. One of those moves was to replace the Eastern Regional Manager with Randall Jefferies. Jefferies had relocated to Atlanta from the home office in Chicago. He was now Mercer's new boss, and that brought an end to the days of hands-off management.

Randall Jefferies had no previous experience as a sales manager, but fancied himself an excellent tennis player. If anyone made the mistake of addressing him as "Randy," Jefferies quickly corrected them. "It's Randall," he would interject.

Randall Jefferies never found a mirror he didn't like. He never missed the chance to take a long look, to make sure every hair on his perfectly gelled head was in place.

Jefferies was ambitious and wanted to make a name for himself as a Regional Manager. He had bigger plans in the company, and this would be his chance to prove himself.

As he travelled with the sales reps in his new region, his style was one of superior knowledge and intellect. In his view, he knew more about the business than the reps or the tennis shop owners. This approach immediately created enormous problems for the sales reps.

"What does that pretty boy, know-it-all, know about my business?" Mercer recalled several of his customers' questioning. That was often followed by, "Don't ever bring that fucking asshole into my store again."

On one unforgettable appointment, Jefferies ignored a female client, thinking that she was only one of the lower paid staff when, in fact, she was the pro shop manager and buyer. When Mercer informed him of that fact, Jefferies tried to make good by inquiring about the due date of her baby. The only problem was that she was definitely not pregnant, just a bit overweight.

They did not leave the store with an order that day.

Each time Jefferies visited customers with a sales rep, the rep would spend the following few days doing damage control. Sadly for Mercer, Jefferies lived in his territory and sometimes got the notion of visiting local retailers on his own. What was the purpose of these store visits, he wondered?

Mercer recalled getting the company memo indicating Chris Peck had left his Los Angeles territory and that the company would conduct a search to fill the open spot. So when the

National Sales Manager called out of the blue one day, asking Mercer if he would be interested in filling the open sales territory in Los Angeles, he had to think it over. He was making a lot of money, living in the low-cost Atlanta market. He had plenty of good friends, the tennis competition was excellent, and after a divorce a few years earlier, he was in a serious relationship. But the thought of working another day under Jefferies was enough for him to accept the Southern California territory.

That was four years ago.

After downing a few more Tsingtao beers and finishing the spring rolls and pho, it was time to say good night and head home.

"Hey Alan, next time you are buying! My numbers are shit right now and you seemed to kill it today," Riley said.

"Oh yeah, it looked like you had all the cute ones eating out of your hand today," Mercer replied. "I don't want to have to tell your lovely wife that you flirt with all the customers just to get the sale. So call it blackmail. You are buying next time!"

"Oh, she already knows that I'm a total slut and will do anything for a sale. She's okay with it," laughed Riley.

As Mercer and Riley stepped out of Lemongrass, they made plans to get tickets for the Los Angeles Lakers and Milwaukee Bucks game later that year.

Born in Wisconsin, Riley was a huge Bucks fan, and the two hadn't missed a game between the teams since Mercer came out west.

"Do you think the Bucks are finally going to win one of these times?" Mercer asked. So far, the friendly get-together had resulted in a Lakers victory each year, so Mercer was feeling confident that the trend would continue for at least another year.

Chapter Six

POST CANYON WAS a popular mountain bike trail system on the northern flank of Mount Hood. Some of the best single-track trails, like Bad Motor Scooter, Lower 8-Track and Toilet Bowl, attracted cyclists from all over the Pacific Northwest.

John Barron and his good buddy Steve Collins were frequent visitors to Post Canyon. The trails offered a mix of mellow to hair-raising technical sections. A full-suspension mountain bike was the best tool to tackle Post Canyon.

After a long summer with little rain, the trails were dusty and riding extremely fast.

John parked his late model Jeep Wrangler Limited at the bottom of the trail along Post Canyon Drive.

After checking over their bikes, they took the gravel road that led them to the long and winding ascent up 7 Streams trail. The final push up 7 Streams was quite steep but then leveled off as they entered the primary hub of the trail system. The long climb provided a nice warm-up for a fun day exploring the extensive network of trails.

John was breathing hard as he reached the top just as Steve yelled out, "Let's hit Lower 8 Track first!"

John followed as he saw Steve disappear into the forest.

After a full morning of climbing and bombing down most of the trails, they decided it was time to head back down the mountain into Hood River for their customary lunch and local craft beer.

"Let's head down Toilet Bowl and hook up to 7 Streams," John called out.

Toilet Bowl got its name from the porcelain toilet that was dumped in the canyon several years ago. Other than the tall weeds growing up through it, the toilet appeared to be in good shape. The descent down this section of trail was fast and flowing.

Close behind, Steve grabbed both brakes hard, as he eventually slid his Yeti SB115 to a stop. Looking back up the trail, his eyes followed a set of skid marks that led off trail into the bushes. John had overcooked the turn, and with the dusty conditions, had missed the turn altogether.

Tracking back a bit, Steve saw his companion about fifteen feet below the trail. Both bike and body appeared to be in good condition.

"You okay?" Steve shouted.

As he dusted himself off, John replied, "Yes, just a little scraped up, but nothing serious. I can't believe I whiffed that turn!"

After a quick inspection, he picked up his Santa Cruz Tallboy and began to make his way back up to the trail.

Pushing his bike up the rugged terrain was difficult, and he tumbled to the ground.

Suddenly, John took a quick step backward and gasped. "Holy fuck!"

"What the hell? Jesus! Steve, get down here!"

∽

Gradually making his way down to his shaken friend, Steve noticed the color had left John's face.

"What is it?" Steve asked.

In response, a speechless John could merely point towards something sticking out of the ground. Hoping it wasn't a snake... Steve hated snakes. He slowly pulled back some of the ground cover to discover what had startled John.

"Oh shit, that looks... human!" Steve screamed.

Upon closer inspection, they concluded they were looking at a human skeleton that had been there for some time.

With no cell service, they climbed back up to the trail and headed back to their car.

Horrified by what they had experienced, they both narrowly avoided the crater-sized potholes that marked the gravel road on their way back down to John's Jeep.

Once back in cell phone range, Steve called the local police.

"I think we've found some human remains up at Post Canyon," he reported to the officer on the other end of the line.

"Yes, we've marked the spot on the trail and can lead you to it. We are parked along Post Canyon Drive in a Silver Jeep Wrangler. Okay, we will wait here for you," Steve said.

Within fifteen minutes, a Hood River Police Department's Ford Explorer pulled up to their Jeep, with mountain bikes now properly stowed on the rear rack. The passenger window opened and the female officer driving the SUV looked over at the two shaken mountain bikers.

"Are you the two who called in the potential human remains up on the trail?" The police woman asked.

"Yes, that was us, and we are pretty certain it is a human," Steve replied.

"I'm Lieutenant Roberts with the Hood River Police." Zandy Roberts said as she turned off the ignition and stepped out of the Explorer and approached the men.

After a brief conversation with Lt. Roberts, John and Steve jumped into the back of the Ford SUV for a ride along a gravel service road to the upper parking area near the trail system hub. The officers decided that would be the best place to access the Toilet Bowl trail.

On a typical Post Canyon outing, they would have already filled their bellies with food and beer at Double Mountain Brewery. There was nothing normal about this outing, and the two mountain bikers hardly noticed their empty stomachs.

Once they reached the hub, John and Steve guided the officers down to Toilet Bowl. One officer secured yellow "crime scene" tape at the access to the trail so other riders didn't disturb the site or impede the officers' work.

After a long hike down just past the toilet landmark, they located the skid marks left by John's twenty-nine-inch tires.

"This is the spot, Lt. Roberts," John noted. "It's just off the side of the trail, about ten to fifteen feet down."

As the officers carefully made their way down the steep embankment, they finally approached the location of the half-buried skeleton.

"That definitely is a human skeleton," reported Lt. Roberts. "My guess is that it's been down here a couple of years. Let's cordon off the area, and I will get on the horn to headquarters to get the forensics team out here."

Because of its small size, the Hood River police department didn't have their own homicide division, but they worked with a nearby forensics lab when cases like this came up. On the rare occasion they needed additional help to solve homicides, they contacted the FBI office in nearby Portland.

Back up on Toilet Bowl, they finally gave John and Steve permission to leave the scene. They rode in complete silence in the back of the police SUV down to their car. Suddenly aware of their hunger, it was time to head into Hood River for some food and beer.

When they set out that morning, they were expecting to find epic riding conditions, not a human skeleton.

As Zandy Roberts waited for the forensics team to arrive, she wondered who the two men had just unearthed. She had handled so many missing persons cases in her few years with the Hood River Police that it was difficult for her to keep them straight. Something in the back of her mind told her she needed to find out who this person was and how their body ended up in the rugged terrain of Post Canyon. She pulled out her cell phone and searched for the name on her list of contacts and pressed the name. The call rang through to voicemail.

"Agent Powell; this is Lt. Zandy Roberts with the Hood River PD. We've worked a couple of cases together. I think I may need your help…"

Chapter Seven

"HEY, JOE. HOW'S it going?" Mercer said into his Bluetooth headset.

He had just left Lemongrass, heading south on Sunset Boulevard before hopping on the 101 freeway.

On the other end of the line was Joe Hamilton. Joe was the Western Regional Sales Manager for Black Label Racquet Sports. He had known Mercer since high school when they first faced off at the California State High School tennis championships. It was Hamilton who had lobbied hard to get Mercer out to California to fill the open sales position when Chris Peck left.

"All good here," Joe replied.

"How was The Racket King sale today?"

While the two were great friends, Joe Hamilton was all about numbers, especially when they impacted his year-end bonus. He had as much riding on the success of Mercer and big accounts like The Racket King, as Mercer did.

"It was great," Mercer reported.

"There was a huge crowd, and a lot of Black Label racquets went out the door today." Mercer added. "I expect a nice order tomorrow when I call Sarge for a fill-in. He seemed thrilled with the day and never had to reach for the shotgun!"

Hamilton laughed. "That is great news. Let's plan to get together later this week, to see a few of your bigger accounts. We've got some new racquet closeout opportunities that I would like to grab before the other regions sell them. Also, if you could set up some doubles practice, that would be great."

Mercer and Hamilton still competed at a high level on the tennis court. Having played together in college, then on the lower levels of the professional tour, they now played on the National Senior Circuit, where they competed for national ranking points. For the past two years, they had been ranked number two in the country. So far, they'd had a good season, and hoped this was the year they reached their goal of being the top-ranked team in the United States in the men's 40 and over doubles.

As the bigger tournaments came up on the calendar, they tried to fit in practice matches after the day's business. With the Pacific Southwest Championships just around the corner in nearby Newport Beach, they could use some practice.

The Pacific Southwest was one of the best Tier 2 national tournaments on the calendar, and they knew the draw would be loaded with some strong local and national talent.

"You got it," Mercer said.

"I'll set something up with the guys over at BJK."

The Billie Jean King Tennis Center in Long Beach was where some of the top players in the area played. It was easy to set up a good match for some pre-tournament practice. They named the public tennis center after the legendary female tennis star, who was born in the city and started playing the sport on the public courts of Long Beach.

Before signing off, Mercer asked. "Anything else going on that I should know about?"

"Not really, but let me know if you see more counterfeit racquets out there," Hamilton replied.

With almost all racquets being made in Taiwan or China, the tennis companies had a difficult time stopping the growing number of fake racquets entering the market.

"I'm dealing with a bunch of these right now, and it seems like the situation is getting worse," Hamilton added.

"Okay. I haven't noticed anything out of the ordinary, but Ted Riley from Head just mentioned that the number of counterfeit racquets was impacting his numbers."

Chapter Eight

Y.K. CHEN WAS just wrapping up his sixteen-hour closing shift at Topstone Manufacturing in Taichung, Taiwan. Chen had worked for the company for twenty-five years. Hours were long and wages were poor. But job security was good, as long as people around the world continued to play racquet sports. His duties included making sure the manufacturing area was clean, and that everything was in place for tennis racquet production to start up early the following morning.

Topstone was the world's largest manufacturer of carbon fiber tennis, racquetball, squash and badminton racquets. In recent years, with lower wages found in mainland China, many of the Taiwanese racquet manufacturers had set up facilities in China. While they still produced most of their high-end racquets in Taichung, Topstone had moved all the mid and lower priced models to their factory outside of Shenzhen.

Topstone produced racquets for most of the leading racquet brands, making it difficult to keep new products under wraps. Keeping visiting Product Managers' wandering eyes from learning what the competition was up to, was almost impossible. Only Black Label had a sealed off area in the plant to maintain some manufacturing secrets from the competition.

What lay beneath the beautiful paint that adorned a tennis racquet was a complex and highly engineered construction of carbon fiber, resin, and generally another aramid fiber, like Kevlar. Many factors influenced the performance of a tennis racquet, including the frame shape, composition, width, head size, flex, weight, and balance. The more subtle influences came from the positioning of the carbon sheets. It was these subtle changes in the lay-up that caused more experienced and professional players to seek certain racquet models.

Topstone was best at maintaining consistency in racquet specifications, so a player could have absolute confidence that every one of his or her racquets would perform the same. Tournament players often travelled with six or more racquets, so tight specs were critical.

Before Chen left for the evening, he grabbed a long, thin racquet box he had filled and sealed the previous evening. Hiding in plain sight, the box had gone unnoticed throughout the day, placed next to other boxes of playtest racquets that were waiting to be shipped to various racquet brands.

Taking a quick look at his knock-off Rolex watch, a gift from his cousin, who often travelled to Hong Kong on business, Chen opened the doorway and stepped through the opening. Inside, a stairway lead to the factory's rooftop. He knew he had just five minutes before security would make a sweep of the factory floor.

The air was heavy and moist as he stepped out into the Taichung night. Upon arriving at the edge of the roof, Y.K. Chen launched the package up and over the factory's exterior fence. Waiting there in the darkness was Tommy Chen, his younger brother.

Y.K. Chen headed back down the factory stairway, while his brother disappeared into the night with the package.

Chapter Nine

AFTER SNEAKING THROUGH their semifinal match at the Pacific Southwest Championships, Alan Mercer and Joe Hamilton found themselves in another close contest in the finals. The semifinal was a rather heated affair, with questionable line calls and unsportsmanlike antics by their opponents. So far, the final was a well-played match against some familiar opponents. Mercer's old buddy, Tucker Burnett from Atlanta, was paired with Peter Dunn from Laguna Beach.

Still on serve deep into the deciding set, the match could turn on any point. Appreciating the high level of tennis being played on the stadium court at Palisades Tennis Club in Newport Beach, a sizable crowd had gathered on this late Sunday afternoon for the tournament's last match.

At one end, the club's bar overlooked the court, making it a popular viewing location. The crowd cheered loudly for club member, Peter Dunn, and his partner Burnett. For this late September tennis match, a light breeze blew off the nearby Pacific Ocean, and conditions couldn't have been better.

With Mercer serving at five games-all, 40-30, Joe gave the signal to poach on a second serve. So far, they had been unsuccessful in winning any second serve points by poaching.

But especially with Hamilton at the net, they played the odds that this time they would convert on such a pivotal point.

With palm open behind his back, Hamilton gave the "go" sign that he would slide across the court as the service return was hit, hoping to have an easy, put-away volley close to the net. Mercer thought about shrugging him off, since that puts a lot more pressure on his second serve, but replied "okay" to Hamilton.

On the receiving end of his serve was Tucker Burnett. Burnett was quite a character and was a regular on the senior tennis tour. Since there wasn't much prize money at this level, players competed for the joy, pride and challenge of earning enough ranking points to claim a high national ranking. The ultimate goal was to win a "Gold Ball," which was awarded to the winner of one of the year's four major championships, the Tier 1 national hard courts, clay courts, grass courts and indoor championships.

Mercer had become friends and a frequent practice partner of Burnett during his years in Atlanta. Since his move to California, Tucker and his girlfriend Jessie had camped out in Mercer's home several times, while Tucker played tournaments in the area.

Burnett, a tennis teaching pro in Atlanta, was a student of the game and studied his opponents closely. Mercer had relied on Burnetts' scouting reports on several occasions when coming across an unfamiliar opponent. Burnett seemed to know every player's strengths and weaknesses. Mercer, a more instinctive and creative player, often made up a game plan on the fly. So having a simple game plan from Burnett had opened his eyes and helped him tremendously, in his pursuit of a Tier 1 national championship and a gold ball.

Mercer was deep into his sixth match of the tournament. He lost in his second-round singles match. With that much tennis under his belt, the rhythm of his serve was perfect.

The ball toss was at the optimal height and placement that would allow him to propel his body up and into the court as he struck the ball. Mercer had hit a well-placed serve into the ad court service box. He hoped it would pull Burnett wide enough to elicit a weak return. Burnett had a beautiful one-handed slice backhand Mercer hoped would be the reply. A slice or underspin return would float a bit, giving Hamilton more time to reach it as he darted across the court to cut it off, resulting in an easy winning volley.

To his surprise, Burnett took a quick step forward to meet the ball early, then drove a well-hit topspin backhand cross court. The sound from Burnett's Wilson Pro Staff racquet was like a cannon being discharged. This was going to be a winner, thought Mercer.

But as Mercer had witnessed many times before, Joe Hamilton had timed his move perfectly, and with his move towards the net, as he crossed the center line, he had cut off the booming returns angle, and was able to stab at it with an outstretched racquet.

The shot from Hamilton was strong enough and placed just beyond the reach of a surprised Peter Dunn.

"Game, Mercer and Hamilton. They lead six games to five. Final set," the official called out.

As the players switched sides of the court, Tucker murmured, in his southern drawl, "That was one hell of a shot. I thought I had that one by y'all!"

In the last game of the match, aided by the shot of

adrenaline from securing the previous game, Mercer and Hamilton were off to a positive start.

With Burnett serving at 15-40, he placed his first serve into the body of Hamilton, but Joe was able to meet the ball in front, and directed it down at the feet of the approaching Burnett. With soft hands, Burnett half-volleyed the ball up Mercer's side of the court, hoping to catch him leaning towards the middle of the court. But Mercer anticipated the shot and protected the open doubles alley on his side. With his back towards the net, Mercer softly feathered a backhand volley cross court, catching Dunn and Burnett, both covering the expected shot down the middle.

The ball crossed the net in what seemed like slow motion, eventually landing a few inches inside the far doubles line.

The chair umpire loudly proclaimed... "Game, Set, Match. Mercer and Hamilton!"

With loud applause, the crowd stood to appreciate both teams, on a well-played match.

Winning a Tier 2 national tournament was nothing new to Mercer and Hamilton, but still felt very rewarding, and would earn them valuable ranking points towards their goal of reaching the number one national ranking. It also gave them a confidence boost before the Men's 40 and over National Hard Courts, which would take place in nearby La Jolla in a couple of months.

"Guess I'm buying dinner tonight," Burnett called out.

Knowing that his good buddy spent almost every cent he earned on traveling to tournaments, Mercer replied, "No, I think I've got this one. We got lucky today, so it's the least I can do."

Chapter Ten

SPECIAL AGENT STAN Powell guided his jet black Crown Victoria out of the Voodoo Doughnut parking lot, into morning rush hour traffic, onto Northeast Sandy Boulevard.

He was on his way to Hood River, his third such trip over the past few weeks, since they had asked him to head up the investigation into the identification of human remains unearthed by some mountain bikers. So far, every clue had led nowhere to determine the identity of the remains, but Stan Powell hoped that their luck was about to change.

It wasn't typical for the FBI to assist in simple murder or missing persons cases, but Stan Powell had other motives for getting involved in this particular case. A couple of years earlier, he had worked a case with the Hood River police that involved staking out an illegal pot farm that was financed by high-ranking organized crime figures. It was then that Stan had the pleasure of working with officer Zandy Roberts. Since then, he had jumped at any opportunity to work with her. Having been instrumental in the take-down of the pot farm, which ultimately led to the prosecution of several high-profile criminals, Stan's boss had given him some leeway when it came to his trips to Hood River. So when Lt. Roberts had called Stan asking him for his help, Stan was more than happy to do so.

With coffee and doughnuts on board, he was set for the hour-long drive through the scenic Columbia River Gorge. Once outside the sprawl of the Portland area, he could expect light traffic on a weekday morning.

Stan Powell had been with the Portland office of the FBI for the past ten years. At just thirty-three years old, he felt his best years at the bureau were still ahead of him. So for now, he was keeping his head down, trying to solve as many cases as possible. He hoped to find some answers to this case, but from experience, he knew he was at the mercy of a lot of variables, as well as the science used to piece together the identity of the mysterious skeleton.

Based upon the location of the shallow grave, the killer didn't want their victim to be found.

Nearing Hood River, Powell passed Multnomah Falls on his right. This stunning 611-foot cascade of water was one of the top tourist spots in Oregon. The beauty and seemingly endless treeline reminded him of home.

Born into a law enforcement family in Essex Junction, Vermont, Powell spent his youth water skiing in the summer and ice fishing in the winter on beautiful Lake Champlain. He also became a champion alpine skier, with plenty of great skiing in his backyard at nearby skiing locations like Stowe, Killington, and Smuggler's Notch.

While most of Powell's childhood buddies were still living in the area surrounding Burlington, Vermont, Stan was determined to be one of the few to experience life outside of the Green Mountain State. After completing his FBI training, the opportunity to work in the Portland office was just his ticket out of Vermont.

Known for its natural beauty, progressive politics, and a vow to "Keep Portland Weird," it was a bit of a shock initially, adjusting to life on the left coast. But over the years, Powell had learned to love his quirky new hometown, rough edges and all.

So far, Agent Powell had been out to Hood River twice since they called him in to handle the skeleton case. As he did with all of his cases, he loved to give them a name. One that would fit an epic serial killer case, like *The Boston Strangler*, *Son of Sam* or *The Zodiac Killer*.

His working name on this case was *The Post Canyon Killer*, based upon the location of the remains.

He had interviewed the two mountain bikers who found the remains, as well as the Hood River police officers, who were able to shed some light on the scene of the grave. For this trip, he hoped to get more information on the identity of the John Doe by visiting the medical examiner's office where the skeletal remains were being stored. He also had a meeting set with Lieutenant Roberts at the Hood River Police Department to look into any cold cases or missing persons' reports that could be linked to the case.

"You Could Be Dancing" by The Bee Gees pumped through the speakers as Powell turned into the parking lot of the Hood River medical examiner's office. Inside, Dr. Sinclair Wooster, a forensic pathologist, greeted him.

Wooster, who was in his mid-sixties, looked to be a very fit man in his forties.

"What is it about these people in Hood River?" Powell whispered to himself.

He figured Sinclair must be another one of the many

outdoor athletes in the area who only worked so he could afford to buy more outdoor sports equipment, or to fund his next adventure.

After a quick hello and brief chat about the upcoming Portland Trail Blazers season, Dr. Wooster guided Stan into the examination room, where a large metal table sat in the middle of the room. Illuminated by the bright overhead lights, Powell could see a complete human skeleton laid out on the table. There were also a few objects on an adjacent table that appeared to be remains of the victim's clothing and shoes.

"So doc, what have you been able to determine about our friend here?" Powell asked.

"Based upon the pelvic bones, I believe we are looking at a male who stood approximately six feet tall." Wooster remarked. "With some initial bone density tests, I'm also fairly certain that the remains are from someone approximately thirty years old. Also, we were lucky enough to find some hair fibers embedded in the recovered clothing that suggest the victim was Caucasian."

"Do you know how long the body has been out in the forest?" Powell asked, hoping to pinpoint the time of the victim's murder and hasty burial.

"It's hard to tell exactly, as our testing of the soil from the gravesite was inconclusive, giving us a range of between two and seven years ago. But one of our interns here is a tennis player, and he recognized that the tennis shoe recovered with the remains was a model introduced about four years ago. It is a Black Label Racquet Sports Predator 7 model, in a men's size 10.5," he said, pointing to what appeared to be an old tennis shoe outsole, with the leather upper long since eaten away by time and the wildlife in the forest.

"So, we have a thirty-year-old male, approximately six feet tall, who played tennis and was buried about four years ago in Post Canyon?" Agent Powell pondered.

"So what killed our tennis player, and what was he doing out in the forest? Or was he just buried there?"

"I wish I had those answers for you, Agent Powell. We are still waiting for some toxicology results to come back. Hopefully that will tell us a little more about how he died. But for now, there doesn't appear to be any major trauma to the skull or skeleton, so it doesn't look to be a violent death."

"Okay, doc. I'm off to meet with Lt. Roberts at the Hood River Police Department to see if they have any matching cold cases for us. When you get those toxicology reports back, give me a call. This has been a big help. I owe you a beer at a Blazers game this season."

"The Blazers' roster looks pretty good. Do you think we will make the playoffs this season?" Dr. Wooster asked.

The Portland Trail Blazers have always been able to field strong teams, but as one of the smaller markets for the NBA, they struggled to attract the biggest stars. In the miracle season of 1977, the team conquered the basketball world by winning the NBA title. Since that remarkable season, fans in Portland have had high hopes for the team, only to see them dashed by another losing season.

"One can only hope, Doc! See you soon."

Chapter Eleven

STAN POWELL HAD only worked a few cases with Lt. Zandy Roberts, but he knew he was really fond of her. Not only was she smart, but at barely five feet tall in heels, she was an athletic dynamo, ready for whatever adventure came her way. Her cheerful smile and awkward laugh, almost a giggle, reminded him of his youngest sister, who had died in a tragic skiing accident in Vermont five years ago.

Powell, a lifelong bachelor, could see himself marrying Zandy Roberts, except for the fact she was happily married to Craig Roberts, the head brewmaster at Full Sail Brewery. Stan had no intentions of being a home wrecker, but he still wanted to get to know her better.

Zandy had grown up in the town of Bend, not far away in Central Oregon. She was an avid rock climber, spending much of her time at the climbing mecca of Smith Rock State Park. She also volunteered for mountain rescue on Mount Hood. It was there that she met her husband, Craig.

Out for a frosty winter snowshoe, Craig had lost his footing after becoming disoriented when a powerful winter storm rolled in. All he could recall was a beacon of light penetrating the winter darkness and then being hauled out of the ravine he had fallen into. To his amazement, once they had reached a safe place to tend to his injured leg, he discovered his savior was the diminutive Miss Zandy.

As part of his wedding vow, he noted that after saving his life, the least he could do was propose to her. Which he did one year later. Now they lived, hiked and adventured together in Hood River with their two German Shorthaired Pointers, Hansel and Gretel.

"Well, hello Agent Powell." Lt. Roberts said with her trademark smile, as Stan stepped into her office at Hood River PD.

"Hello to you, Lieutenant. I brought doughnuts!" he declared, as he held up a pink box with the Voodoo Doughnut logo printed on the outside.

"I know… kinda cliche," he said. "But I've got your favorite Bacon Maple bar!" he added with a grin.

Opening the box, it quickly filled the room with the scent of sweet, gooey dough and sugary frosting.

"Any Voodoo Dolls in there?" she asked, while she approached the open treasure chest of doughy delicacies.

"Of course. I couldn't miss those," he beamed, then pointed to the chocolate-covered dough, in the shape of a voodoo doll.

"Well, then I guess we may have to dig up some more bodies out here, so you will keep coming back!"

As they dove into the box of doughnuts, Zandy said, "I just got the report from Dr. Wooster. Sounds like we are looking for a cold case that would lead us to the identity of our six foot tall, white male, in his thirties. Oh, and he is a tennis player. Sound about right?"

"Yep, that's our guy." Stan replied, as he wiped some maple frosting from his chin.

❧

For the next several hours, they dug through the large file boxes of cold cases and missing persons' reports Zandy had pulled together before their meeting. After setting aside all the relevant files that matched a case with a thirty-year-old white male, Stan noticed one more unopened box.

"What's in this box?"

"I contacted the local DMV and wrecking yards, in case our John Doe left behind a car somewhere," she said as she lifted the lid on the remaining box. Then she replaced the lid, and said, "But this can wait until the morning. Are you planning on staying the night?"

"Uh… I guess I am now," he answered. Not the least bit sad about the prolonged stay.

"Great! Go ditch those clothes and put on some hiking gear," she said. Knowing that in this part of the country, one must always be ready for an impromptu hiking session.

"I'm going to pick up the dogs and meet some friends at Syncline for a hike. I'll swing by the hotel and pick you up. Are you staying over at the Hood River Inn?"

"Yes, that works," Powell replied.

"After the hike, we'll drop by Full Sail and see what Craig has been brewing up today."

"Sounds excellent! See you at the hotel."

Chapter Twelve

AGENT POWELL STEPPED through the front door of the Hood River Police Department. He was up early, having grabbed a quick breakfast in town, followed by a short walk along the Columbia River, to check out the early morning windsurfers who were already out on the water. Still thinking about the great evening out with Zandy, her husband, and their friends, he felt energized for the day in front of him.

"I could get used to this," he said to himself, admiring the department's relative calm compared to his frenetic Portland office.

"How's your arm feeling this morning?" A smiling Lt. Roberts greeted him as he stepped into her office.

"I hope Hansel didn't do too much damage during our hike," she giggled.

"That dog of yours sure likes to be out front, doesn't he?" Powell responded while massaging his right shoulder. "The shoulder was fine once I popped it back into its socket. Now I know why you gave me his leash to hold!"

᎗

For the next few hours, they went through the box of DMV

and local wrecking yard records, hoping to find a vehicle that was abandoned by their John Doe.

Because of the remote location, and the number of hiking, snowshoeing, and cycling trails, it wasn't uncommon for adventure seekers to disappear into the wilderness, often leaving a car behind at a trailhead. On the occasion where the owner was never found, or had turned up dead, they usually returned the abandoned vehicle to the next of kin. For those discarded on the side of the road, typically with license plates and VIN numbers removed, they ended up at a nearby wrecking yard or sent to auction.

"Nothing seems to stand out to me in the DMV files, but I am curious about a few located at a wrecking yard in The Dalles," Lt. Roberts said. "It might be worth a drive out to take a peek."

"I'm not seeing anything either, but always welcome a wild goose chase," Powell replied.

"Great. Let's take my HRPD truck. They tend to get a little jumpy around the Feds out there," Zandy said, as she gathered up her notes and files.

The Dalles was situated twenty-five miles east of Hood River and was recognized as the end of the Oregon Trail. A dam was constructed there in 1957 by the Army Corps of Engineers to control the flow of the Columbia River.

The Dalles Dam was one of the ten largest hydro-power dams in the country. Native American tribes had battled local government since its completion, claiming that the dam ruined much of the fishing in the area that was crucial to the survival of their tribes. From Powell's perspective, the tribes had plenty of reason to fight against the dam.

Today, The Dalles was a sleepy town, marking the transition

point between the wetter and greener part of the state, with the dryer, browner side. Most businesses made little money, one of those being The Dam Wreck, owned by the notorious Grizz Mason.

※

A weathered metal sign with several bullet holes in it marked the driveway entrance to The Dam Wreck. Zandy steered her Ram 1500 4x4 off Highway 197 onto the gravel driveway that led to the remote wrecking yard.

Located a few miles from town, the only sounds they heard when they stopped at the front gate was the wind that was blowing strong enough to whip up several dust devils that dotted the horizon.

They were greeted with another bullet riddled sign that announced:

ABSOLUTELY NO TRESSPASSING. WE SHOOT FIRST & ASK QUESTIONS LATER.

A rusty intercom sat on a post next to the gate. Lt. Roberts pushed a dusty button and waited for a reply. Moments pass before she tried again. This time, calling into the microphone, "This is Lt. Roberts, with the Hood River Police Department. We would like to look at some vehicles in your yard."

Moments later, the box on the post crackled to life.

"I'm busy. Go away," a man's voice said.

"Sir, we won't be long. We just want to look at three vehicles that may be linked to a homicide," Zandy pleads.

"Don't know nothin' bout any homo-cides, lady!" the voice answered.

"Okay, we can just waste each other's time by getting a warrant. Who knows what permit violations the judge might find while digging into your business?" she said, while still maintaining her composure. "Plus, if you send us off, we'll have to drink the two growlers of beer we brought for you," she added.

"What kinda beer you got? If it's not that hopped-up yuppie piss water, you can come on in."

On the recommendation of a deputy at the station, Zandy had her husband fill up two forty-ounce growlers, with Session Lager, as a peace offering to the wrecking yard owner. While Session was an excellent craft beer, it appealed to a wide range of tastes.

"No, none of that crap, just some amazingly tasty lager," she responded.

"Well shit, I'll be the judge of that! I'll be right out," a much cheerier voice was heard through the intercom.

Moments later, in a cloud of dust, a Polaris Ranger four-wheel ATV came skidding to a stop on the other side of the gate. An old junkyard dog, that hadn't been bathed in years, jumped out of the passenger seat, followed by a large, bearded man in overalls, that also hadn't seen the inside of a washing machine in a while.

When the gate finally swung open, Lt. Roberts and Agent Powell stepped inside to greet the large man, who appeared to be in his mid-forties, though it was difficult to say because of the thick beard that obscured much of his face.

Before Stan could speak, Zandy extended her right hand to greet the imposing bear-sized man, and in her left hand, revealed her HRPD identification.

"I'm Lt. Roberts, and this is Deputy Powell," she said, with a quick glance towards Agent Powell.

Stan took the cue and nodded in the man's direction,

knowing it would be best to not identify himself as a federal agent.

He eyed her ID. With a quick smirk, the giant said, "I'm Grizz Mason. I own this piece of shit," he said, gesturing towards the wrecking yard. "You said somethin' bout a murder?"

Most visitors to the yard were people looking to restore an old car, hoping to find a cheap part they could pull off one of the many wrecks on his yard. So a murder investigation was something to get excited about.

"Yes, we are investigating some remains that were found near Hood River. We believe the person was murdered and buried in the forest around four years ago. We think he may have left a vehicle behind, so we hope to find it here," Zandy said, while she stared past Grizz at the enormous mountain of wrecked cars.

"Hmmm…. four years you say? That would be on the back lot," Grizz said, as if he had an organized system for keeping track of his inventory.

"Here is the paperwork on the three vehicles," she said, while she handed over the documents.

"If you can take us to them, we won't trouble you with anything else," she added.

"Right. You said somethin' bout some growlers?" Grizz said, while he looked over the two law enforcement officers.

"Of course. Deputy, can you go fetch those from the truck?" she declared with a wry grin, clearly enjoying their little charade.

"Yes, Maam," Agent Powell replied instantly, while strolling back to the truck.

After delivering the two growlers of Session Lager to

Mason's ATV, they jumped back in the truck to follow the four-wheeler to the back lot location on the sprawling property. Along the way, they passed a sea of twisted, rusty hulks of metal that were once fully operational cars, trucks, minivans, and other vehicles.

"Don't get many visitors to this part of the yard, 'cept for vultures," Grizz said, referring to those he considered cheapasses who picked over the dead metal bodies that littered his yard. "Let me grab the crane and pull down them vehicles for you. I'll put 'em in this clearing for y'all."

After some doing, Grizz had assembled the three wrecks, and arranged them in the open space in the back lot.

"Right. So here y'all have the ninety-nine Honda Odyssey," pointing to the carcass on the left.

"This here be the oh-one Ford Explorer." Motioning to the one in the middle, which actually looked in decent condition, minus the wheels, a few side panels, and most of the interior of the SUV.

And finally, Grizz Mason pointed to the burned-out shell on the right and said, "That bucket of ash is an oh-two Toyota 4Runner."

"Right. I'll leave y'all to it. Just come by the office when you're done," he said, as he and his old dog hopped back into the ATV, which was now carrying the precious cargo of two fresh growlers of brew.

✥

With Grizz Mason out of their hair, Lt. Roberts and Agent Powell were left to pick over the three wrecks.

"Let's go through the Honda Odyssey first," Zandy said.

"It was abandoned four years ago at the Cooper Spur

campgrounds, which is located on the northeast side of Mount Hood. Some local hikers had noticed it on multiple occasions, before notifying the local authorities," she said.

With no license plates or VIN number, Zandy and Stan picked through the mini-van, looking for clues that would tie it to their John Doe. They bagged and recorded some samples that would be sent to the lab for analysis.

Moving on to the Ford Explorer, Zandy noted, "This Explorer was dumped in the parking area at the Klickitat Trailhead."

"The trail is located on the Washington side of the Columbia River, and is popular with mountain bikers," she added. "It too was discovered about four years ago, with the owner never being located."

Again, they picked through the interior, and bagged more samples for the lab. There were several food wrappers and empty beer cans in the SUV, that they might be able to connect to the owner, or perhaps were left behind by someone living in the vehicle, when it was abandoned at the Klickitat trail.

Finally, they approached the rusted hunk of metal that used to be a Toyota 4Runner.

"They found this beauty last year at the bottom of Lost Lake, which is on the Southeast side of Mount Hood. Because of recent drought conditions, the low water level allowed some fishermen to hook onto this big metal fish! When the salvage crew pulled it to the surface, they estimated it had been submerged for about three years, so it fits our timeline," Zandy reported.

"Well, from the looks of it, someone didn't want it to be found, so it could be tied to our case," Stan replied.

With not much remaining but a burned-out frame of an

SUV, they dug through what they could. Surprisingly, there was still a glove compartment with a door partially attached.

"Can I borrow your flashlight for a second?" Powell asked, while peering into the glove compartment.

"Sure. Did you find something?"

"Not sure, but it looks to be a piece of paper stuck in the back."

With a pair of tweezers, Stan was able to grasp a partially burned piece of paper. Carefully pulling the fragile piece of paper towards him, he hoped he might be holding the remains of a vehicle registration card.

"I'm not 100% sure, but it could be a small fragment of a vehicle registration, business or insurance card. I'm not sure how it survived the fire and being submerged in the lake for three years, but I want to get this to the FBI lab in Portland to see if they can pull up any writing on the card."

Before they finished up with the Toyota, they stored the paper card, along with some odd melted objects that were stuck under the metal frame of the driver's seat.

"Let's go see our large friend Grizz, and get the hell out of here before he finishes up that beer," Powell said.

"I'd like to get these samples back to Portland tonight. But something tells me I'll be back out this way soon."

"Good. Don't forget to bring doughnuts!"

Chapter Thirteen

"HI LILY. HOW are you?" Alan Mercer asked the store manager at The Tennis Spot, in Fountain Valley.

Lily Nguyen responded in a thick Vietnamese accent, "I'm always good when you come by the store."

Lily, a slender twenty-five years old with long jet-black hair that matched her perfectly painted fingernails, had used some of her hard-earned salary to enhance certain physical assets.

Mercer couldn't keep his eyes off her tight-fitting Nike t-shirt with a plunging neckline, which left little to the imagination.

"What do I have to buy today?" Lily joked.

She knew the drill. When the sales reps came by the store, they wanted to write an order. For Alan Mercer, he usually did write an order, but he also enjoyed the time spent with Lily.

Lily was a breath of fresh air as she glided around the tennis shop. Quite different from most of the other shop owners. His rapport with Lily had always been fun and somewhat flirtatious. But Mercer was trying his best to resist the temptation.

A few years earlier, he could not resist his urges, and began an affair with Lisa Weldon, a tennis facility manager in Atlanta. While his marriage had reached its end, he still felt guilty that his relationship with Lisa had started before his divorce was finalized.

Lisa was also small, with an athletic build and a voracious appetite for sex. She couldn't get enough, which suited Mercer just fine. If he had a type, Lisa checked all the boxes.

Once his divorce was finalized, Mercer and Lisa became more open with their relationship, often taking trips to Destin, Florida, a popular vacation spot on the Florida panhandle. They would get in plenty of time in the sun, a bit of tennis, some great seafood, and a lot of love-making. It became a game for the couple to see how many times they could have sex in one day. With assistance from a little blue pill, Mercer was up for the challenge.

After his first marriage had fallen apart, Lisa was everything Mercer was looking for in a partner, and he often considered asking her to be wife number two, but there was just one issue. Lisa had a substance abuse problem. She liked to drink, and take prescription painkillers, and would become a monster when under the influence. Frequently, Lisa would scream at Alan while out in public, accusing him of not loving her. Within seconds of being a fun-loving, caring person, she would flip a switch and became her version of Dr. Jekyll and Ms. Hyde.

For four years, Mercer encouraged professional help and a healthier lifestyle. Meanwhile, he overlooked the verbal abuse, and even asked her to move out to California when he relocated. But with no one else in her life in California, Lisa became increasingly aggressive towards Mercer. He finally worked up the courage to send Lisa packing back to Atlanta. To help ease his guilt, he sent a nice sized check, along with the plane ticket.

"Why don't you just write an order, and send it to me to check?" Lily asked, bringing Mercer back to his thoughts about getting into some trouble with the young and hot Miss Lily.

"You got it, Lily," he replied. "I'll put together a holiday season order and put in your tennis ball booking order for next year."

The front door of the small shop opened, and an older Vietnamese gentleman walked into the store, carrying a covered bird cage. The man nodded hello to Lily, then disappeared behind the curtain that concealed the back of the store.

This wasn't the first time Mercer had witnessed the mysterious bird cages moving in and out of the store. Rumor among the tennis reps was that Lily's father, Duke, was running an illegal exotic bird operation out of the back of the store. Birds came in from around the world, and sold for several thousand dollars each. Clearly, The Tennis Spot wasn't staying in business based only upon their tennis sales, Mercer thought.

Despite his desire to respond to Lily's flirtations, Mercer decided it was best to wrap things up before he lost the battle with his conscience.

"Lily, I'm running a bit late, but really appreciate your business. I will email the proposed orders over to you tonight."

Mercer gathered up his sales samples and headed for the front door, just as another bird cage entered the store. Following the birdcage was a customer with a Black Label racquet that had some serious damage to it. The head of the racquet was folded over, creating an L-shape to the racquet. Sensing that this may involve a phone call to him eventually, he decided to stick around and offer support to Lily.

Lily and the young man with the broken racquet spoke to each other in Vietnamese.

"Alan, can you take a quick look at this racquet and see if I should send it back to Black Label for a replacement?" Lily asked.

"Of course. Let me see what is going on with it."

Mercer knew what the warranty team at Black Label would search for, so he could usually determine whether it was worth the expense of sending the racquet in.

"How did the racquet break?" he asked the young man.

"I just hit an overhead, and the racquet exploded!" he answered, adding the word exploded, to make for a more dramatic description of the event.

Mercer had heard this story before, so he always looked over the broken racquet for signs that it had come in contact with the court, the fence, net post or something else that would cause it to fail. He also checked the stringing of the racquet to make sure it was done according to proper specifications.

After a brief examination, Mercer didn't see any of the usual signs of abuse. Other than the folded over racquet head, the racquet was in pristine condition. But then something caught his eye. While the racquet looked perfect, the small holographic decal on the side of the frame looked odd.

To help protect against counterfeit racquets entering the market, each racquet had a unique holographic decal attached to it. When viewing the decal at various angles, you could see images that were hidden when viewed head on. The decal on this racquet didn't seem to have the same depth and detail that Mercer had noticed on other Black Label racquets.

Recalling his conversation with Joe Hamilton, Mercer considered that the racquet might be a fake.

"Sir, if you could excuse me for a minute, I'd like to speak with Lily about getting your racquet replaced," Mercer said.

"Sure, that would be great. I'm going to run next door and grab a boba tea. Do you want anything?"

While he loved boba, Mercer declined, "No, thank you."

Once the man had left the store, Mercer asked, "Lily, did he buy the racquet from you?"

"Yes, of course," she replied.

"There is something not quite right about this racquet. I think it might be a counterfeit."

Somewhat defensive, Lily responded, "Well, I bought the racquet from Black Label, so how did I get a fake?"

"I'm not sure, but I would like to take the racquet and check into it some more. If you can just give your customer a new racquet off your wall, I will arrange to send you a replacement. I also want to take a quick peek at some of the other Black Label racquets you have in the shop, to make sure they are okay." Mercer added.

After looking over the racquet wall and not finding any others with the same odd decal, Mercer took his notes, and the broken racquet, and excused himself.

"Thank you, Lily! I will be back in touch later this evening."

Chapter Fourteen

JACK SHARP WAS on his second bourbon & coke, while relaxing in the Delta Airlines Crown Room, at Portland International Airport, or PDX, as it's referred to by Portlanders. After a brief trip to Los Angeles, Sharp was on a layover before his flight to Taipei.

While not in his job description, he insisted on visiting the manufacturing sites, where they produced Black Label racquets. He was looking forward to the scheduled meetings he had for the trip, but he also was excited about the meetings that didn't appear on his travel itinerary.

Jack Sharp's life was a lie. In fact, Jack Sharp wasn't even his real name.

His life had been built on a series of smaller lies that made for one enormous lie. As with many afflicted with such narcissistic personalities, it all began with a simple lie that then led to the next one. For Jack Sharp, only he knew when the lying started, but it was hardly a secret to those who knew him. It was a long chain of lies that led him to his position as General Manager at Black Label Racquet Sports. Continued lies would keep him there. That, and the inner circle he had put in place in the Black Label Racquet Sports management team, which he created to protect him.

In high school, Sharp, who was then living under his given name, Jack Shapiro, tried unsuccessfully to make the varsity tennis team, landing on the junior varsity instead. During his senior year, occasionally they inserted him into a varsity match for a meaningless doubles match.

In his freshman year at the University of Southern California, he walked into the men's tennis coach's office, expressed his desire to "walk-on" to the team, and stated that he had been a four-year varsity letterman at Marina High School in Los Angeles' South Bay.

USC was a perennial top-ranked team, with national champions from around the world filling the roster. Shapiro's resume did not impress coach Gene Tessler. He had heard this story before. But as he did with all of those who tried to walk onto the team, he set up a match with the lowest ranked player on the team; he figured if they couldn't beat him, they would have no shot at playing on the team.

After the 6-0, 6-0 drubbing, coach Tessler advised the young Jack Shapiro that perhaps he should focus on his studies while a student at USC. But he should come out to watch and support the team.

On the resume he submitted to Black Label Sporting Goods for the sales rep position in Los Angeles, he indicated he was a member of the varsity tennis team during his four years at USC.

In his role as a racquet sports sales representative in Los Angeles, Jack had found his calling. He was now at the top of the mountain in his tennis community, loving that he represented the number one brand.

His style was to bully his customers into buying more and more product, even though he knew it wasn't always in their best interest. He would use his sizable promotional budget to buy off upset customers, instead of using the budget to promote the grassroots efforts in the community, as was intended. The local retailers found that if they wanted Black Label products, they needed to play Jack's game. If they didn't, they would be left on the outside looking in.

He built some powerful alliances with some of the store owners who had similar aspirations of being the big dog in Southern California tennis.

With impressive sales index numbers, his Regional Manager, Joe Hamilton, mostly left him alone.

Hamilton, like many others in the company, had fallen under the spell of Sharp, and tried to adopt the same bullying practices in other territories in the western region. All the other sales reps in the region did their best to resist the Jack Sharp way of doing things. Many of them had spent several years fostering close relationships with their retail customers. They would not throw it all away by playing Jack's game.

In just his third year in the territory, they honored Jack Sharp with the prestigious Jack Armstrong Award, which is offered to the top sales rep at Black Label Racquet Sports. Named after hall of fame tennis player Jack Armstrong, who played most of his remarkable career using Black Label racquets, it was the most important award given out each year by Black Label.

Jack Sharp had reached the number one position, with the number one brand. But he wasn't satisfied. He had bigger plans for himself.

"Mr. Sharp, your flight to Taipei will board in a few

minutes, with First Class boarding first," said the smartly dressed female attendant, inside Delta's Crown Room, as she leaned over to refresh his drink.

"Great! Are you coming along for the ride?"

"No, Mr. Sharp, not this time. I'm off to Paris in the morning. But maybe I will see you here another time," she replied.

"Oh, that's too bad. We would have had some fun in Taiwan." Sharp said, as he drained the last of his drink.

The flight to Taipei was long, so better prepare for it, he thought.

Chapter Fifteen

ALAN MERCER WAS constantly on the move, so he looked forward to his Monday office day. While it was anything but relaxing, it provided a day without having to negotiate the brutal Southern California traffic, or having to grab a quick lunch, often a Subway sandwich. Sweet Onion Chicken Teriyaki on wheat was his current favorite.

With the laundry in the washer in the background, Mercer spent Mondays catching up on paperwork, returning phone calls, setting up the week's appointments, and analyzing the weekly sales index report. Depending upon how the report looked, Mercer would spend some time calculating what actions to take for the rest of the year. Fortunately, he was having another good year. Not his best, by a long shot, but good enough to keep management happy… at least he hoped.

Mercer was still feeling the ill-effects of the weekend, having been invited to a party at a house in Venice Beach on Saturday night. He had been startled awake by a pounding headache. It was Sunday morning, and he was wrapped in the jersey sheets of his female companion, whom he'd met the night before at the party. In the few years since moving to the Los Angeles area, he had made his way into the "L.A.

Scene," mostly though his tennis friends, who happened to be high-profile attorneys, agents, or were in some way connected to the entertainment industry. The seemingly never-ending parties often took place at the homes of Hollywood's elite, with plenty of alcohol, drugs, and scantily clad men and women. While he passed on the drugs, Mercer rarely resisted the drink and beautiful women. It was this appetite that landed him in his bedmate's Playa del Rey apartment.

In the direct path of departing flights from LAX, the engines of the departing jumbo jets were like jackhammers crashing against his skull. Realizing he had a late morning USTA mixed doubles league match, he quietly excused himself, with the promise of connecting again soon.

Mixed doubles was not his best form of tennis, but he really enjoyed the camaraderie of his USTA team.

He suffered through the match as best he could. Fortunately, his partner was on fire and they were able to pull out the victory. Mercer declined all alcohol at the post-match team gathering. He thought about never touching the stuff again, but that usually only lasted until the next party.

Running down his to-do list, it was time to call his Customer Service Rep, Abigail Johnson. Abby was his eyes and ears at Black Label's corporate headquarters. He could not be successful at his job without her.

Abby was just twenty-four-years old, and was hired straight out of college, where she had played number one singles on the University of Wisconsin women's tennis team. Having grown up in Chicago, she was well acquainted with Black Label Sporting Goods' history as a sports giant. She had always dreamed of working for Black Label, and her plan was to work in the player promotions department, where she would work with the company's sponsored professional and top junior players. When she picks up, Mercer swore he could hear her smirk even before she opened her mouth.

"Hey Abby! How's your day going?"

"Well, I was wondering if you were going to call today, or just sleep all day," Abby said sarcastically.

She had been working with Mercer since she started at Black Label, and was aware of his west coast lifestyle and reputation for partying a bit too excessively. She never missed a chance to play the mom role, even though she was several years younger than Mercer.

"What famous actress did you play tennis with, or do something else with this weekend?" she asked, looking for a bit of dirt on her favorite sales rep.

"Oh, I was mostly well behaved, from what I remember," he laughed. "No actresses came to any harm. But I ran into that actress from *The Karate Kid* at a party, and we talked tennis for a bit," he said, leaving out the actress's name, to see if Abby knew who she was.

"What? Elisabeth Shue? I love her!"

Mercer knew that life as a CSR could be dull sometimes, so he always enjoyed ruffling Abby's feathers, with a story from life in "Hollyweird."

"So, what's going on there today?" Mercer asked, hoping to move off the subject of his personal life.

"I just got off the phone with Smeagol. We reworked his next accessory pre-book order, and moved up the ship date," she said, sounding somewhat annoyed.

Abby had given the nickname to the owner of Topspin Tennis, one of Mercer's accounts. He was constantly on the phone with Abby, and his high-pitched voice reminded her of the ghoulish Gollum character from *The Lord of The Rings*.

"You know, he always asks about you when I go to see him… my precious?" Mercer said, as he slipped into his best Smeagol voice.

"Oh gross! Smeagol can keep dreaming!"

"Alright then. I'll let him know you are open to the idea," he joked.

"Ugh… Alan, I'm going to kill you!"

"Hey, while I've got you in a good mood, can you check on a racquet serial number for me? I picked up a strange racquet from The Tennis Spot in Fountain Valley."

"Sure thing. What's the number?"

"It's BL371978," Mercer read the number off the decal on the broken racquet.

After a few minutes, Abby came back on the phone once she'd checked the computer database. "That number doesn't come up in our system."

"That's strange. Lily claimed she got the racquet directly from Black Label," he said, while wondering how the counterfeit racquet got into her shipment.

He remembered bringing over a few racquets from another store. Perhaps that's how she got it?

One duty of being a successful tennis sales rep that wasn't written in the job description was the constant shuttling of tennis equipment from one store to another. Sometimes Mercer wondered if he could open his own tennis shop with just the product that was in his SUV on any given day. Helping stores get rid of slow selling products, or getting a racquet for a special customer was all part of the day's work.

"Alright. Can you send out a Velocity Tour 95, in a 3/8 grip, to Lily, on my promotional account?"

"Sure. I'll get it shipped out today," Abby replied.

"Thanks Abby. I've got to run. I'll call you if I find out anything more about this mysterious racquet," he said, while trying to recall which store he might have gotten the racquet from.

"Okay. Say hello to Elisabeth Shue for me," Abby giggled as she said goodbye.

Chapter Sixteen

HAVING GROWN UP in Southern California, Jack Sharp thought the Chicago summers were brutally humid, but there was invariably a slight breeze that would afford some relief. As he stepped out into the lifeless air of Taichung, Sharp recoiled from the pungent stench of Taiwan's primary industrial city. Thankfully, he thought, this was his last day of the trip and would fly home to Chicago in the morning. But first, one final meeting.

After a full day in meetings at Topstone Manufacturing with Peter Shin and his team, he left the Hotel National for the short walk to The Fat Cat, an American-style bar. Located in the Central District of the city, it was one of the few bars that didn't offer traditional karaoke.

He loathed the evenings when the proprietors of the nearby factories would insist on drinks and karaoke until late into the evening. For this meeting, he was in charge of the agenda, so he sought out the sleepy bar, known for pouring a stiff drink.

Lynyrd Skynyrd's "Freebird" was playing on the jukebox as he found a table in the back of the bar. He ordered a Moscow Mule and waited for his guest.

Settling into the oversized, black leather chair, Sharp

couldn't help but reveal a slight grin as he took a pul, potent drink. His plan was coming together nicely, he th

The new Element-5 racquet lineup he reviewed a stone was looking great. He had no input into the design or performance of the new racquets, but would take full credit if sales took off. He felt he had to give each new line of racquets his blessing.

They would present the new Element-5 racquets to the sales reps at the upcoming sales meeting in Utah. Sharp was always excited to introduce a new technology, as it would provide a big initial sales boost, as their network of retailers would have to replace the old models with an entire range of new Element-5 racquets.

With the new racquets shipping in January, deals were being made each day to move the remaining inventory of the current Velocity-X models.

He loved being in the powerful position of approving or declining all deals.

Sharp knew his team would be pleased, and Black Label would maintain their position as the number one tennis brand. With his team in place, or as he called them, "The Inner Circle," Sharp felt confident he could finally run the company the way he wanted. His Inner Circle would protect him from attacks from the outside. They were all doing too well financially to question his motives.

Since stepping into the role of General Manager, he lobbied hard to appoint Bill Cashman as the company's new Vice President. With "Cash" Cashman in place, he could protect him from the company's owners and top management. This was the critical move in his plan.

He then promoted Randall Jefferies to National Sales

Manager. He knew Jefferies wasn't the sharpest knife in the drawer, but he would do whatever Jack demanded with no questions asked.

To head up product development, Jack had tagged his close friend and ally, Tom Saltz. Tom had served as the Western Region Technical Representative, back when Jack was in the field. The two formed a tight bond in those days and shared their love of a fine cigar.

Last but not least, was his Executive Assistant, Valerie Little. Having previously served as his Customer Service Representative, he knew Valerie would be a loyal member of his inner circle. She had a sickly child, with mounting medical costs, so the extra financial support from being by Jack Sharp's side was all she needed to surrender her soul to the cause.

Just as he was about to signal for a refill, a young Taiwanese man approached his table.

"Mr. Sharp? My name is Tommy Chen. I am Walter Chen's son. He apologizes for the change in plans, but he would like you to come with me. I will take you to him."

"That's not what we had agreed upon," Sharp said, with a look of disdain on his face.

"I am very sorry for the change in plans, but my father has some good things to show you. Could you please come with me?"

"Well, for fuck's sake. This better be good," Jack said, as he fished some New Taiwan Dollars out of his wallet and dropped the bills on the table.

Jack climbed into the back seat of the Lincoln Towncar, which was parked in front of The Fat Cat, while Chen entered the front passenger seat, and nodded to the driver to proceed. For the next forty minutes, the Towncar bobbed and weaved through the busy Taichung streets, which were filled with a dizzying array of scooters, bicycles and other cars.

From the back seat, the view out of the window was a video game of vehicles, trying to reach an unknown destination, with apparently no rules to guide them. With the free-for-all taking place outside his comfortable Lincoln, Jack reached for the bottle of *Maker's 46* Kentucky Bourbon, in the back seat mini bar.

As they reached the industrial Shalu District, which was northwest of the city, the streets became less crowded, and darkness took the place of the Central District light show.

The Towncar slowed as it pulled up to the gated entry, where a machine gun armed guard triggered the large metal gates to open, as he waved to the familiar driver.

The gold lettering on the plaque outside the factory gate was a series of Chinese characters, or Hanzi, followed by the English translation, Green Dragon Manufacturing.

At this hour, the factory was quiet and dark, except for a small office building situated next to the main factory production building. As he exited the rear of the car, Jack couldn't help but notice the stark contrast between the clean and modern appearance of Topstone Manufacturing, with the distressed and down-trodden shambles of Green Dragon. The faded green paint that covered the outer walls of the factory buildings was peeling badly, and in need of a fresh coat or two.

Green Dragon Manufacturing was owned by Walter Chen and managed by his adult children. Once a thriving manufacturing facility, Chen did not have the foresight of his competitors, and had neglected to secure property in China for a second plant. As most manufacturing jobs jumped to the mainland, Green Dragon was left on the outside looking in.

A stylishly dressed older gentleman presented his hand to Jack as he arrived at the main entrance.

"I'm so sorry for the change of plans, Jack. But I thought it would be best if I could show you the results of our work."

Slowly accepting Walter Chen's hand, the Maker's 46 had taken the sting out of Jack's anger.

"I'm just happy to have survived the trip out here. I thought Chicago drivers were bad!"

With a laugh that turned into a brief bought of coughing, Walter replied, "It takes a bit to get used to driving in a sea of motor scooters. We've found the best strategy is to give them a gentle nudge with your car. Most often, they will move out of your way." He grinned, revealing a set of gold-capped front teeth.

"So what is it you want to show me, Walter?"

"I think you are going to like this. Let's move to the showroom," he said, as he extended his arm towards an open door.

Inside the spacious showroom was a long conference table in the center of the room. On the table were seven tennis racquets. As Jack stepped up to the table, he recognized that these were perfect replicas of the new Black Label Element-5 racquets. The same models he saw that day at Topstone.

"Very nice," Jack said with a smile as he inspected the new K-Six-One Tour racquet.

"Thank you, Jack," Walter said, as he shot a quick glance towards his oldest son.

"Yoshi, can you show Mr. Sharp what else we have for him?"

Standing next to the showroom door, Y.K. Chen flipped the light switch that illuminated the back of the room. There, another table sat, with several tennis racquets on it.

As they approached the table, Jack noticed that these were racquets from Black Label's major competitors, Wilson, Babolat, Head and Prince. He did not recognize the racquet models.

Sensing his bewilderment, Walter stepped closer and said, "These are the new models that will begin shipping in January."

He took a moment to gather his thoughts, but Jack quickly understood what it meant for him to be able to undercut his competitors with their own products. He and his inner circle would be able to sell knock-offs of Black Label racquets to his select network of dealers, and he would be able to sell other brands too, essentially cutting the other companies out of the picture. All the money would funnel into his secret bank account. Jack finally looked towards Walter and said quietly, "It's going to be an excellent year!"

Chapter Seventeen

WITH AS MUCH rainfall as Portland gets, one might think Agent Stan Powell would barely notice the drops of rain that streamed down the windows outside of his office. But after a long, dry summer, the early November rain signaled the beginning of the rainy season. Stan took a minute to enjoy the scene from his downtown Portland office.

On sunny days, which didn't happen that often, Powell could see the majestic Mount Hood looming on the horizon. He expected it would be a while before he saw it again.

His thoughts drifted to the unsolved Post Canyon Killer case that had been on his desk for the past few months.

As if on cue, the intercom on his desk sparked to life. "Agent Powell, you have a call from Dr. Wooster holding for you on line three."

Stan quickly punched the button on his phone. "Hey Doc Wooster! I hope you have some good news for me."

"Hello there, Stan. I guess that depends on what you consider being good news." Dr. Sinclair Wooster said, from his lab in Hood River.

"Maybe good news for you, but not so good for our John Doe," he added.

"Our toxicology analysis found traces of Tetrodotoxin, or TTX, in the hair samples that were recovered with the remains. TTX is one of the most lethal poisons on the planet. A single milligram, an amount that would fit on the head of a pin, is enough to kill an adult, even one the size of our victim."

"So how would TTX get into our victim?" Stan asked.

"TTX is most commonly associated with pufferfish. About two hundred people per year die from Fugu poisoning, because of pufferfish not being prepared properly. Almost all of the deaths occur in the Indo-Pacific region. To see a case involving TTX in Hood River leads me to believe that the toxin was injected into our victim. Either that or he ate the Columbia River's first and only pufferfish." Dr. Wooster reported.

"What happens to a person injected with TTX?"

"If the dose was considerable, our victim would have been paralyzed almost instantly, then basically suffocated within minutes," Dr. Wooster responded.

Taking a moment to absorb the news, Agent Powell deduced, "So we are definitely looking at a homicide. Is there any way to trace TTX back to its source?"

"Unfortunately, there is no way to determine where the TTX came from, but it isn't a synthetic toxin produced in a lab. Someone with knowledge of the poison would need to extract and store it prior to injection."

"Okay doc, this is a big help, and your timing is perfect. The lab here is presenting their findings on some samples we pulled from a few abandoned vehicles to me this afternoon. Hopefully, something will help us identify our guy."

"The Trail Blazers season has started, so just say the word, and it's my treat for a home game!" Stan says, as he signed off with the forensic scientist.

With this new information, theories circulated through Agent Powell's thoughts.

"How did the Post Canyon Killer get his hands on pufferfish toxin?" He whispered to himself.

"Guess I should call Zandy Roberts with the news."

Chapter Eighteen

THERE WAS A longer than usual wait at Killer Burger, so Agent Powell had increased his pace on his walk back to FBI headquarters. The steady rain was a refreshing change, and for the first time in a while he had thrown on his trusty Outdoor Research waterproof rain jacket.

One thing he appreciated about Portland was the absence of umbrellas. Portland residents simply didn't use them. Use of an umbrella was a signal that you were from out of town. Waterproof jackets and footwear were all that locals needed to shield themselves from the elements.

With the taste of his peanut butter, pickle, bacon burger lunch still on his tongue, Stan Powell pushed through the headquarters front door security on his way to the lab. He was looking forward to hearing what the FBI scientists had learned about the three abandoned vehicles.

Inside the lab's empty conference room, Powell took a seat at a table in the middle of the room. On the table was a laptop, a projector and a sealed two-foot by two-foot cardboard box. A three-ring binder, with Case #40806, and Special Agent Stanley Powell, listed as the agent in charge of the investigation printed on the outside. Before he had a chance to open the binder, Agent Wendy Newton walked into the room.

Newton, in charge of the Portland lab, took her job seriously. Never skipping a step, agents working out of the Portland office relied heavily on the labs' findings. They had helped solve an untold number of tough cases.

The bureau had tried to lure Agent Newton to head up the main lab in D.C., but she refused to leave the Pacific Northwest.

"Good afternoon Wendy. How is your day going so far?" Stan asked, while she took a seat on the opposite side of the table.

"Oh, you know, just the usual blood spatter analysis, gunshot residue study, and a few other less appetizing cases," she replied.

"Hopefully, my case is fairly appetizing. I'm still trying to digest my lunch!" Stan laughed.

"Yes, your case definitely is of the more palatable variety, and pretty interesting."

With the press of a button, the laptop computer came to life, and an image was projected on the screen at the far end of the room. The photograph was of the rusted, burned-out hunk of metal that was once a Toyota 4Runner.

"Let's start with the samples collected from the Toyota," Agent Newton said while she faced towards the screen.

"As you may recall, the vehicle suffered serious fire damage and the three years being submerged in Lost Lake didn't help to preserve any evidence as to the cause of the fire. But what we can conclude from the pattern of the burn is that the SUV was still on fire when it entered the water. This may be the stroke of luck that we are looking for."

"Oh? How is that?" Powell asked.

"It appears the SUV was pushed into the lake, head first, with the water extinguishing the fire in the front of the vehicle, before it could burn everything. As a result, the glove compartment wasn't entirely destroyed, which allowed you to recover the small part of a business card. But more about that in a minute," Wendy said, as she advanced the PowerPoint to the next slide.

Powell recognized the melted objects that were found under the front seat framing.

"Those are the melted rubbery objects. Did you figure out what they are?"

"Yes. We analyzed the rubber, and found that it is natural, as opposed to a synthetic rubber that is produced in a lab. If you look at the next image, you see that under a microscope, we found some fibers embedded in the rubber," she added, while gesturing towards the screen.

"With a bit of effort, we were able to extract some fibers and found them to be both nylon and wool. Using these three elements, natural rubber, nylon, and wool, our conclusion is that these objects were once tennis balls."

Agent Powell raised his hand, with palm facing Agent Newton, as if he intended to push the pause button, while he gathered his thoughts.

"Did you say tennis balls?"

"Yes, and not just any ordinary tennis balls," she answered, excited to have found something of interest.

"There are two main types of tennis balls, the cheaper balls that you find at Costco, which are labeled 'Championship' balls. While they still use a natural rubber core, the cover is made of 100% nylon, and uses a non-woven needle-punch process of attaching the fibers to the cover. It's a less expensive ball, and better players prefer not to use them."

"The premium balls, found in most tennis stores, use a natural rubber core, often with a proprietary blend of added elements, designed to change the feel of the ball when it hits the racquet strings. These balls use a woven felt cover that is made of nylon and wool. The higher the wool content, the better the ball will play," Newton said.

"Wow! I had no idea there were different types of tennis balls. Is there any chance to narrow it down to the exact model of the ball?" Stan asked.

Agent Newton opened the cardboard box that rested on the table and pulled out six cans of tennis balls, lining them up on the table, with the brand and model name facing Agent Powell.

"These six fit the specifications of the tennis balls found in the 4Runner. They are all premium balls that feature a natural rubber core and a woven felt cover made of nylon and wool."

His eyes on the cans of balls, Agent Powell said, "Knowing you and your lab rats, something tells me you have narrowed it down even further."

With a wry smile, Candy replied, "You wouldn't believe the rabbit hole I went down to learn all about this stuff! They know me by my first name over at the Portland Tennis Center," joked Wendy.

She returned her attention to the projected image, then continued. "The can on the left is the Pro Penn model, made by Head/Penn Racquet Sports. It is the only ball made in the USA. Our analysis of the fibers found in the balls from the SUV shows that they don't match up to the American sourced materials. So we can safely rule out the Pro Penn ball," she concluded.

"The next three models are all made in the same plant in the Philippines, using the same materials."

"The Dunlop Grand Prix ball, which is the top model for Dunlop, and considered one of the best playing and longest lasting balls on the market."

Pointing towards the next can, she continued, "As the official ball of the French Open Championships, Dunlop sells a limited number of Roland Garros balls, which come in a four-ball metal can. Same materials as the Grand Prix, but a higher wool content, and a lighter regular duty cover, which are ideal for use on clay courts."

"The next model is another limited production ball, sold under Dunlop's sister brand, Slazenger. It is the official ball of the prestigious Wimbledon Championships. Again, it has a high wool content cover."

As she picked up the fifth candidate, a black plastic can, with White and Gold lettering on the label, Agent Newton said, "This is the U.S. Open ball, made by Wilson Racquet Sports. It is the official ball of the largest professional tournament in the United States, the U.S. Open. And while the Dunlop and Slazenger balls fit all the same specifications, the Wilson ball is almost an identical match to the melted balls that were found in the Toyota."

"So this looks to be your winner?" Stan asked.

"I said almost," Agent Newton replied.

She then picked up the pewter-colored plastic can with a large black label graphic and optic yellow lettering on it.

"This is the Black Label Pro Tour ball. We were able to isolate the fourteen compounds used in the making of the rubber core of the melted tennis balls we found in the Toyota. They are an exact match to the Black Label Pro Tour tennis ball," Agent Newton said while tossing the can of balls to Stan.

Stan removed the lid from the Black Label can and took out one of the optic yellow balls and tossed it in the air, rubbing the soft cover with his thumb as he cradled it in his hand.

With the pieces coming together in his mind, Agent Powell considered the coincidence of finding Black Label tennis balls inside an abandoned vehicle, found close to the skeletal remains in Hood River, where they found Black Label tennis shoes with their unknown victim.

His focus returning to Agent Newton, Stan said, "Please tell me you found something on that piece of burned paper we pulled from the glove compartment."

∽

Wendy pressed the return button on the MacBook Pro's keyboard. An image of the burned business card appeared on the screen.

"Again, we got lucky that the fire didn't entirely consume the glove compartment, which helped to preserve a portion of a business card," Wendy said.

"Using a technique called Infrared Reflected Photography, where we use an infrared light source to pull up the images on the burned card, we could recover some of the print on the card."

Advancing one slide forward, a new image of the burned card appeared. This new image revealed distinct letters and numbers.

Leaning forward in his chair, Stan narrowed his focus and asked, "Those images still look difficult to make out. Can you make them clearer?"

With another press of the return key, an enhanced image of the text appears. The text was now relatively clear.

∽

TS

K

GER

ROW

90292

TS.COM

∽

"That is pretty disappointing," Stan said, hoping that the card would have revealed a person's name. "Is there anything else that could be helpful in identifying our victim?" Stan asked.

"I'm afraid that is all we could pull from the piece of paper. Not a lot to go on, but hopefully the information will prove useful," Wendy replied. "We did find two items in the samples that you collected from the Toyota that may be of interest."

"At this point, anything will be helpful. I feel like I've been treading water on this case for a while. I could use a break," Stan said.

"Funny that you mentioned water. The two items we found were sand and wax. The sand is representative of what you would find at any beach. The wax contained special elements that let us narrow it down to a popular brand of surf wax. The wax found in the Toyota is Mr. Zog's Sex Wax. The wax is used to coat the deck of a surfboard and provide traction between the surfer's feet and the board," Wendy reported.

"Black Label Pro Tour tennis balls, Mr. Zog's Sex Wax, beach sand and a partial business card. That's a pretty good start. I think things are starting to come into focus. Too much is lining up to be a coincidence," Stan said, as he realized that this new information might be the big break he was looking for.

"I just recovered some letters and numbers and became an expert on tennis balls and surf wax," Agent Newton replied. "It's up to you to figure out what the missing information is, but I know that's the sort of thing you like to do."

◈

Over the next two hours, Agent's Powell and Newton combed over the items found in the other vehicles from the salvage yard. While they uncovered some interesting information, nothing linked the vehicles to their victim.

◈

"Once again, you and your team have worked miracles. I've got some work to do, but this points me in the right direction," Stan said, as he gathered his notes and copy of the case binder, then stood to leave.

"Oh, Agent Powell, one more thing. Do you have a dog?" Wendy asked.

Not expecting the question, he responded, "No, would love to, but just too many crazy hours in this job. Why do you ask?"

"Well, we had to test a lot of tennis balls, but still have some left over," Wendy said, as she playfully tossed a ball in his direction.

∽

Back at his desk, Stan checked his voicemail. His ears perked up at the sound of Lt. Zandy Roberts' voice. She was curious about the outcome of the lab meeting and was offering to help. Apparently, she was a bit bored, as Hood River was in its slow season.

Chapter Nineteen

TRAFFIC AROUND LAX was consistently dreadful but during the Thanksgiving holiday, it was a nightmare.

Alan Mercer was crawling towards the terminal seven baggage claim to pick up his good buddy, Tucker Burnett, and his girlfriend Jessie. They would enjoy Thanksgiving together, and the guys would practice for the Men's forty and over National Hard Courts, which started in just a few days at the La Jolla Beach and Tennis Club.

Mercer always enjoyed the company of Tucker and Jessie. They liked to see many of the more touristy areas of Los Angeles that he normally stayed away from. He just knew not to schedule anymore hikes in the Santa Monica mountains, where on a previous visit, they nearly stepped on two rattlesnakes while hiking on the narrow trails in Topanga Canyon.

∽

After a fun few days of holiday festivities and some focused practice sessions, the three made their way down to La Jolla, a city just north of San Diego.

The men's forty and over hard courts were the ultimate challenge on the Senior Tennis Circuit calendar, attracting all the top players from around the country. This late in the season, there was always a lot at stake for those fighting for ranking points. For Mercer and his doubles partner, Joe Hamilton, they sat at number two in the rankings, close behind the team of Hawkins and Jacobs from Texas, who had finished number one the previous two years. With a good result in La Jolla, and then at the year-end Fiesta Bowl in Phoenix, Mercer and Hamilton had a shot at finishing the year at number one.

While his focus was on doubles, Mercer also liked to play singles. He knew that the additional time on court sharpened his game and got him used to the conditions.

In his third-round singles match, Mercer trailed five games to love in the third and final set. His thoughts drifted back to exactly twelve months earlier. When following a bout with the flu, he ran out of gas, and lost his first-round singles match six-love in the third set.

On the change of sides, Mercer was determined to get one game to avoid being bageled in the final set yet again.

Sitting in his chair while he toweled off, his former college teammate T.J. Smith sat down outside the court and offered his support.

"Come on Mercer, you've been in tough spots before. You've got this!"

With a smile, Alan turned to his old buddy and their eyes met. Mercer knew exactly what T.J. was referring to.

Back in college, they used to play highly competitive and stressful challenge matches between other members on the team. The results would set the lineup for the upcoming season. To add to the mental and physical stress, their coach would make these matches the best three out of five sets.

In his sophomore year, Mercer had found himself down

two games to five in the fifth set against Smith. This, after losing a challenge match 7-6 in the fifth set just two days earlier. Somehow, on this day, Mercer was able to find another level, and mount an improbable comeback against Smith by winning the final five games of the match.

Anything was possible, Mercer thought as he strode to the baseline to serve.

Thrilled to get on the scoreboard in the final set, Mercer was finally able to hold serve.

Not budging from his courtside seat, T.J. Smith continued to offer his support, and was there once again to witness another epic Alan Mercer comeback.

Suddenly, Mercer found himself in what tennis players call "The Zone," where everything seemed to work. His opponent was the number ten player in the country, but on this day Mercer was the better player, and found a way to squeak out a thrilling final set tie-break.

With less than twenty-four hours to recover, Mercer was badly outclassed by the number three seed in the quarterfinals. But the excellent result would move his singles ranking into the nation's top fifteen: his highest ever.

In the semifinals of the doubles, after playing some of their best tennis of the year, Mercer and Hamilton faced their old college teammates, T.J. Smith and Rob Gibson. In the other semifinal, the nation's top team of Hawkins and Jacobs from Texas looked to make it through to the finals, and hopefully would face off with Mercer and Hamilton in a match that could determine the number one ranking for the year.

Brimming with confidence, Mercer and Hamilton felt good about their chances in the semis, but the match turned into a fairly routine win for Smith and Gibson. With everything going their way all week, absolutely nothing worked for them in this match. The only good news was that the Texas team also lost, setting up a battle for third place and the bronze ball the following day.

At dinner that evening, Tucker Burnett drew up a game-plan for Mercer and Hamilton, but mostly did his best to lift their spirits after the resounding loss early that day.

"On the points serving to Hawkins on the ad side, go with the I-formation, and put the serve on his backhand. He loves to drive the return cross court, but struggles to hit down the line. Also, mix up your serves on Jacobs, but keep most into the body. You've got this!" Tucker pleaded.

The match for third place was tight all the way through. The team from Texas broke serve to go up five games to four in the final set. With Jacobs serving for the set up 30-love, Mercer and Hamilton found one more streak of magic just when they needed it most.

They rattled off twelve of the final thirteen points to snatch the bronze ball with a 7-5 victory in the third set.

Feeling like they stole something and got away with it, Mercer and Hamilton collected their bronze prize, showered, and headed for a celebratory dinner with Tucker and Jessie.

Before they left the club, they caught the last points of Smith and Gibson, winning the final match to claim the gold ball.

"Still some work to do to get that gold ball," Mercer said to himself.

Chapter Twenty

AGENT POWELL WELCOMED the morning sunshine that was shining through his office window as he read over his notes on the Post Canyon Killer case. Stan savored the last drops of the *Hair Bender* blend he picked up at Stumptown Coffee Roasters on his way to the office. He was waiting for Lt. Zandy Roberts to arrive. They would spend the day together working on the investigation, and hopefully would get closer to confirming the identity of their mysterious John Doe.

Stan looked up as he heard a gentle knock on the open door of his office. Standing there was the always smiling Zandy Roberts, holding a white cardboard box.

"Well hello there, Lieutenant," said Powell, as he rose to welcome her into his office.

"What, no Voodoo?" he inquired, noticing the absence of the signature pink box of Voodoo Doughnut.

"No sir. I wanted to show you my sophisticated side, so I went with Blue Star Donuts," she said, as she opened the box, allowing the sweet scent of fresh donuts to permeate the room.

"Any Blueberry-Bourbon-Basil ones in there?"

"Of course. Those are my favorite too," she said, as she placed the open box on his desk.

"Welcome to the humble home of the Portland office of the FBI. Did you have any trouble getting through security?"

"No, I told them I was D. B. Cooper, and they just waved me through," Zandy said with her signature giggle.

"Great. I was hoping to solve that case one day!" Stan laughed.

The 1971 hijacking frequently made the Portland newspapers, as every nutcase in the Pacific Northwest claimed to know who the infamous Cooper was, and where he and the $200,000 in ransom money landed when he parachuted out of Northwest Orient Airlines flight 305 just north of Portland.

"So, what fun do we have in store for today?" Zandy asked while taking a seat in the chair facing Stan's desk.

"I'd like to review the notes we have so far and start making some phone calls. I figure between the two of us, hopefully we can find out something more about our guy by the end of the day."

"Great. What do we have so far?" Zandy asked.

"Our meeting with Dr. Wooster tells us we are looking for a six foot tall, white male, who is around thirty years old. We know our victim was injected with or ingested TTX, or Pufferfish toxin, approximately four years ago, and buried in a remote location at Post Canyon. We also believe that the Toyota 4Runner that was discovered at the bottom of Lost Lake is most likely his."

Agent Powell then added, "Someone went to a lot of trouble to make sure this guy was never found. Most likely, the killer or killers are still out there."

He slid a piece of paper across the desk. Zandy picked it up and could see the magnified image of the burned business card from the Toyota's glove compartment.

"It looks like we don't have much to go on here," Zandy said.

"What makes you think that this is his business card?"

"Even if the business card was not our victim's, the identity of the card owner could help us figure out who he is," Stan said.

"What have you figured out so far about the information on the card?" Zandy asked, while holding up the sheet of paper.

"The zip code on the card is for a Marina del Rey address, in the Los Angeles area. This makes sense, given the fact that we also found beach sand and surfboard wax in the SUV. I think our search starts by contacting tennis shops in Los Angeles."

Powell then removed two more sheets of paper from a folder and handed one to Lt. Roberts.

"What's this?" Zandy asked.

"I thought we could call some tennis stores in the Los Angeles area to see if we can find someone who had dealings with our guy. These lists have the names and numbers of all the tennis shops in the area," he said, while holding up the list of tennis shops.

"I've split up the list of stores, and have you set up in the office next to mine. Let's make some calls and see what we find."

"Sounds great," Zandy replied, as she grabbed an orange-olive oil donut from the Blue Star box, and headed for the empty office adjacent to Stan's.

∽

For both Stan and Zandy, the first few calls were unsuccessful, as the stores were not open yet, or had simply gone out of business. One store owner who answered the phone had only just taken over the business, and already regretted his decision to do so.

"The damn internet is killing us, and the tennis companies are doing nothing to protect the little guy. Pretty soon, we will all be out of business," the store owner reported.

"Manhattan Beach Sports. How can I help you?" The young man answered, on the other end of the call.

"Hello. This is Special Agent Stan Powell from the FBI. I am looking for someone who might know a tennis sales rep that called on your store around four years ago."

"No shit… FBI? I've only worked here for about a year, but I bet Bodhi would know who you're looking for."

Happy to have made some progress, Powell asked, "Great. Could you put Bodhi on the phone?"

"I think the surf sucked this morning, so he should be in the back of the store. Let me go see if he's here. Hold on for a bit," the man said.

Agent Powell appreciated the choice of music being played while on hold, and sang along to Motley Crue… "don't go away mad, just go away"… a very welcoming tune, Stan thought, as he formed an image in his mind of the Bodhi character. Must be a fan of the Keanu Reeves, Patrick Swayze classic, *Point Break*?

"Yo, this is the Bodhisattva. What can I do you for today?" The man's voice said through the phone.

"Hello Bodhi, this is Special Agent Stan Powell, from the Portland office of the FBI."

"Yah right bro, and I'm Serena Williams," replied the amused Bodhi.

"Okay… Serena? I really am an agent with the FBI field office in Portland, Oregon. I will gladly text over my credentials," Stan said.

"Whoa! So you must know Johnny Utah. He was a Fibie,"

Bodhi said, confirming Powell's suspicion about his fondness for the Reeves and Swayze surf film.

"Bro, is this about that surfboard I bought off the dude in Hermosa? I was totally suspicious that it was stolen!"

"No Bodhi, this isn't about the surfboard. I am hoping you can help me with some information about someone you might know."

"No way, bro. The Bodhi is no snitch!"

"No Bodhi, that's not the type of information I'm looking for. I am trying to track down the identity of a sales rep, that might have called on your store a few years ago. Do you think you can help me with that?"

"Bodhi has needs. What's in it for me? Is there some kind of finder's fee?"

Realizing that besides surfing, Bodhi had spent a lot of hours watching detective movies, Agent Powell replied, "Well, if something pans out from the information you provide, I can swing lunch sometime."

"Right on, bro! What can the Bodhi do for you?"

"I believe you had a tennis sales rep, or someone working for a tennis company, call on your store. It would have been about four or more years ago. The person was a male, age thirty, and stood about six feet tall. Does that sound like someone you know?"

"Dude… that sounds like Sasquatch!" Bodhi replied.

"Squatch was our Black Label Racquet Sports rep. He got canned, or just left, and dropped off the planet. He was a cool dude."

"Do you know his real name?" Powell asked, wondering if everyone in Southern California went by a single word nickname.

"Yeah, dude's name is Chris Peck."

"Why did you call him Sasquatch?" Powell asked as he jotted down the name.

"Dude was from somewhere like Washington, or someplace up north. Lived in the woods. When he came down here, he wanted me to teach him how to surf. I told him that Sasquatch don't surf, if you know what I mean?"

"Did you teach him how to surf?" Stan asked.

"Yeah, he was getting pretty good, too," Bodhi answered.

"This may seem like an odd question, but do you have a preference for the brand of surf wax you use?" Asked Stan.

"Ha. Bodhi only waxes his sticks with Mr. Zog's. That shit is real!" Bodhi replied.

"Do you know why he dropped off the planet?"

"No man, the dude just disappeared. Got a letter from Black Label saying he moved back home. I tried calling him a bunch of times, but the dude just ghosted me. I was pissed!"

"Do you know where he lived?"

"Sasquatch had an apartment in Mariner's Village up in Marina del Rey. No surf up there, so I told him he needed to move down this way."

"So you never heard from him after he left?"

"No man, nothing. Rumors were out there that he was into some illegal shit, but that's the usual crap that Black Label put out there whenever they let a sales rep go."

"So you don't think he was into any illegal activities?"

"Sure, Sasquatch liked to burn a few bowls of chronic, but that's pretty chill. Dude was a solid motherfucker."

"Bodhi, is there anything else you can tell me about Chris Peck?"

"No man, what did he do, rob a bank or something?"

"No, nothing like that. Right now, I am looking for information. I'll be making a trip down your way in a week or so. It would be great to meet in person, if that's ok?"

"Sure, bro. Don't forget, you owe me lunch. There's a killer fish taco shop down the street."

"You got it, Bodhi. Tacos are on me. I'll be in touch soon," Powell said as he hung up the phone.

Looking over the words he had scribbled on his notepad, Stan narrowed his gaze to the name that he had underlined three times… Chris Peck.

Chapter Twenty-One

TWICE EACH YEAR, the entire sales force and management team from Black Label Racquet Sports gathered for their national sales meetings. These meetings signaled the launch of new products that were introduced to the sales team for the first time. The meetings typically lasted about four days and provided an opportunity for the entire team to socialize and bond over the successes and failures they've had since they last assembled.

One sales meeting each year would take place in Chicago near the company headquarters. They would hold the other meeting at a remote location, which allowed everyone from the corporate office to let down their hair a bit more and celebrate with the sales reps. For a sales rep who spent most of their time on the road working alone, gathering with the other reps and inside team was always a highlight of their year.

Alan Mercer was waiting at the baggage claim in the Salt Lake City airport when he saw his counterpart from Phoenix, Dan Sims.

"Hey Danny Boy, how the hell are you?" Mercer greeted his old friend.

"Mercer. Your bastard! I can't believe they invited you

back, especially after the last sales meeting!" Dan said as they embraced in a bear hug.

"Well, I guess they couldn't find anyone else who is dumb enough to take my job," Mercer said.

"I hear you. I certainly wouldn't want your territory out in the wild west. I'll take my territory any day. It's much less cutthroat, and management doesn't bug me too much."

As they did at most sales meetings, Mercer and Dan Sims would be roommates. After some trial-and-error rooming with other reps, the two found they had similar sleep schedules, and neither one was a notorious snorer.

Mercer recalled his first Black Label meeting where he had roomed with the rep from New York. His roommate would roll back to the room, about two or three o'clock each morning, and in a drunken state, would call his buddies back in New York. Mercer could tell that his New York friends were just as annoyed at the calls as he was, as he tried to sleep just a few feet away from the drunken rep.

Having collected their Black Label Sports luggage from the baggage carousel, the pair made their way to ground transportation and the shuttle pickup area.

"Have you ever been to Snowbird before?" Dan asked.

"No, but looking forward to it. I've never skied Utah, but hear the conditions are spectacular."

At this year's meeting, Black Label was providing the team with an additional day on the slopes for some fun in the snow.

❦

Mercer was doing his best to ignore the pounding headache as he walked down to the opening general session of the meeting. Mercer always needed a day or so to acclimate to the higher altitude. The meetings were being held at the Cliff Lodge, with the Snowbird ski resort right out of its back door.

The opening session was always exciting, with a mix of theatrics, technological wizardry, and imagery, as they unveiled the new product line for the first time. Designed to get the reps excited, the launch of the new Element-5 tennis racquet line was perfect, and on par with previous launch presentations.

Mercer still held as his favorite the Astro Carbon launch, which included some impressive smoke and pyrotechnics, along with the product manager dressed in a full astronaut suit. That meeting was also memorable, as all the new hires had to wear a white baseball cap with FNG embroidered on it in large red letters. If someone discovered an FNG's not wearing the hat, he or she had to buy drinks for everyone in the room. The meeting was in hot and sticky Florida, so by the end of the sales meeting, Mercer's hat was a swampy mess.

Along with the product launch, the general session included presentations from the Racquet Sports General Manager, Jack Sharp and the Vice President, Bill Cashman. Sharp gave all the usual sales updates, always imploring the sales team to reach even higher.

Since joining the racquet sports side of Black Label, Bill Cashman had not made any friends. Coming from the Team Sports side of the company, he brought his abrasive personality to the most successful and profitable category in the Black Label Sporting Goods family. He openly disregarded the history of those in the room, who were the reason why the company was the top racquet sports brand.

As per usual, Cashman proceeded to let the air out of any excitement and positivity in the room, as he painted a gloomy picture with his plans for the sales force. In his view, the current tennis reps were all making too much money, and there would be changes coming to correct this serious injustice. A collective groan from the reps could be heard as Cashman continued his threats to their livelihoods.

Knowing that Mercer lived in one of the more expensive territories, Dan Sims leaned over and whispered, "You going to be able to afford to live in LA?"

"I guess I'll just live in my car. I'm in it most of the time anyway," Mercer replied with a wry smile on his face.

After a quick break to stock up on coffee, tea and snacks, the reps split into regional meetings. There was a Regional Sales Manager for each of the three regions, East, Central, and West. Mercer and Sims headed towards the western region breakout session, hoping their manager, Joe Hamilton, could offer some reassurance following the news of the Cashman Plan.

Joe Hamilton anticipated the upcoming storm of questions coming his way, so instead of starting off by discussing the new Element-5 products, he guided each of the west region reps to their assigned seats in the U-shaped set up. At each seat sat a binder with the rep's name on the cover.

"So, I know you all have some questions about the new compensation plan that Bill mentioned," Joe said.

"Yeah, what the fuck?" Cole Bundy shouted.

Bundy was the rep in the San Diego area. He was a hard-charging rep who had made some questionable deals in order to get the sale. Bundy was also one of the most outspoken, with a short fuse and no filter when he spoke. He always exceeded sales forecasts, but the upper management team saw him as a thorn in their side, as he always questioned their decisions.

"Hold on, Cole. If each of you opens up your binders, you will see your new pay structure and bonus program," Hamilton said.

Black Label paid each of the reps entirely on what they earned in commissions and bonuses. Some key products would receive higher commission rates than others, but in general, the rep's income was directly related to how much they sold and how good they were at making bonuses, by hitting company set goals.

The conference room was silent for a few minutes, while the reps studied the new Cashman Plan.

"So basically, that fuckhead lowered my commission rate on the best-selling products, and gave me absolutely no shot to hit my bonuses," Janice Owens said.

Janice serviced the Rocky Mountain territory and was one of Black Label's longest tenured reps.

The other reps nodded in unison and looked to Hamilton for any sign of help.

"Look guys, I know this isn't ideal, but it's what we have. I'm getting pinched too, if that makes you feel any better," Joe said, while he looked towards the ground, afraid to make eye contact with the angry mob assembled in front of him.

"We've got some great new products, which will help all of our numbers," he said, trying to turn the discussion in a positive direction, but Joe knew that he no longer had any say-so in the rep's compensation packages. Cashman had taken on that responsibility.

"I bet Cashman isn't taking a pay cut! I've got kids depending on me. This is not fucking cool," an agitated Cole Bundy said. "I want to talk to that S.O.B. if he isn't too much of a chicken."

"Unfortunately, Bill has already left to go back to Chicago, so he won't be around to take your questions. But Jack Sharp and I will sit down with each of you individually over the next few days to discuss any questions you have," Hamilton said. "Now, let's turn our attention to the new Element-5 products."

⌘

With the rest of the day focused on learning about the new products, it went by quickly. Mercer especially appreciated the time allocated for sharing ideas between the reps. There was a wealth of experience gathered in the room, so he loved the open discussion with his counterparts about how they could overcome various obstacles in the selling process.

At the end of the first day, Joe Hamilton approached Mercer. "I've got most of the other reps scheduled to sit with Jack and me tomorrow. I have you scheduled for seven o'clock the following morning."

"Great. Nothing like starting off the day on a positive note," Mercer replied.

The next day included more meetings, along with an off-site play test session at a nearby indoor tennis club. The response to the new racquets was mostly positive. But lurking in the minds of each rep was how much their already stressed-out accounts could absorb.

It was a never-ending cycle of pushing in new products, while trying to help the retailers move out of older products. The reps were already expecting the kick-back coming from shop owners, who accused companies like Black Label of simply slapping a new paint job on a racquet, giving it a new name, and claiming it had groundbreaking new technology.

⌘

After a long day, Mercer and Dan Sims were tuned into *Sports Center* in their room when they heard a knock on the door.

Mercer jumped off his bed to get the door. Opening the door, he found it was Steve Hudson, the rep in the Pacific Northwest.

"What's up, Steve?"

"Can I come in?" Steve asked. He was visibly upset about something.

"Sure, come on in," said Mercer, as he shot a glance at Dan, who looked puzzled.

"Cole Bundy is gone! They fucking fired him," Steve said.

"Wait... what? We just saw him at dinner," Dan said.

"He had his meeting with Jack Sharp, and it didn't go well. They came into our room and escorted Cole off the property. They said they were going to put him on a plane back to San Diego tonight. He wasn't even allowed to gather up his stuff. Valerie Little came in just now to get his luggage."

"Who the hell are they?" Mercer asked.

"It was Randall Jefferies, Tom Saltz and Valerie Little. They had a hotel security guard with them."

"Oh, crap!" Mercer said, still numb by the thought of his fellow rep being removed from his room. "I've got a seven o'clock meeting with Jack and Joe in the morning. I'm going to try to reach Cole on his cell, and see if I can find out what happened," said Mercer, as he picked up his phone and dialed Cole's number.

After a few moments, Mercer pulled the phone away from his ear.

"It goes straight to voicemail."

Chapter Twenty-Two

A CUP OF Earl Grey tea usually brought some comfort to Alan Mercer, even on his most stressful days. Just the soothing smell of bergamot was enough to bring down his pulse rate. After a sleepless night, he made his way down to the Cliff Lodge kitchen, a good thirty minutes before they opened at six o'clock. He was able to persuade the kitchen staff to serve him some hot water and an assortment of teas. They probably noticed the look of desperation on his face, along with the dark bags that had formed under his eyes.

He tried hard to put the previous evening's events out of mind. Mercer gathered his thoughts for his upcoming meeting with Jack Sharp. He and Jack have always had a contentious relationship. Mercer always felt that Jack was jealous of his friendship with Joe Hamilton. He imagined that in Jack's mind, Mercer posed a threat to his position as the top sales rep, when Jack was still working in the Los Angeles territory. And now Mercer was blowing away all of Jack's old sales records, since moving to LA. But one incident that defined their relationship happened while Mercer was still the rep in Atlanta, and Jack was out west.

To commemorate the 50th anniversary of their famous Jack

Armstrong Autograph tennis racquet, Black Label launched a limited-edition Jack Armstrong model. Instead of being made of wood like the original, the new model was a graphite racquet that was painted to look like wood. Black Label's plan was to only produce two thousand racquets worldwide, with each one being numbered in the series. Because of the limited production, Black Label set a high price tag on the racquet, and everyone thought the racquet would be popular with collectors and tennis geeks.

The sales reps did such a good job of selling in the limited-edition Armstrongs that the Black Label management team elected to produce another two thousand racquets, diminishing the value of those racquets that were already sold. It was a complete nightmare for the reps. The bigger nightmare came when the racquets didn't sell at retail. Customers didn't want to pay extra for a wood paint job. So, the reps had to get creative in order to help their accounts move the Armstrong duds.

To his surprise, Mercer received a call from Jack Sharp, who had an account in Los Angeles that was holding an event with Jack Armstrong as the special guest. Armstrong, who was in his late eighties, lived in the area and remained involved in the local tennis community. Sharp's customer saw the event as an opportunity to make some sales happen by having Armstrong sign the new limited edition racquets, and sell them for $500 each. To help bolster his inventory, he had Sharp gather as many of the racquets as he could from other stores. The stores were happy to get rid of them.

Mercer got with Jimbo Johnson, owner of Big Serve Tennis, who had twenty of the racquets sitting in his Atlanta stores. Jimbo was thrilled to have Mercer gather up the racquets and ship them off to Sharp's customer, who would send a check to cover the cost of the racquets and shipping. The only problem was that the check never arrived, and Jimbo was pissed. When Sharp finally returned Mercer's call to get the payment sent to his customer, Sharp was anything but helpful. He said it wasn't his problem and that he wouldn't ask his customer to send a check. Despite his repeated efforts to solve the issue with Jack, Mercer ultimately had to make things right for Jimbo by covering the $4,000 loss, using his promotional budget.

How many other store owners and reps did Sharp and his customer screw over in the deal? Mercer would never know, but he knew he wasn't the only one. There was no love lost between him and Jack Sharp.

∞

At seven o'clock, Mercer walked into the second-floor conference room at the resort, where he found Joe Hamilton and Jack Sharp sitting at one end of a long table. They waved him over to come join them.

"Good morning, Alan. Sleep well?" Joe asked.

Taking a seat at their end of the table, Mercer replied, "Honestly, not great. We got a knock on our door from Cole's roomie last night. We know about him being fired."

"I figured you would have already heard the news," Jack casually interjected, as if he were sharing the news about someone who was late for their tee time. He continued, "We had uncovered some disturbing information about Cole, and when we confronted him with it last night, he became violent. Therefore, we felt the only recourse was to have him removed immediately."

Looking straight at Jack, Mercer tried to imagine Cole Bundy doing something "disturbing" enough to get him fired, let alone turning violent. While he understood Cole could put together some questionable deals, he always recognized his neighbor to the south as an upstanding family man, without a violent bone in his body.

"What sort of things was Cole doing?" Mercer asked, while anticipating the answer.

"We are not at liberty to answer that question at this time. But this could benefit you, so let's talk about that instead," Jack said, putting an end to the discussion about Cole Bundy.

Sensing his friend's concerns, Joe waded in. "With Cole gone, we would like you to take over some of his accounts in South Orange County. We have yet to decide how we will adjust his old territory, but you would gain a few key customers."

Already stretched to his limit, with the largest territory in the company, Mercer wasn't jumping for joy at the prospect of even more work.

"Okay, just let me know who I need to call on."

"We also need you to hit some bigger numbers this next year. You've been doing a fair job, but should do a lot better," Jack said.

Wondering what Jack meant by doing a "fair" job, Mercer knew that while this hadn't been his best year, he had always been near the top in Sales Index, and continued to grow sales in the territory.

"Yes, I've seen my bonus plan. Pretty aggressive," Mercer replied without emotion.

He didn't want to give Jack the satisfaction of seeing his anger at the new Cashman Plan, which the reps had already renamed as the "Impossible Dream Plan."

Mercer decided against bringing up Cole Bundy again.

He felt it was best if he ended this meeting before he, too, got violent.

"Anything else you need from me, just let me know," Mercer said, as he flashed Joe a sarcastic smile. Not pleased by the lack of support.

Mercer looked at his watch and decided he had a few minutes before the first morning meeting sessions began. Plenty of time to phone Cole to see if he made it home.

Chapter Twenty-Three

LOOKING FORWARD TO the following day of skiing at Snowbird, Mercer and the rest of the western region gathered for dinner at the Aerial Grill, the main restaurant inside the Cliff Lodge. The mood was not the usual boisterous one, but most were doing their best to put Cole Bundy out of their minds and enjoy the traditional gathering on the last evening of the meeting. The western region would have the highest bar tab at this year's meeting, as the wine and cocktails were going down faster than the downhill skiers on the mountain, just outside the restaurant's window.

Mercer enjoyed a Late Harvest Zinfandel from Bella Winery, one of his favorite Sonoma County wineries, when he felt a hand on his knee that was slowly inching upwards to a more sensitive area. With a flash of panic, Mercer looked around the table, but realized that nobody was aware of the situation going on below the dinner table. To his right was Janice Owens, who continued gently massaging Mercer's upper thigh.

Mercer was well aware of Janice's reputation for finding her way into the beds of many of the other reps and some of the management team. While starting to show signs of her age, and the pressures of being a Black Label Racquet Sports rep, Janice was full of energy and was one of the most fit and well put together women on the Wilson team. She didn't need to try too hard to attract a sales rep to jump into the sack. But Mercer was not in the mood and felt that becoming another notch in Janice's bed post would send him down a hole that he might not be able to climb out of. With his self-esteem already at an all-time low, Mercer wanted more than ever to settle into a serious relationship, and stop the bed-hopping routine that had become his life.

Mercer's gaze connected with Dan Sims, who sat directly across the table from him. Rubbing his left ear, Alan had given Dan their private signal. Even with a few glasses of wine in him, Dan recognized that Alan desperately needed help. They have used the signal to get out of uncomfortable situations at past meetings.

"Alan, are you able to help me fix the buckle on my ski boots?" Dan said as he stood up from his seat. "I figure we should do it now, before dinner arrives, and we drink too much wine."

A fairly lame excuse, but Mercer replied, "Sure Dan, let's take care of it now, so we are ready to ski some fresh tracks in the morning."

As he pushed back his chair, Janice's hand quickly recoiled, in time to avoid anyone knowing about the party going on under the table.

※

Later that evening, while smoking cigars with his Inner Circle, Jack Sharp's burner phone vibrated, signaling an incoming message. Putting down his drink, Jack glanced at the phone. It was a message from Walter Chen at Green Dragon.

First shipment of racquets leaving by sea today.

✧

The day on the slopes was a lot of fun, but Mercer just wanted to go home. He was bothered that he had yet to reach Cole Bundy. He knew the tennis industry was small and recognized Cole would have trouble replacing the income he needed to support his family. If he hadn't heard from Cole by the time he got home, Mercer was planning to drive down to San Diego and check in on him.

Chapter Twenty-Four

STAN POWELL WAS back in Hood River, this time for a brief stop to pick up Zandy Roberts on their way to interview Chris Peck's family in Winthrop, Washington. Armed with the information they got from Bodhi at Manhattan Beach Sports, they were able to confirm with the Mariner's Village apartment manager that Chris Peck lived there four years ago, and had skipped out on his lease. Also, with a bit of digging, they could match the dental records from Chris' Los Angeles dentist with those of their John Doe. Stan was pleased that Zandy had convinced her superiors to let her make the trip to Winthrop. She had successfully argued her case that the investigative experience would pay dividends down the road.

They were now 100% certain. The remains found buried at Post Canyon were those of Chris Peck, the former sales rep for Black Label Racquet Sports.

With the "Sasquatch" tip from Bodhi, Powell and Roberts were able to trace Peck's past to the north central Washington town of Winthrop. Much like Hood River was to Portland, Winthrop was an outdoor escape for Seattle residents, well known for its network of groomed cross-country ski and mountain bike trails that stretched throughout the entire Methow Valley.

Chris' mother, father and older brother ran the area's top sports shop, Methow Valley Sports, which focused on snow sports in the winter, then turned into a bicycle shop in the summer, when mountain bikers and gravel cyclists descended upon the area.

Stan had reached out to the parents with information about their missing son, who they figured long ago was dead. The confirmation, though devastating, seemed to provide the family with the catharsis they desperately needed. On the phone, they sounded excited to get an update from Agent Powell and were looking forward to his visit.

※

East of The Dalles, Stan guided his FBI-issued Jeep Grand Cherokee onto Highway 97, which would take them through beautiful central Washington, and would put them back in the Columbia River Gorge as it twisted and turned its way north. Eventually, the road would place them east of the North Cascades National Park and into the glorious Methow Valley.

Stan had his best road trip music prepared for the lengthy drive, with a mix of classic rock, reggae, and some other surprising music genres that he hoped would impress Lt. Roberts. But the upbeat music and his best jokes didn't seem to bring out the usual laughs and cheerful response from Zandy. She didn't seem to be herself.

"So, is it the music or my jokes that have you bummed out?" Stan asked.

It took a moment for the question to register, then Zandy snapped out of her mental fog.

"Oh, I'm sorry for dragging down the mood. The music is awesome. I especially like that you tossed in some Oasis! The jokes could use some work, but the bar was already set pretty low," she answered.

"I've just got some stuff going on at home. Not a big deal, so I promise to be better company."

"Okay, if you want to talk about it, I've been told that I'm a good listener," Stan said, happy to see the smile return to her face, even if it seemed forced.

He hoped maybe she would open up to him on the trip. But for now, he would do his best not to pry.

❦

After a long day on the road, the sun had dropped beneath the surrounding mountains by the time they pulled into the Observatory Inn, a remodeled gem of a hotel that used to be the only room in town situated above the old saloon. While still a small town, Winthrop had experienced some growth in recent years, as it was well known for its world class outdoor sports.

While checking into their rooms, Stan asked the hotel clerk for a good place to eat dinner.

"Oh, it's a perfect evening to go to the Old Schoolhouse Brewery. Just make sure to get a table on the back deck overlooking the river. It's very romantic," the clerk said, as she noticed a red hue come across Zandy's face. The clerk added, "It's just a short walk up Riverside Avenue, on the other side of the street."

"Great. Let's drop our stuff in our rooms and meet back downstairs in five minutes," Stan said.

Still a bit embarrassed by the clerk's comment, she replied, "Make it ten minutes. I want to get out of these work clothes."

❦

Stan thumbed through a cross-country ski brochure in the hotel living room, when his attention turned to Zandy as she descended the hotel's main staircase. Dressed in skin-tight, weathered jeans and a sweater that hugged her small, athletic body, Stan couldn't help but notice how drop-dead gorgeous she was. They both threw on Patagonia down jackets as they exited the hotel for the short walk to the restaurant.

Usually there was more snow on the ground at this time of year, but it had been unseasonably warm, and the streets were mostly clear of snow and ice, which provided them with a nice opportunity to stretch their legs after several hours in the car.

Upon arrival at the Old Schoolhouse Brewery, they were guided to the back deck, where under heat lamps and small lights strung overhead sat a scene out of a travel magazine. Their table was only a few feet from the fast-moving Chewuch River. The hotel clerk was right about it being romantic, thought Zandy, as Stan pulled out a chair for her.

After they looked over the menu for a few minutes, a young waiter with one arm in a cast ambled over to take their order.

"You folks decide on some food and drink?" The waiter asked.

"Yes, I'll have the fish and chips, and a pint of the Hooligan Stout," Zandy answered.

"Excellent! And for you, sir?"

"I'll have the BBQ burger, medium-well, and the garlic fries. To drink, let's try the Ruud Awakening IPA."

"Great guys, I'll get those food orders in, and be right back with your drinks."

"That's a pretty impressive beer order, young lady," Stan remarked.

"What can I say? I'm from an Irish family. We just love our stout."

"You are just full of surprises. I'm looking forward to learning a bit more about the mysterious Zandy Roberts on this trip."

"Oh, am I now under investigation, Agent Powell? I better be careful not to drink too much and reveal too many of my secrets," Zandy laughed.

Stan was happy that he could bring out her smile and laugh again, and wondered why he had never found someone like Zandy. All the good ones turned out to be married, he thought.

Balancing the beers on a tray, the waiter placed it on the table without spilling a drop.

"Here you guys go. The stout for the lady, and the IPA for the gentleman."

"That must be tough to do, with one arm in a cast," Zandy asked. "Did you have a skiing accident?"

"Thanks, I'm getting pretty good at it, but anything over four beers, and it's trouble. I was out on a fat tire bike with some friends and hit a pretty icy section on the trail. Ended up wrapped around a tree."

"Ouch! That sounds awful," Zandy said.

Raising his glass of hazy brew, Stan looked into Zandy's eyes.

"Cheers! Here's to our meeting with the Peck family tomorrow, and to finding out who killed their youngest son. And to a nice evening together, in this beautiful spot."

"Cheers to you as well. I could get used to this kind of business trip. We make a pretty good team, so I'm confident that we will solve this case," Zandy said.

"Speaking of being teammates, I've got to take a trip down

to Los Angeles next week. I could sure use some help. Do you think you could join me?" Stan asked, hoping that Zandy didn't misinterpret the invite, but was curious to see her reaction to it.

Blushing again, she replied, "Now I know why you are still single. Is that how you ask a girl out on a date?"

"Wow, that bad? I guess I don't date a lot, now that you mention it. Most of the women I meet get freaked out when they hear that I'm an FBI agent."

"So, no one has ever passed Agent Powell's interrogation?"

Usually not one to feel comfortable discussing his personal life, it surprised Stan at how easy it was to talk with Zandy.

"I was engaged once, but let's just say that things didn't work out. And that's a story best left for another time."

"Hmmm… look who the mysterious one is now. Okay, you were easy on me earlier by not prying into my home situation, so we can come back to this when you are ready," Zandy said, as she took a drink from her stout, leaving a foam mustache on her upper lip.

"So, what do you think about our little date to Los Angeles?" Stan asked and was now the one with the red tint to his face. He wasn't sure how Zandy felt about him. He just knew that he really liked her. For now, he told himself to give her some room, but that wasn't going to be easy.

"I don't think the department will pay for my trip, but they've been after me for not taking a vacation in a while. I could certainly use some time away from Hood River, so yes, I would love to come with you. See, that wasn't so hard, was it? There's hope for you yet."

Chapter Twenty-Five

AFTER A BREAKFAST of steel cut oatmeal, fresh baked muffins, and spicy chai tea at the Rocking Horse Bakery, Stan and Zandy arrived at Methow Valley Sports. The store was located just off the main road and had a fleet of fat tire bike rentals parked out in front of the store. With the rise of this new winter sport, the locals had designated several miles of trails so that cyclists didn't disrupt the cross-country skiers, who didn't appreciate cyclists ruining their magnificently groomed trails.

Expecting their arrival, a tall, bearded man stepped out of the store. His muscular build was on display by the skin-tight cross country apparel he was wearing.

"Agent Powell? Lt. Roberts? Did I get that right?"

"You sure did," Powell replied.

"I'm Quinn Peck. I'm Chris' big brother," he said, and presented his hand to greet the law enforcement officers. "Mom and Dad are inside the store. We all really appreciate you coming up to Winthrop to meet with us."

Stan knew that this was the moment in the investigation where he began to think of the victim as not just a pile of bones, but as a living person. A brother. A son.

"It's our pleasure to be here. I just wish it were under better circumstances," Stan said.

"Me too. Please come on inside."

Inside the store, they were immediately immersed in a vivid display of the latest cross-country ski gear from brands like Fischer, Salomon, Rossignol, and Madshus.

"Wow, what a great store," Zandy said.

"Thank you. Do you cross-country ski?" Quinn asked.

"Yes, we've got some good tracks on Mount Hood, but nothing like the trail network you have up here."

"I've tried a few times, but I'm pretty bad at it," Stan said.

"Maybe I'll give you some lessons this winter," Zandy said, with a wink towards Stan.

Mary and Norman Peck, Chris' parents, welcomed Stan and Zandy to their store.

"Thank you both for coming. We've waited so long for some answers to what happened to our son. Let's head back to the office, so we won't be disturbed. Can I get either of you something to drink?" Mary asked.

"No, thank you. We've just filled up at your local coffee shop and bakery," Zandy said, while rubbing her belly in delight.

Agent Powell and Lt. Roberts spent the next hour bringing the Pecks up to speed on the status of their investigation, starting with the chance discovery of Chris' remains at Post Canyon.

"Can you tell us the last time you had contact with your son?" Powell asked.

"It was just before he went missing, over four years ago. He called us out of the blue to tell us he was leaving Black Label and would drive home in a few days," Mary said.

"It really surprised us, because we knew how much he

loved his job. We were concerned that there was something terribly wrong in California, and that was the reason he was coming home," Norman added.

"So he gave no reason for the sudden change? According to one of his customers, the letter sent to the tennis stores by Black Label said that he had decided to go back home. No other reason was given, but this customer speculates they let Chris go," Powell said.

"The only thing he said was that something had changed at Black Label. Something he didn't think was right, that he would tell us more when he got home in a few days," Mary said. "That was the last time we spoke with him."

"When we didn't see him or hear anything from him after a couple of days, we called the local Sheriff's office to ask what we should do," Norman said. "They assured us he was probably just upset, and that he would turn up in no time."

"Days led to weeks, then to months, and finally to years, with nothing. The police could not find any trace of him. Chris had just simply disappeared," Mary says, wiping a tear from her cheek. "With the help of his cell phone provider, we found that the last signal from his phone had pinged a cell tower near Leavenworth, which is in central Washington."

"Do you have any idea how he would have ended up in Hood River?" Zandy asked. "Was he familiar with the area, or know anyone who lived there?"

"We don't think he knew anyone there. When driving back from Los Angeles, as you know, once you reach Portland, you have a choice whether to continue north towards Seattle, or take the road less traveled, by driving through the gorge. Knowing Chris, he would always take the road less traveled," Mary said.

"So the fact that his cell phone was recorded near Leavenworth means he would have driven through Hood River."

Quinn, who had been quiet, removed his glasses, rubbed his temples, then looked towards the two visitors. "I called the Hood River police shortly after Chris disappeared, then drove the route he would have taken, just to see if I could find any signs of my brother," Quinn said. "Have you contacted Black Label yet? As much as we tried, they were absolutely no help. They told us that Chris had suddenly left the company, with no reason given. I think that's a load of bullshit! Something was wrong, and they were putting up a wall to hide it from us. Chris wouldn't just up and quit unless there was something bad going on. There is something not right about this. I don't believe Chris just wandered off and got killed by some random stranger. I know in my heart that he was killed for a reason."

"We have yet to get much information from Black Label. I spoke with the head of Human Resources, but didn't mention that we were working on a murder investigation. They only provided me with some basic facts about Chris' start and end dates with Black Label. I plan on paying them a visit soon," Powell said.

"You need to talk to that asshole, Jack Sharp. He's the General Manager. The prick would barely give us the time of day when we were trying to find Chris. It was like he had already forgotten about Chris and just wanted us to go away!" Quinn said.

"Look, I don't normally like to share these kind of details, but feel you needed some answers. Because of the rare toxin we found in Chris' remains, we tend to agree with you that this wasn't just a random killing. We too think that your brother's death was planned," Powell said. "Now that we have spoken to you, we feel we are just at the starting point with our investigation. I will use all the FBI's considerable resources to find out who killed Chris."

∽

They spent the rest of the morning getting more background information on Chris and shared more details on the investigation.

After thanking the Pecks again with a promise to keep them informed, Stan and Zandy left Methow Valley Sports for the long drive home just as the weather shifted, the sky darkened and a heavy snow began to fall.

Chapter Twenty-Six

MERCER RUSHED THROUGH terminal one at LAX, trying desperately not to miss his flight to Phoenix. He was on his way to the Fiesta Bowl, the year's final major tournament on the senior tennis calendar.

Mercer arrived at most tournaments a day or two before his first match, so that he had time to get used to the playing conditions. But this time he was only playing doubles, and had had a hectic schedule leading up to the tournament, so he made the short flight to Phoenix on the morning of their first round match that afternoon.

He would meet Joe Hamilton and Dan Sims at Sky Harbor airport. The two had been working together the past few days, presenting the new Element-5 products to the tennis retailers in the area. Sims would take them straight to the tournament site, so they could get a light warm-up before their match.

Mercer and Hamilton were currently ranked number two in the nation, and would need to win the tournament to secure enough points to overtake the top-ranked team of Hawkins and Jacobs, the top-seeded team in Phoenix, who hoped to hang onto the number one ranking for the third straight year.

As he settled into his window seat, Mercer took a few deep

breaths and closed his eyes. He hoped to calm his nerves after a frenzied dash through the airport. His thoughts drifted back to the days following the sales meeting in Snowbird. He had flown home and called Cole Bundy's wife Trish. She was thrilled her to hear from Mercer, and also extremely worried about her husband.

Bundy had made it home to San Diego after he was terminated and ushered out of the hotel, taking a taxi home from the airport in the early dawn hours. He had talked little to his wife about the events in Snowbird, choosing to shut himself in his office for most of the day. She wasn't sure that Cole wanted any visitors, but welcomed the idea of Mercer driving down to their house.

When Mercer arrived at the Bundy home in San Diego, Trish gave him a big hug and directed him to Cole's office. Entering his office, Alan didn't like what he saw or smelled. Clearly, Cole hadn't shaved or bathed in a few days. His hair was a greasy nest of tangled strands. Mercer's friend's life seemed to have unraveled, and he was despondent. While he perked up a bit when Mercer arrived, he became agitated when he recalled the events of the previous week in Utah.

Bundy had confronted Jack Sharp during their sit down at the sales meeting, upset about the new Cashman Plan. But that wasn't what caused things to get heated. Bundy quizzed Jack about his recent trip to visit some of Bundy's customers without his knowledge. He accused Jack of going behind his back and working his own deals.

Company policy indicated that members of the management team wouldn't visit a tennis store without the local sales rep present. But according to an employee at one of the San Diego retailers, Jack Sharp had indeed met with the owner of one of his largest accounts.

In their meeting at Snowbird, Jack had denied the allegations and told Cole that he should just drop it. Cole was already fired up, and now the GM was lying to his face. He couldn't just let it go, and continued to press Jack with questions about the purpose of his meeting. Finally, Jack had had enough. He fired Cole on the spot and told him to leave on the earliest flight in the morning. Jack later changed his mind when he ordered his goon squad to remove him from his hotel room.

Mercer had additional questions for Cole about Jack's secret meeting in San Diego. Why was Jack in California? Did he visit any stores in his territory too? Whatever the answer was, Cole was determined to find out why Jack had lied about being in San Diego. He would not let this go.

Mercer assured Cole that he would come visit again soon, and that he was there to help whenever he needed it.

~

The captain's voice, announcing their descent into Phoenix, crackled over the plane's speaker system, pulling Mercer out of an uneven sleep. With the top ranking on the line this week, he reminded himself to focus on what was in front of him, and to enjoy the week in Phoenix. Being around the other players would be a pleasant distraction from the ongoing pressures at Black Label Racquet Sports.

~

The first-round match was a struggle for Mercer and Hamilton. They barely made it on time and had difficulty adapting to the playing conditions in the desert. The ball flew a lot faster in the lighter, drier air. These fast conditions suited their games well, but adjusting from the heavier Southern California conditions took a handful of lost games. To make matters worse, they were both playing with the new Element-5 racquets. The new models were very similar to their old racquets, but it still took a while to adjust to the new equipment. So, while they played poorly, they were happy to find a way to win their opening match.

From there, they improved each match, including a convincing win in the semifinals over their old buddy Tucker Burnett and his partner. As good as Tucker had been with helping Mercer and Hamilton find the right strategies against other teams, he could not solve the problems they presented on the court.

With the final scheduled for the next day, Mercer and Hamilton joined Tucker, Dan Sims and his wife for dinner and drinks at The Old Town Tortilla Factory in Scottsdale. At one time during the evening, the conversation shifted to Cole Bundy. Up to this point, Joe had offered little information about the meeting in which Sharp fired Cole.

"I tried to calm Cole down, and also convince Jack that he was making a mistake by firing him," Hamilton began. "But the truth is, Jack never liked Cole, and was just looking for an excuse to get rid of him."

"Who does Jack like?" Sims asked. "Seems like he thinks all the reps are bad."

"Honestly, I think he only likes the younger, inexperienced reps who don't rock the boat, and he feels he can control. Oh, and it helps if you are a pretty female," Hamilton answered.

"Sounds like the plans at Black Label are to replace all of us old-timers with younger, inexperienced reps who they can pay a lot less," Mercer said.

In the Fiesta Bowl final, Mercer and Hamilton would once again face off against their rivals from Texas, Hawkins and Jacobs. The winner of this match would end the year ranked number one. The tournament director had done an excellent job of promoting this fact, producing a large crowd that gathered at the center court to witness the important battle.

The excellent play from their semifinal match carried over to the final, as Mercer and Hamilton blitzed through the first set. But in the second, they were down a break of serve late into the set. The weight of the top ranking magnified each missed shot, and the pressure continued to escalate. The team from Texas recognized this and soon found their groove.

After fighting back to level the second set at five games all, Mercer and Hamilton dropped serve to see the Texas duo serving again for the second set at 6-5. The play from both teams had been exceptional, and those gathered around the court eagerly anticipated a third set.

On the change of ends, Mercer spent the break focusing on his breathing; he worked to clear his mind of all outside pressures. He had recently started taking yoga classes and found the practice helped him stay focused and centered on the tennis court.

From that point on, Mercer was a man possessed. He moved effortlessly about the court, unencumbered by the gravity of the situation. Winning shots began flowing off his Element-5 racquet.

They broke serve to get into a second set tie-break. Mercer ended the match a few points later with a perfectly placed topspin lob on match point.

Game, set, match, and year-end number one ranking, for Mercer and Hamilton!

※

Mercer was relaxing at his gate that evening, standing by for his flight home to Los Angeles. He reflected back on the crazy year. He was extremely proud of his efforts on the court and felt like he would have a great sales year at Black Label Racquet Sports. But there was the uncertain feeling that his days at Black Label were numbered. As one of the more seasoned and highest paid sales reps, his time might be running out.

Chapter Twenty-Seven

A LIGHT SNOW fell as Dustin McCabe maneuvered his Sprinter van through the maze of warehouse buildings that made up The Freeport Center in the town of Clearfield, Utah. Located twenty miles north of Salt Lake City, The Freeport Center was a major shipping hub for over seventy large companies.

Though it was a beehive of activity during the day, the roads were now empty, as McCabe backed his van up to the dimly lit warehouse door around two o'clock in the morning. The sign next to the large roll-up door read Trojan Horse Logistics. With temperatures in the mid-teens, McCabe moved quickly as he entered the side door to the leased distribution facility.

Inside, McCabe turned on the overhead lights, illuminating rows of orange metal storage racks that stretched to the ceiling. Almost all were completely filled with brown cardboard boxes. Each box had information printed on the outside, showing the product model name, the size and quantity, along with the manufacturer's name. Also stamped on each box, "Made In Taiwan."

Over the next hour, McCabe pulled down several boxes, each time checking off the list that was attached to his clipboard. Once he had checked off the last item, he unlocked the roll-up door and pressed the UP button on the metal box just to the side of the door.

The door lurched upward, and the freezing air blasted into the warehouse. Carefully lowering himself to the ground as not to slip on the icy asphalt, McCabe opened the back doors of the Sprinter, and began transferring flattened cardboard boxes onto the loading dock floor. After he transferred the last of the boxes, he closed the van, and climbed back into the warehouse, then pushed the DOWN button, and the door began to close.

McCabe grabbed a tape gun off the shipping station table and began reassembling the flattened boxes. He paid close attention not to get them mixed in with the other boxes he had just pulled down from the storage racks. Checking his watch, he still had time to transfer the contents of the sealed boxes into the newly assembled boxes and deliver them on time.

Opening the first box, he rubbed his hand across the Green Dragon logo that was printed on the box and pulled out a stack of Black Label Element-5 tennis racquets. McCabe carefully placed the racquets into one of the awaiting boxes. He repeated this process until all the racquets had been transferred. He then broke down the empty Green Dragon boxes and deposited them into the large recycling bin.

Double checking the filled boxes while he sealed them, McCabe made note that the racquets were in their appropriate boxes, as he checked the Element-5 model name against his checklist. Now in boxes marked with Topstone Manufacturing on the outside, McCabe placed the sealed boxes onto the loading dock to move them into his van.

After loading the van and closing up the warehouse, McCabe drove through the icy darkness to the Black Label

Sporting Goods distribution center, located a short distance away.

He checked his watch again, noticing that his timing was perfect. Black Label, in an attempt to reduce costs, had just replaced their twenty-four-hour security team with a new group that rotated between Black Label and a few other nearby companies. This new system meant there were times when the Black Label distribution center was without manned security. The security schedule changed each week, so that would-be thieves were unable to track the security guards' schedule. The security company sent the schedule to Black Label's Vice President, Bill Cashman, each Friday. He only shared it with his Director of Operations in Clearfield, Dustin McCabe.

※

McCabe put the last of the boxes away, into the Black Label storage racks, and made sure he had mixed the newly transferred boxes in with the others holding the same Element-5 racquet models. He looked one more time at his watch, and smiled when he realized now he made these transfers much faster than when he first started, less than two years ago.

Thinking back to those early days, he knew how good his luck had been. He was now making more money than he ever imagined and felt secure in his job. It had been a couple of tough years, after being fired from his last job on charges of sexual misconduct. But then his old fraternity brother from USC called with an amazing opportunity.

After locking up, McCabe jumped back into his van and pulled out his phone. As he typically did after each transfer was completed, he sent a quick text to his old frat brother to let him know that all went according to plan.

Scrolling through the address book on his phone, McCabe found the name he was looking for and pressed his finger on the name Jack Sharp.

Chapter Twenty-Eight

ZANDY ROBERTS WAS a fearless mountain climber and outdoor adventure seeker, but that calm demeanor evaporated the minute she stepped foot onto an airplane. In the short two-hour flight from Portland to Los Angeles, she had been on the edge of her seat, and had clutched Stan Powell's forearm at any sign of turbulence. Stan was a bit amused at the sight of his travel companion's discomfort, but was also glad to be there to lend some support.

Zandy could finally relax when the Alaska Airlines Boeing 737 touched down at LAX.

"Sorry about your arm. I hope I didn't leave any marks," Zandy said with a sheepish grin on her face.

"No worries. I think I'll only need to be in a cast for a few weeks," Stan said with a big smile, showing off his perfect teeth.

"Ha ha, you are so funny," Zandy said, and punched Stan on the shoulder.

"Wow! Who knew flying could be so painful?" he said.

The pair would be in the Los Angeles area for only a couple of days, but were hoping to move further along in their case to find out who might have wanted to kill Chris Peck. They had a meeting scheduled with the manager of Mariner's Village that morning, and would then drive to Manhattan Beach to meet with Bodhi. They also planned on meeting with a few more of Chris Peck's customers before returning to Portland.

∽

Mariner's Village was located in Marina del Rey, just north of LAX. They made the short drive in their rental car, passing through the Ballona Wetlands on their trip up Highway One, before turning into Marina del Rey, Southern California's largest marina.

At the very end of the marina, alongside the main channel that led boats in and out of the Pacific Ocean, Mariner's Village was just a short walk to Venice Beach. The sprawling property was a lush, tropical jungle with a full host of amenities, to serve the needs of their residents.

After parking the rental car, Stan and Zandy made their way to the leasing office, where they were greeted by the cheerful receptionist, who quickly led them back to the Property Manager's office.

They spent the initial part of their meeting briefing Jenna Levelle on the status of the investigation. Miss Levelle was a sharply dressed woman in her forties, and based upon her sharp tan lines and muscular legs, Powell imagined her leading a peloton of cyclists on a fast group ride or demolishing the field at a local criterium race.

She offered them some herbal tea, and they happily accepted.

"That is the most horrible story. Poor Mr. Peck!" Jenna said after Stan and Zandy completed their briefing.

"I had no idea. I was so mad at him for skipping out on his lease, but now I feel just awful. Poor man."

"So you said Chris skipped out on his lease? Did he leave any belongings behind?" Zandy asked.

"No. It was the strangest thing. We received a call from his next-door neighbor, who was annoyed that some movers were in Mr. Peck's unit, making noise early one morning. We went to check into it and found four rather burly gentlemen removing Mr. Peck's furniture and other belongings. When I confronted one of them, he told me that Mr. Peck had suddenly moved back home, and hired them to move his stuff."

"Did they tell you where they were moving his things to, or did you notice the name of the moving company?" Stan asked.

"They did not say where the forwarding address was. I told them that Mr. Peck still had two more months remaining on his lease, and that he owed us $4,800. One guy reached for his jacket and pulled out a stack of $100 bills. He counted out $5,000 and handed it to me. I was dumbfounded!" Jenna said.

"So, do you even know if they were actual movers?" Zandy asked.

"When I asked for identification, one man handed me a business card. I remember thinking it was an awful name for a moving company. It was… let me think… oh, yes, it was Four Horsemen Moving Company. Pretty apocalyptic if you ask me," Jenna said.

"Do you still have the card?" Stan asked.

"No, but I will save you the trouble of looking them up. After they left, I realized I needed to send them a receipt for the two months lease payment. But when I called the number on the business card, it reached an out of service number. The address on the card was to a vacant parking lot in Inglewood."

They finished up their meeting with Jenna and got a quick tour of Chris' old apartment. The current tenants had given their approval for them to enter, so no warrant was needed. The unit was a nice one-bedroom with a loft and a massive storage space. Stan could see how this space would work for a sales rep, with the extra space to store samples, demo racquets, and other items.

After a tour of the property, Stan thanked Jenna for her time then excused them, as they had another meeting in Manhattan Beach.

On their way back to their rental car, Stan got an excited look on his face and began rubbing his hands together.

"Are you ready for some fish tacos?" he laughed.

∽

As they pulled into the parking lot of Manhattan Beach Sports, their rental car smelled like the inside of a taco truck. Bodhi had given them specific instructions that they were to stop at *Fishbar*, in the El Porto part of town. There they loaded up on a mix of Baja style and blackened Cajun fish tacos. It took every ounce of their willpower to not dive into the bags of tacos.

Entering the store, the woman behind the front counter directed them to the back of the store to the tennis section. There, they entered a tennis player's dream, as a full wall of racquets sat surrounded by rack upon rack of tennis apparel and accessories. Behind the tennis counter sat two Wilson Baiardo stringing machines.

With his back to them, a tan, long-haired man in flip-flops and board shorts was holding court with a woman and what appeared to be her teenage son.

"So bro, do you want to hit some gnarly spin like Rafa, or are you more of an all-court maestro like Fed?"

"Uh… I guess I'm more of a Rafa Nadal guy," the teenager replied.

"Hell yeah! Rafa's the GOAT! Let's hook you up with the Babolat Aero Drive, and string it up with some RPM Blast. You're going to be rippin' the cover off the ball!" The man said. "And Mom, he's gotta have at least two sticks if he's going to be playing tournaments."

The woman nodded, and the man grabbed a couple of bright yellow Babolat racquets off the wall, and made sure he got the correct grip size for the teenager.

Once the mother and son had left the tennis area, Stan said, "That was impressive. I was ready to buy a couple of racquets! You must be Bodhi?"

"Stan the man! How the hell are you?" Bodhi said, as he approached Stan, and gave him a bear hug, to his surprise. "Woah, and who is this goddess?"

"Hello Bodhi, I'm Lt. Zandy Roberts. It's nice to meet you," she barely finished, when she too was embraced in a warm hug from Bodhi.

Apparently Bodhi didn't shake hands, thought Stan.

Unable to keep his eyes off of Zandy, Bodhi asked, "Do you surf?"

"No, I'm more of a climber and snow sports kinda girl."

"You would be a real shredder. I'd have you up on the board your first time out," Bodhi said while he admired Zandy's athletic figure.

"Okay, maybe on our next trip down we can give it a try," Zandy said.

"Stan, those tacos smell outrageous. Let's go to the office in back and chow down. The surf was going off this morning, and we smoked a few bowls after, so I'm super famished!"

"Sure thing, Bodhi," Stan said with a laugh, amused that

Bodhi wasn't bothered by bragging about smoking pot in front of two law enforcement officers.

While they were enjoying the tasty fish tacos, they brought Bodhi up to speed on the investigation.

"Bro, that's fucked up! Why would somebody kill Sasquatch? He was super chill, and wouldn't hurt a flea," Bodhi said.

"That's what we are trying to figure out," Zandy said. "Do you know if Chris had any problems with money or drugs?"

"Nah, he was rollin' big time, making some good coin with Black Label, and never touched anything stronger than weed. Those pricks at Black Label got their usual rumor machine going big time, saying Sasquatch had some drug problems, and bullshit like that. Total crap!"

"Has that happened before?" Stan asked.

"Yeah, they burn through reps out here every couple of years. Sasquatch only lasted about a year. Every time, they spread wild nonsense about the rep, after they fire them. The only time they didn't was when Jack Sharp moved to headquarters. Never trusted that dick. Can't believe he's running the company now."

Remembering what Quinn Peck had reported about Jack Sharp, they both jotted down his name in their notebooks.

"So, who is your Black Label rep now?" Zandy asked.

"Dude's name is Alan Mercer. Super cool cat. A monster on the tennis court. His nickname is "Federer of the Forties." He totally kicks ass on the senior tennis circuit. He took over when Sasquatch left, so he's probably due for the Black Label axe pretty soon."

"Do you think you could give us Alan's phone number?" Stan asked. "We'd like to meet with him while we are in town."

"Sure, anything to help. Alan was just in the store yesterday. Usually comes by a couple of times a month."

Bodhi got Stan the contact information for Alan Mercer, and they talked a bit more about Bodhi's surfing lessons with Chris Peck, but then it was time to move onto their next appointment.

"Bodhi, you've been a great help. I will be in touch if I have more questions, and will let you know when we have more information to share," Stan said.

"Stan the man, you can call on Bodhi anytime. I'm ready to get into some Special Ops shit. Go undercover, whatever you need." Then Bodhi gave Stan another big hug.

Turning to Zandy, he grabbed on tight for a much longer hug.

"You two lovebirds come back down here, and let Bodhi teach you how to surf. You will be hooked."

"You got it Bodhi," Zandy said, as they turned and headed for the door.

Chapter Twenty-Nine

MERCER'S PHONE RANG constantly, all day, every day, but this was the first time anyone from the FBI has ever called him. Agent Stan Powell was in town from Portland and wanted to meet with him. Bodhi had given him his phone number. With his schedule for the following day keeping him in the Long Beach area, Mercer had agreed to an early breakfast meeting at Chuck's Coffee Shop.

~

It was a magnificent late winter morning, so Mercer grabbed an outside table at Chuck's. Chuck's Coffee Shop was a Long Beach landmark, located in the Belmont Shore part of town, just a few steps from the Pacific Ocean. Their signature breakfast dish, the Weasel, was two scrambled eggs with homemade chili on top.

Alan recognized Agent Powell and Lt. Roberts instantly as they stood out in their business attire among the other more casually dressed diners.

"Agent Powell?" Mercer asked.

"Yes. Very pleased to meet you, Alan. This is Lt. Zandy

Roberts. Thanks for picking a great spot for breakfast. Dining outside this time of year is a real treat for us Oregonians."

"You both are in for a fantastic breakfast. Ever have a Weasel before?" Mercer asked.

"No, but I'm afraid to ask what that is," said Zandy.

"Well then, I guess it will be a surprise," Alan replied.

They ordered three Weasels, then started into their coffee and tea, and settled into a comfortable spot under the warm Southern California sunshine.

"Thank you for meeting with us on such short notice," Stan said. "Bodhi said you might be able to help us."

"So, you met the one and only Bodhi?" Mercer asked.

"Yes, we sure did. Does he hug you when you go to see him?" Zandy asked.

"Every time," Mercer laughed. "Tell me how I can help. You mentioned it had something to do with Chris Peck?"

Stan and Zandy recounted to Mercer about the discovery of Chris' skeletal remains in Hood River, and brought him up to speed on where their case currently stood.

Absorbing the shocking news, Mercer rubbed his forehead and lowered his head.

"Oh, my god. That is awful. I guess that must be why I've never heard from him," said Mercer, his voice trailing off.

"Do you usually stay in contact with former sales reps?" Zandy asked.

"No, only a few. The current management at Black Label does a good job of torching the reputations of their former reps, so they just seem to fade away. I guess they don't want them ending up working for a competitor?"

"Did you know Chris Peck very well?" Stan asked.

"Yes, we hung out a fair amount at sales meetings. I was

the Black Label Racquet Sports rep in Atlanta when he was out here in California. Chris was a pretty talented tennis player, so we often ended up on the same court when testing the new racquets at sales meetings."

"When was the last time you spoke with Chris?" Zandy asked.

"Probably at the sales meeting before he left. I think it was in Chicago. He seemed to be doing okay. His numbers were always pretty good, so it was a big surprise to me when he left. But I know that this territory can eat you up, especially if you are from a small town in Washington."

"So, you never spoke with him after you found out he was leaving?" Stan asked.

"No, I didn't. I tried calling him several times, but he had already left Los Angeles by the time I heard about it."

"You ended up taking over this territory. What did Black Label management tell you about the reason behind Chris' departure?" Zandy asked.

"I received calls from our National Sales Manager and from Joe Hamilton, the Regional Manager out here. They both wanted me to move from my territory in Atlanta to take over this one. I have roots in California and have known Joe Hamilton for a long time, so it was a good fit. They didn't say much about Chris, so I sort of figured he just got homesick. The rumors were that he got into some drugs and money problems, but I try not to pay attention to the rumors."

"Did any of the tennis shops say anything about Chris when you first moved out?" Stan asked.

"To tell the truth, I stepped into a bit of a nightmare when I came out. I had left all of my sales samples and demo racquets for my replacement in Atlanta. I was told that Chris had done the same for me. Black Label rents a storage unit to store some equipment for a professional tournament we sponsor. Chris' samples and demos were supposed to be waiting for me in the storage unit. But there was absolutely nothing, just the tournament equipment. So I had to request new samples and demos, in order to do my job," Mercer said.

"But then, phone call after phone call started coming in from pissed off tennis retailers. They all had the same complaint; they had received large shipments of Black Label products that they never ordered. Between the missing samples and the mysterious orders, I figured Chris had sold his samples and placed the bogus orders to get one last big commission check before leaving town. I was told by Black Label management to have the stores keep the shipments and to use my promotional budget to help the complaining stores net down their costs with free goods. So it was a double whammy for me. No commission on those big orders, and I burned through a lot of my promo budget. It took a while to get past it."

"Do you know if Chris had any problems with the Black Label management team?" Zandy asked.

"The regional manager here is great. Joe is very supportive of his reps and knows how to put together deals to help grow sales. His pay and bonuses depend on how well we all do, so he is super motivated," Mercer said.

"How about from the home office?" Stan asked.

"The customer service team is amazing. We couldn't do our jobs without them. The product and promotions teams are also great to work with. But a shift in upper management took place about five years ago, which isolated the upper management team from the sales force. We all got the feeling that we were expendable, and slowly being cut out of the picture."

"How so?" Zandy asked.

"The new management team has removed certain perks and incentives, and continually makes it more difficult to earn a living doing our jobs. But it is more than just that. For example, we recently had our sales meeting at the US Open in New York. Each rep could invite a few of our key customers to attend and enjoy the tournament. There was a big party scheduled a few days before the tournament started. It was in a cool two-story warehouse in the meat-packing district. All of our sponsored players were there. We're talking about some of the biggest names in our sport. The sales reps were super stoked to get to mingle with our heroes. But that never happened. Our GM, Jack Sharp, kept the reps on the ground floor while the pros and retailers partied upstairs. It was a real gut-punch for the reps. It really showed us where we stood."

"Yes, we've heard a few stories about Jack Sharp. Seems like a man with an agenda," Stan said.

"For someone who used to be a sales rep, he sure doesn't like us very much. He's like the kid in a game of marbles who wants to take all the marbles and go home," Mercer said.

"That doesn't sound like ideal leadership qualities. Why do you stay at Black Label?" Zandy asked. "Do you think this is why Chris Peck left?"

"I ask myself that question often, but I love my job. I enjoy helping our customers. I love having a hand in growing the game of tennis. At the end of the day, the current tenants in their ivory tower will have their day of reckoning. Black Label Sporting Goods has such a great history as a company. One day good leadership will return. I may not be around to see that day, but in the meantime, I will always make sure my customers get the best possible service. I really wish I had paid more attention to the situation with Chris. Did I miss something?"

The waiter stopped by to clear the table of three empty plates.

"What did you guys think of your first Weasel?" Mercer asked.

"Not something I would eat every day, but it was delicious," answered Zandy.

"Alan, I know you have a busy day, so we won't keep you any longer. We really appreciate your help, and will be in touch again soon. You have my card if you think of anything else," Stan said.

"It was nice meeting you both, and thank you for picking up breakfast. I hope you can find out who did this to Chris. Enjoy your time here in California, and safe travels home."

"We have a few more stores to visit today, as we try to piece together Chris' life in Los Angeles and what his last days were like," Stan said.

Back at his SUV, Mercer took a few minutes to reflect on his breakfast meeting. *Chris Peck murdered? Why would someone want him dead?* he thought. *Was this somehow connected to his position at Black Label?*

Chapter Thirty

MERCER SPENT THE day visiting a handful of tennis retail stores, getting an initial read on the sales of the new Element-5 racquets. So far all signs were positive, and he could confirm some of his backup orders. Quantities were even bumped up on some orders.

As was typical with a new racquet launch, Mercer and the store buyer, who was usually the owner, would put together an initial shipment of the new racquets. At the same time, Mercer would enter one or more backup orders with future ship dates. It made for a bit more work on Mercer's part, but it helped Black Label with planning production, and also put Mercer's clients in line for racquets coming in from Taiwan or China. If an account didn't place backup orders, it would risk losing out if a particular racquet became a hot seller. When that happened, the store owner would call Mercer to see if he could hunt down the racquet from another store.

As the store owners gained confidence that Mercer was going to take care of them, if they became stuck with slow selling products, they would often let him write the orders and just send the orders to the store owner for approval. He was constantly working with his customer service rep to adjust future orders. They made a good team, and were able to keep the product flowing and the customers happy.

※

Throughout the day, Mercer just couldn't shake the image of Chris Peck and the thought of him being murdered. Why? Who?

On his drive home, he pressed the speed dial button for Joe Hamilton.

"Hey, what's going on?" Hamilton said over the Bluetooth speaker.

"I got out to see most of the Long Beach and South Bay accounts today. All seem to be starting off well with Element-5. I'll be adding some racquets to my backup orders. So things are looking good on that front."

"That's great! Your sales index is up over 130%, so it looks like another good year. Let's keep it going," Hamilton said.

"Hopefully those numbers are good enough for Jack Sharp," Mercer replied.

"That is the top index in the company, so I would think so," Hamilton said. "But I've seen the number one guy get axed before, so I guess nobody is ever safe."

"Thanks. I feel much better," Mercer laughed.

"Oh, before I forget, Patty wants to invite you down for a little barbecue and get together with some friends. Apparently, she wants you to meet someone. But don't blame me, I've never met her," Hamilton said.

Joe's wife Patty, along with their teenage daughter Samantha, had always been on the lookout for the perfect woman for Mercer.

"I don't know. I haven't had much luck with blind dates.

I know Patty and Sam are looking out for me, but I'm not so sure about this," Mercer said.

"You know my wife isn't going to take no for an answer. So I'll tell you what, I will get us a good practice match that day so the trip down won't be a total loss."

"Let me think about it, and get back to you," Mercer said, thinking maybe he should leave the matchmaking up to Hamilton's wife and daughter. He certainly hadn't been doing a very good job of it on his own.

"So, now that we have that out of the way, the big news of the day is that I had a breakfast meeting with the FBI this morning," Mercer said. "Chris Peck is dead, and they think he was murdered!"

"What? When did it happen?" Joe asked.

"They think it was during his trip home to Washington, after he left Black Label over four years ago," Mercer responded.

"Do they know who did it?"

"No. That's what they are doing down here. They got my number from Bodhi. I guess they are trying to piece together his life in Los Angeles, to see if that will help them find some answers. But it seems like a bit of a long shot, if you ask me."

"So, do they have any theories on who might be involved?" Hamilton asked.

"No, at least nothing they shared with me. It's not like they deputized me."

"But they didn't give you any indication of why they came all the way down from Oregon? That's a long trip just to poke around. They must have some evidence," Hamilton asked.

"Joe, I think you've been watching too many true crime shows on TV." Mercer chuckled.

The phone was silent for a while, as Hamilton pondered the news that Mercer had just delivered.

"What did you tell the FBI?" Hamilton asked.

"Just that I didn't believe the rumors about the drugs and money problems. Also, I told them about the bullshit that went down when Chris left the territory and I took over. But mostly, I told them it did not surprise me he left Los Angeles, and that he was a good guy."

"Did they say what they were going to do next?" Hamilton asked.

"Other than Bodhi, I guess they were meeting with some other accounts of his. I wouldn't be surprised if they make a trip to Chicago to see what they can find out from Jack Sharp," Mercer said.

"Alright, keep me in the loop if you hear more. I've got to jump on another call. Don't forget about the meetup that Patty is working on. You don't want her showing up on your doorstep and dragging your ass down here," Hamilton laughed.

"Okay, okay. I'll let her know soon."

Chapter Thirty-One

A WEEK HAD passed since Agent Powell's trip to California with Zandy Roberts. He somehow survived the flight home to Portland with only some minor arm discomfort, as Zandy clenched his arm at any hint of turbulent air.

Now Agent Powell was relaxing in the main lobby at the Black Label Sporting Goods Company headquarters in Chicago. He was slated to meet with Jack Sharp to see what he could find out from the head of the Racquet Sports division. Stan was sad that Zandy couldn't get away for another trip. He had enjoyed her company and thought the two made a great team.

During their last night in Los Angeles, Stan and Zandy had dinner on the patio of the Wildflower Cafe in Redondo Beach. Navigating the confusing network of the southland freeway system made for a long day. They had traveled to a few more tennis stores, which only added to the mystery of Chris Peck's disappearance and sudden departure from Black Label Racquet Sports.

They were both exhausted but enjoyed some wine with their meals.

"This wine is going to my head," Zandy had said. "I must say, I'm happy I joined you on this adventure."

"I'm glad you did too," Stan replied

"I feel like I owe you some answers," Zandy said. "I know I told you that I had some things happening at home."

"Zandy, you don't owe me anything. You can tell me what's going on only if you want to."

Tears had welled up in Zandy's eyes and rolled down her cheeks. "I caught Craig cheating on me," Zandy said, the words difficult for her to form.

"Oh shit! I'm sorry. What the fuck is he thinking?" Stan said, as his disbelief turned to anger.

Stan learned that night that Zandy's husband had been having an affair with the Assistant Manager at the brewery. At first, Zandy had tried to get past it, but struggled to forgive and forget.

"I think you know that I have feelings for you," she had said. "I don't know what's going to happen with my marriage, but I feel like it is over."

Stan was surprised to hear Zandy admit her feelings towards him. "I think it's pretty obvious that I have feelings for you, too. I've been feeling guilty about some of my remarks towards you. I know that you are married and want to respect that, but you are just so easy to talk to and I know I can come off as a bit of a flirt," Stan had said.

Zandy had reached across the table and placed her hand on his. "The flirting is from both sides. We do fit together nicely. I just need some time to sort through this," she had said.

Stan had assured her that she should take as long as she needed and that he was there for her. But he finally had a sense of where he stood with her. She liked him.

∽

Snapping out of his daydream, Stan sank into the comfortable leather chair and surveyed the array of Black Label Sporting Goods' latest products on display in the lobby.

Founded in 1920, as the Great Lakes Manufacturing Company, they started out by making tennis and musical instrument strings, as well as surgical sutures, utilizing animal by-products. Then in 1920, William Black Jr. was appointed President, and renamed the company the William Black Company. Rebranded the Black Label Sporting Goods Company in 1940, Black Label produced tennis and other racquet sports products, as well as golf, football, baseball, soccer and volleyball equipment. Since 1992, it had been a subsidiary of the German group, AMG Sports.

While he waited for his meeting, Stan reviewed his notes from his recent trips to California and Washington. The name Jack Sharp had come up several times during his meetings. He looked forward to meeting the Black Label Racquet Sports GM, who had not been overly helpful to this point. In fact, it had taken the threat of a warrant before his Executive Assistant agreed to the meeting.

"Agent Powell?" A stylishly dressed woman inquired as she neared the waiting area in the main lobby.

"Yes, I'm Stan Powell. You must be Valerie Little?" Stan said as he rose out of his chair.

Valerie Little was a beautiful woman in her mid-twenties. She dressed in the latest designer threads, and preferred to wear dresses and high heels whenever the Chicago weather allowed, as they showed off her long, toned legs. She wore more makeup than she needed, but she knew her boss liked it when she was all dolled-up.

"Has anyone offered you a coffee or other beverage yet?" Valerie asked.

"No, not yet," Stan replied.

"Well, let's get you up to Jack's office and grab something on the way."

"That sounds great. Thank you."

On the way upstairs, Stan took the opportunity to chat with Valerie.

"Did you know Chris Peck well?"

"No, not really. When I was working in Customer Service, he wasn't one of my reps. I only get to meet the reps at Sales Meetings, but I'm always so busy at the meetings, so I have little time to talk."

"So no impressions of Chris?" Stan asked.

"Oh, he was pretty cute, but other than that, I can't tell you that much about him."

Valerie gently tapped on Jack Sharp's office door and cracked it open to peek inside.

"Jack, Agent Powell is here for your meeting."

"Yes, bring him in."

Standing to greet the FBI agent, Jack Sharp reached across his desk to shake hands.

"Agent Powell, welcome to Black Label Racquet Sports."

"Thank you very much. It's quite a place you have here; an athlete's paradise," Stan said.

"Do you play tennis, Agent Powell?" Sharp asked.

"Not since high school. I was on the JV team, but honestly, I wasn't very good. University and work got in the way, so I gave it up. I'd love to play again, so hopefully someday soon," Stan replied.

"Well, if you do, just reach out to Valerie, and she will get you set up with some equipment," Sharp said.

"That is very kind of you. Thank you." Stan said, wondering to himself if Jack Sharp had just tried to bribe him with free tennis equipment.

"So how much do you know about Black Label?" Sharp asked.

"I'm familiar with a lot of the products, and have owned a few Black Label footballs and basketballs over the years. I was a big Billy Simpson fan when I was younger, and remember him playing with his steel Black Label tennis racquet."

"Very good, so you know a bit about our company," Sharp said.

Feeling like he had just received a "C" grade on his Black Label Sporting Goods exam, Stan said, "I'd like to know more."

"So, you're here to talk about Chris Peck? What an awful situation, and quite shocking. I can't think why anyone would want to harm him. And you're pretty sure it wasn't a random act?" Sharp asked.

"The circumstances of his death point us to the overwhelming likelihood that it was a pre-meditated murder," Stan replied.

"Well, I feel like you've wasted a trip to Chicago, Agent Powell. I really don't know how I can help you."

"Maybe so, but I want to make sure I cover all the bases. I've spoken to several of Chris' former customers, and even had a pleasant chat with your current sales rep in the area, Alan Mercer. Oh, and Chris' family was also very helpful in filling in some holes."

"Then what can I tell you about Chris Peck?" Sharp asked, having quickly lost interest in this meeting.

"What sort of sales rep was Chris?" Stan asked.

"Average at best. He was too nice and didn't know how to work a deal," Sharp replied.

"So was he fired?" Stan asked, as he focused on Sharp's facial expressions, for a reaction to his question.

With no variation to his expression, Jack replied, "No, he simply quit. I don't think he could handle the pressure of a territory like Los Angeles. Having once been the rep out there, I know it can be challenging. In all honesty, it was a mistake putting Chris in that territory."

"According to many of the store owners I spoke with, they seemed to like him," Stan said.

"Being a good sales rep is more about being liked by your customers. His numbers were decent, but he wasn't working the deals like I used to. You simply can't leave opportunities on the table, or your competitors will take them."

"When Chris went missing after leaving Black Label, his family criticized your efforts to help them find him," Stan said.

"Look, I'm running the largest brand in our sport. I have a lot of responsibilities here. I don't have time to search for a former employee who has gone on a walkabout to find himself," said Sharp defensively.

"A moving company called Four Horsemen Moving showed up at Chris' apartment the day he left Los Angeles. Did Black Label hire the moving company?" Stan asked.

"No. It's not our practice to move sales reps. That is up to them."

"There are rumors Chris got into some trouble with drugs and money. Do you know anything about that?" Stan inquired.

"I wouldn't be surprised. As I said before, it's a tough job, in a difficult territory. There are a lot of temptations, and easy to get in with the wrong crowd. Perhaps that's where you should focus your investigation. Most likely drug related, or he owed someone some money?"

"Maybe so, but we like to cover all possibilities and not jump to conclusions based upon rumors," Stan said.

"Did Chris have any problems with anyone on the Black Label Racquet Sports management team?"

"No. My team is a very skilled and professional group. I would have known if there were any problems."

"Have you ever been to Hood River?" Stan asked.

"No, I have not, and I'm not sure what that has to do with anything," Sharp responded angrily.

"Like I said, just exploring all possibilities," Stan said.

"I would like to access the travel records for your management team. Should I ask Ms. Little for those? Oh, and I would need your travel records too."

"I'm not in the habit of giving out information on my team, so you better come with a warrant if you even want to speak with anyone on my team," Sharp said.

"Good to know. I'll do that," Stan said.

"Now, if you'll excuse me, I have work to do. Valerie will escort you out."

As Stan exited the building, he smiled, knowing that he had made Jack Sharp a little uncomfortable with his questions. He felt like this would not be the last time their paths crossed. Something was telling him he needed to know more about Jack Sharp's past.

Chapter Thirty-Two

THE OJAI TENNIS tournament, known to locals as "The Ojai," was first held in 1896, in the small Ventura County town, just eighty miles north of Los Angeles. It was now the oldest and largest amateur tennis tournament in the United States.

Alan Mercer had a long history with the tournament, first having played in the junior event at thirteen years old. At fifteen, he and his doubles partner won the eighteen and under title for one of the most cherished titles of his entire tennis career. Since players needed to be invited to play, each year Mercer would call Mrs. Thacher, one of The Ojai's organizers, to request a place in the draw. She was always interested in Mercer's tennis, and they would have a friendly chat during their calls.

Mercer last played The Ojai a few years ago in the men's Open division, but still made the trip to the tournament every April. As a sponsor of the tournament, Black Label Racquet Sports hosted a tennis exhibition one evening, a mix between a rock concert and a professional tennis match. Black Label brought in some of their sponsored professional players to help make it a memorable evening for both players and spectators.

For the rest of the tournament, Mercer would help run the tournament desk for the women's Division III college division.

As he sent a singles match out to an open court, he heard a familiar voice call out to him from behind.

"Hey Mercer! They aren't paying you enough."

Mercer turned to see his friend, Cole Bundy, smiling back at him. He was thrilled to see a smile on Cole's face. A big turnaround from their last meeting at the Bundy's home.

"Holy smokes! They'll let anyone in here," Mercer replied, then shared a long hug with Cole.

"What brings you to The Ojai?" Mercer asked.

"I'm helping coach one of the D3 schools in our area. Now that I have a lot of time on my hands, the coach invited me to help with the team. It's been good to get out of the house," Bundy replied.

"Well, you look great! It's awesome to see you. Are you going to be around for a few days?" Mercer asked.

"Yes, I'm staying in Ventura at the Pierpont Inn. Do you have time for a hit and dinner later?"

"Let's do it. I'll be finished here around five o'clock. Let's hit a few, and then head over to The Ojai Tortilla House for dinner," Mercer said.

"Perfect. Looking forward to it."

※

After a full day of working at the tournament desk, then a good workout on the court with Cole Bundy, an ice cold Corona was a welcome sight as he and Bundy sat down to enjoy some burritos and beer.

Mercer raised his bottle and said, "Here's to seeing you out of the house."

"Cheers! Great to get out on the court with you today," Bundy said. "As much as I hated my ending at Black Label, I've got to say that I don't miss the constant pressure of the job."

"I'm sure it's been a big change, but I'm happy to hear that you can slow down a bit. It's pretty much the same story at Black Label. Element-5 is doing well, but they always expect more," Mercer said.

"So, Alan, I have to tell you about a call I got the other day. Do you remember Cari?" Bundy asked. "She was the intern that came out to Snowbird for the sales meeting."

"I think I remember her," Mercer replied. "Was she the blonde girl who worked with the promotions group?"

"Yes, that's her. She called me out of the blue, looking for advice. Apparently, on the last night of the sales meeting, Jack Sharp and a few others in upper management gathered in Sharp's suite at the hotel for a little post-meeting party. Cari was told to come up to his suite under false pretenses and then got caught up in a bad situation. According to Cari, they made her play drinking games, and then offered money for each article of clothing she removed. Before the nightmare was over, Sharp had groped her, and told her they would give her a full-time job at Black Label, if she would join him in his bedroom. She was only able to escape by using the excuse of needing to use the bathroom," Bundy said.

"Holy shit!" Mercer said as he pondered the gravity of what Bundy had told him. "Did she file a complaint with HR?"

"She immediately left the resort, and later contacted Human Resources, to lodge a sexual harassment complaint. At the direction of HR, she was told not to return for the remainder of her internship. She has heard nothing from Black Label since. So, she called me to ask what she should do. I guess she felt like I would be sympathetic to her situation, since I had just been fired."

"Did she say who was in the suite, along with Jack?"

"It was Randall Jefferies, Tom Saltz, Dustin McCabe from the Clearfield Distribution Center, and oddly, Valerie Little. They were all involved and nobody tried to stop it."

"Jesus! What are you going to do with this?" Mercer asked.

"I'm thinking about it, but plan on helping Cari out if she'll let me. Jack Sharp has been a bully his entire life. It's time someone stood up to him. Firing me wasn't the only mistake he made in Utah."

∽

On his way back to his hotel, Mercer checked his voicemail. His jaw hit the floor when he heard the voice of Jack Sharp.

"Alan, this is Jack Sharp. I hear you spoke with an FBI agent recently. I'm calling to tell you that you are not to have any further discussions with them. Everything should be directed to me."

Mercer realized that in over four years working the largest territory in the company, it was the first time he had received a call from Sharp. And this is what he called about? What the hell was going on?

Chapter Thirty-Three

MERCER WOKE EARLY, he wanted to get on the road before traffic got too bad. He had planned to visit a few customers in the Westwood and Brentwood areas on his way home from Ojai. He looked forward to sleeping in his own bed that night.

His first stop was at Westwood Tennis, which was near the UCLA campus. They had a reputation as being the best racquet stringers in Los Angeles. Mercer couldn't remember a time when he'd been in the store when both racquet stringers weren't busy the entire time. Because of their location, the store got a lot of Hollywood, Beverly Hills and Santa Monica tennis players, along with a steady stream of UCLA students and faculty.

"Hey John, how's it going?" Mercer asked John Fleming, the owner of Westwood Tennis, who stood behind one of the Babolat stringing machines—his usual position in the store.

"Alan, I'm glad you came in today. I've got a strange situation going on with some new Element-5 racquets."

"Oh? What's going on?"

"I have a customer who bought five Element-5 Tour 95 racquets from Brentwood Tennis Center. He brought them to me for customizing and stringing. I needed to add some weight to the racquets, so I removed the bumper guards and placed some lead tape on the frame. When I tried to install new bumper guards, none of them would fit. I thought that maybe the bumpers were the wrong ones, but I was able to install one on a racquet I had here in the shop. So, I think there's something not right about these racquets. They are different from the ones I have here in the shop," Fleming reported.

Fleming walked down his side of the long glass counter and pulled out five Black Label Element-5 Tour 95 racquets, arranging them on the counter in front of Mercer. All the racquets had lead tape at various positions on the frame, to match the weight and balance that the player was searching for.

Fleming and his team were expert racquet customizers, and their work was impeccable. If they were incapable of installing a new set of grommets and bumper guards, there must be something wrong. But just to make sure, Mercer attempted to match up the holes in the racquet head with the ones of the new bumpers. The holes didn't match.

Thinking back to his visit to the Tennis Spot in Fountain Valley a few months back, he checked out the holographic decals on the racquets, then compared them with the racquets that Fleming had on his racquet wall. They didn't match. All five of the Element-5 racquets that were purchased at Brentwood Tennis Center were different.

"John, I think these are counterfeits. I've seen this before, and that's the only explanation I can come up with. I think the fake racquets have a slightly different drilling pattern, so the real bumpers and grommets won't fit," Mercer said, placing the stack of racquets back on the counter.

"I was thinking it must be something like that," Fleming said.

"Let me call Black Label Customer Service, and see if they can pull up the serial numbers on these racquets. It should only take a few minutes to confirm," Mercer said.

"Okay, I've got some racquets to string. Just let me know what you find out."

⌘

Just as he had suspected, Abby Johnson, his Customer Service Rep, could not track down any of the serial numbers on the suspicious Element-5 racquets.

"Okay, John, it looks like we don't have those serial numbers in our system, so I think we are right. Somehow, your customer got hold of some counterfeit racquets," Mercer said.

"So, what should I do for my customer?" Fleming asked.

"I'm having five replacement racquets sent to you via overnight delivery, so you will have them tomorrow morning. After I leave here, I am going to see Mark Stephens at the Brentwood Tennis Center. I will see what he knows about these racquets."

"Okay, thanks for sending the replacement racquets. Let me know what you find out at Brentwood."

⌘

The Brentwood Tennis Center was a very popular tennis facility in the upscale community overlooking the Pacific Ocean, surrounded by multi-million-dollar homes. Mercer often noticed the paparazzi at the park that surrounded the tennis courts, as they stalked the many actors and actresses who routinely visited the park and tennis courts.

The small shop at the tennis center was filled with tennis equipment and apparel. Black Label Racquet Sports signage and Point-Of-Sale displays were arranged throughout the shop.

With several of the tennis pros at the facility on Mercer's Advisory Staff, they moved a lot of Black Label product through the shop.

"Hey Alan, how are things?" Mark Stephens asked as he welcomed him into his shop.

"Things are good, Mark. Thanks. I just spent the week in Ojai for the tournament. UCLA won the men's PAC 12 tournament, so your boys did well and should be tough to beat at nationals."

After taking a footwear fill-in order and confirming a tournament tennis ball order, Mercer pulled the five Element-5 racquets that he picked up at Westwood Tennis out of his bag. Mercer spent a few minutes bringing Mark up to speed on the situation with the suspected counterfeit racquets.

"So you are sure they are fakes?" Stephens asked as he picked up one of the Black Label racquets.

"Yes, it looks that way. Any idea how they got into your inventory?"

"No idea. I get all of my shipments straight from Black Label," Stephens answered.

"Do you mind if I check some of your racquets in the shop to see if I find any others?" Mercer asked.

"Oh, that's okay. I've got most of my back stock in a storage unit. I can check them, and let you know what I find," Stephens replied.

"Alright. If you are sure. I don't mind checking for you," Mercer said.

He was used to spending a lot of time in the back storage rooms of tennis shops counting Black Label products for his customers. Many of them didn't have the time to take regular inventory counts, so the only way Mercer would get fill-in orders from some of his customers was to find out for himself what they needed.

"It's not a problem. I've got to do a quick inventory, anyway," Mark answered, quickly handing the racquet back to Mercer.

"Great. Let me know what you find out. It looks like we are seeing an increase in counterfeits. I'd like to find out how they are getting into the stores," Mercer said.

Mercer promised to follow up and then excused himself. He hoped to pick up a quick Subway sandwich before his next appointment.

∽

After Alan Mercer had left the shop, Mark Stephens sent a text message to Jack Sharp's burner cell phone: WE HAVE A PROBLEM. CALL ME ASAP.

Chapter Thirty-Four

STAN POWELL WAS back at his desk at the Portland FBI headquarters. He was going over his notes from his meeting with Jack Sharp at Black Label headquarters when a large gentleman filled his doorway.

"Hey Stan. You ready to meet?" The giant figure asked.

"Yes, come on in, Sherlock," Powell replied.

William "Sherlock" Cahill was the top sleuth in the Portland office. When it came to digging up a suspects most well-hidden secrets, nobody did it better than Cahill. When he wasn't unearthing a persons' darkest, deepest secrets, Sherlock was home on his Xbox for hours on end. He favored the *Halo Series* and was somewhat of a legend in the Portland gaming community.

"Who's in your crosshairs today?" Sherlock asked as he took a seat.

"I need you to do what you do, and find out whatever you can about a man named Jack Sharp. He's the GM at Black Label Racquet Sports."

Over the next half hour, Powell brought Agent Cahill up to speed on his case. Something in the back of Stan's mind told him that Jack Sharp was not being completely honest with him. So he pulled out his secret weapon in the search for answers.

"Let me go to work on Mr. Sharp, and see what skeletons I can find," Cahill said as he got up to leave Agent Powell's office.

◈

Alan Mercer talked with Sarge Turner on the phone every Sunday evening to get his weekly orders, and frequently visited the Racket King store. So when he retrieved a voicemail from him on a Tuesday requesting he call back immediately, he knew Sarge was upset about something. Most likely, Black Label management had threatened to cut him off if he didn't raise his prices. But whatever it was, Mercer never delayed when returning his calls.

"Hey Sarge. It's Alan Mercer calling. How's your day going?"

"Oh, hey Alan. Well, fuck. I'm pissed off at Black Label, and you aren't going to like this."

"What's going on Sarge? How can I help?"

"Well, that's the problem. You can't help. You aren't driving right now, are you?" Sarge asked.

"No. I'm at home. What's up?"

"You know I'm good friends with Rick at Tennis Superstore? Well, he had a visit from your National Sales Manager, Randall Jefferies, today. As usual, Randall was full of himself and puffing his chest out, telling Rick how to run his business. To show just how powerful he is, he told Rick that he was going to be in Southern California for the next few days because he had to fire his sales rep in Los Angeles." Turners' voice trailed off to nothing but silence from the other end of the call.

"What?" Mercer finally yelled.

"Alan, that's what he told me. It's total bullshit. You do a great job representing Black Label. Why would they want to let you go?" Sarge said, trying to show some compassion for Mercer. He had been down this road before when companies decided to replace good sales reps for no apparent reason.

"Crap, Sarge. They probably want to give the job to someone they can pay half of what they pay me. I've heard nothing from Jefferies, so I'm not sure when he plans to tell me?" Mercer said, the tremble in his voice betraying his emotions.

"Well, that pompous prick better not set foot in my store," Sarge said. "I'm really sorry to have to give you this news, but I wanted to give you a heads-up. And listen, you should come work with me. I need someone to handle our online business."

"Thank you Sarge. I really appreciate the heads-up, and will let you know about helping you at The Racket King. I just need some time to figure things out."

"No problem Alan. The offer is available to you whenever you want."

"Thanks again Sarge. I'll call you after I talk to Randall Jefferies," Mercer said, and ended the call.

Sitting in his office, Mercer buried his head in his hands, and tears began to flow. Black Label Racquet Sports had been his life for the past ten years. Is this how it was going to end?

After a while, anger replaced Mercer's sadness. How can they fire me? What is the reason? Mercer wondered.

He checked his email and found a new message from Randall Jefferies. It said nothing, except that he needed to meet with Mercer the following morning at the LAX Hilton Hotel, during his quick stop in Los Angeles.

"Really?" Mercer said out loud. "That fuck!" Tomorrow

was his birthday, and he was taking the day off to play golf with some friends.

"Fuck him. If he's going to fire me, he's going to have to wait," Mercer yelled as he backhanded the cans of Black Label tennis ball cans that were arranged on his desk. The cans clattered loudly on the concrete floor of his office.

Mercer then replied to the email that he was unavailable the next day, but could meet him the following morning.

For the next several hours, Mercer's anger fueled his efforts to dig through sales index reports he had kept over the past ten years. His efforts showed that there was only one sales rep in the company who had maintained a higher average sales index during that period. And at 132% index, he was currently far and away the top rep in the company.

Looking around his office, which was filled with Black Label products and memorabilia, Mercer was once again overcome with dread, and the tears began to fall.

Chapter Thirty-Five

THE LARGE GLASS doors opened in front of Mercer as he stepped inside the LAX Hilton Hotel, located a short shuttle ride from the Los Angeles International Airport. At the far end of the expansive lobby, Mercer recognized Randall Jefferies sitting at a small table. As usual, Jefferies was overdressed, and his perfectly gelled hair showed that he spent a considerable amount of time in front of the mirror that morning.

As Mercer approached Jefferies, he could tell that the National Sales Manager was nervous and very much on edge. Gone was the look of arrogance replaced by a slightly panicked expression on his cleanly shaven face.

"Alan, have a seat," Jefferies said, while motioning to the empty chair on the opposite side of a small table.

Jefferies handed Mercer a file folder and said, "Please read the enclosed letter."

So much for idle chit-chat, thought Mercer, as he accepted the folder. But he knew to expect nothing more from Jefferies. He must have forgotten how much Mercer had done for him when he moved to Atlanta to become the Southeast Regional Manager. Mercer knew it stung Jefferies' sizable ego when he moved to Los Angeles, thus leaving a region that the great Randall Jefferies managed. Perhaps he was enjoying this payback, Mercer thought.

Mercer turned his attention to the folder in his hands. He opened it and read the brief letter.

∽

ALAN MERCER,

YOUR EMPLOYMENT AS A SALES REPRESENTATIVE FOR THE RACQUET SPORTS DIVISION OF BLACK LABEL SPORTING GOODS IS HEREBY TERMINATED, EFFECTIVE IMMEDIATELY.

ENCLOSED WITH THIS LETTER IS A MEMO THAT EXPLAINS YOUR SEVERANCE PACKAGE, AS WELL AS INSTRUCTIONS ON RETURNING ALL COMPANY EQUIPMENT AND MATERIALS TO BLACK LABEL.

BEST OF LUCK IN YOUR FUTURE ENDEAVORS.

JACK SHARP

GENERAL MANAGER, BLACK LABEL RACQUET SPORTS

∽

"This is total bullshit, Randall! What is the reason for firing me?" Mercer demanded, knowing that Black Label surely needed to show some justification for firing him.

Nervously looking down at the table, Jefferies said, "I'm sorry, but I cannot discuss that with you."

"What?" Mercer blurted out. "For ten years, I've busted

my ass to be one of the very best reps in the company. When asked to take on a new territory, I didn't complain. I had to clean up the mess left by the previous rep and turned the Los Angeles region into the highest volume territory in the company. And this is what I get?"

Jefferies shifted in his chair and said nothing.

Mercer shook his head in disgust, then looked directly into the eyes of the National Sales Manager. "So let me get this straight. I'm currently the top sales rep in the company. My accounts like me. I get great reviews each year from my regional manager, and I don't even get to know why I'm being fired?"

"I'm not allowed to answer that question. I can only recommend that you read and accept the severance plan," Jefferies said, with a blank expression, and then stood and walked towards the exit.

Every muscle in Mercer's body was prepared to launch at Jefferies and pummel the shit out of him. But he somehow resisted the urge to do so. Instead, he gave him an earful as he walked away.

"This is unbelievable, even for you! You can't even answer a single question? You really are a spineless fucking asshole!"

∽

The hotel lobby buzzed with activity as tourists and business travelers came and went, but nobody noticed the former sales rep for Black Label Racquet Sports, who had been sitting alone at a small table for the past hour.

Paralyzed with dread, Mercer struggled to come to terms with the events of the last few days. Just two days ago, he was working a job that he loved, focused on having his best sales year ever. Now he was left to wonder what came next. His entire identity for the past ten years had revolved around being "Mr. Black Label."

"Who is he now?" Mercer pondered.

He finally gathered the strength to pull himself out of his chair and headed for the hotel's sliding glass doors. Beyond those doors, an uncertain future awaited Alan Mercer.

∽

As he drove home, Mercer pressed the speed dial button for Joe Hamilton. Hamilton answered on the first ring.

"Hey, I just heard the news from Jack Sharp this morning. I'm so sorry. Are you okay?" Hamilton asked before Mercer could say a word.

"No, I'm not okay. So, you did not know this was coming?" Mercer asked.

"Not at all. It completely caught me off guard. I tried to change Jack's mind, but he wasn't listening to anything I said," Hamilton replied.

"Since when does the GM fire a rep without consulting with the rep's manager?"

"You know how it is, Alan. Since Jack took over the GM role, he's been calling all the shots. He does whatever he wants."

"Did he at least tell you why I was fired? That ass, Jefferies wouldn't answer a single question."

"He just said he didn't like the way you ran the territory. He wants to give someone else a shot at it. I think he wants to bring in one of his people; someone he can control. Sort of like he's done with the upper management team," Hamilton said.

"This just isn't right, Joe! You can't fire your best sales rep for no reason. I think I'm going to talk to an attorney friend of mine about this."

"Look Alan, I know you're upset right now. Take a few days to gather your thoughts, but take that severance package. It's a good one."

"Joe, I'm going to sign off now. I just pulled into my driveway. I'll call you tomorrow."

"Alright, that sounds good. Alan, I'm really sorry about all of this," Hamilton said into his phone, but wasn't sure it registered with the person on the other end.

❧

As Mercer reached for the door handle to his house, he was alarmed to find that the door had been jimmied open and the lock was hanging askew. He slowly stepped inside and discovered that most of the house appeared to be untouched, but when he entered his office, he realized the intruders had made off with almost all of his inventory of racquets, including the five Element-5 Tour 95s that he picked up at Westwood Tennis the other day. The thieves had tossed his desk and file cabinet, leaving papers all over the floor.

Mercer's hands were shaking as he grabbed his phone and dialed the police. While on hold, he said to himself, "What a day. What a shitty day!"

Chapter Thirty-Six

JACK SHARP WAS feeling better about the situation with the counterfeit Element-5 racquets. He had an absolute fit when he found out about the error with the drilling pattern. But it had been almost three weeks since Alan Mercer had identified the issue with the racquets at one of his accounts and then had questioned Mark Stephens about it.

He had immediately contacted Dustin McCabe in Clearfield to halt the shipping of counterfeit Element-5 Tour 95 racquets, and then laid into Walter Chen at Green Dragon. How could they have made such a costly mistake?

With new replacement grommets and bumper guards for the Green Dragon racquets now on hand, they had been able to send those to the selected accounts that carry the racquets. Green Dragon had remedied the problem with their racquets, so going forward, the racquets would match up to the real ones.

But most of all, Sharp was delighted with the changes in the Los Angeles territory. Alan Mercer was no longer around to stick his nose into his counterfeit racquet scheme. He now had someone in the territory that reported directly to him and was loyal to him. Jack Sharp was once again pulling the strings in the largest territory in the company, and his new rep would keep an eye on Alan Mercer to make sure he wasn't causing anymore trouble.

※

Over the last couple of weeks, Mercer had been overwhelmed by the outpouring of support from his fellow sales reps, his customers, and friends, who were shocked at the announcement of his termination. He'd already had a few job offers from other tennis brands who would love to have him represent them in the territory. But at the moment, his heart wasn't in it, and he was not committing to anything long-term. He was leaning towards helping Sarge Turner on a short-term contract just to get himself out of the house.

His tennis buddies had been getting him out on the court for some tennis therapy. A good friend at the tennis brand, Tecnifibre, had sent him some racquets, knowing that Mercer would no longer want to play with a Black Label racquet. So far, Mercer was impressed with the Tecnifibre T-Fight racquets and their multifilament strings.

He hadn't been good about returning phone calls. For the first time in ten years, he enjoyed not having to return every call immediately. He did speak with Joe Hamilton, Cole Bundy, and Dan Sims regularly. After consulting with his attorney, Mercer took Hamilton's advice and accepted the generous severance package.

Bundy was still fired up about taking down Jack Sharp, and had been hinting at some interesting dirt that he had dug up.

Both Dan Sims and Mercer's Customer Service Rep, Abby Johnson, had been reporting in frequently. The Black Label rumor mill had started up, with reports that Mercer was involved in an illegal trans-shipping network that put him at the center of a plan to ship Black Label products to retailers outside of his territory, including to overseas locations… a practice that was forbidden at the company.

Amused by the creativity of the person who came up with the rumor, Mercer already noticed people pulling away from him as a result. Maybe it was time to get out of the tennis industry? *Maybe it was finally time?* Mercer pondered.

Chapter Thirty-Seven

"YOU HAVE SOMETHING for me?" Stan Powell asked, as he ducked inside the office door of Sherlock Cahill's lab space.

On the front of the door, a sign read: DO NOT DISTURB. MASTER CHIEF AT WORK.

Stan laughed at the tribute to the hero of the *Halo* game series.

"Yes, I do. Enter at your own risk," Sherlock said, as he cleared a mountain of papers off a chair.

"Sorry about the mess. I don't get too many visitors."

Cahill then tossed a few empty Red Bull cans into the overflowing wastebasket beside his desk.

"I've got some good stuff on your friend Jack Sharp. I think you are going to like it," Cahill said. "To start, Jack Sharp isn't his real name. He changed it several years ago. His real name is James Henry Shapiro, but he has always gone by Jack."

"Do you know why he changed his name? Usually, that is done when someone has something to hide," Powell asked.

"That seems to be the case here as well. Our Mr. Shapiro was quite the lying narcissist in his youth. He would tell his version of the truth in order to step over anyone in his path to success. Growing up in a home of modest financial means, friends who were all from well-to-do families surrounded him. Jack wanted what they had, money and power."

"Sounds like he got what he was looking for. Being the GM at Black Label Racquet Sports has status and a big paycheck," Powell said.

"But our young Jack Shapiro made some mistakes along the road to success. Mistakes that, if found out, could bring down his house of cards," Sherlock replied.

"Tell me more."

"Jack was only an average student in high school. While I couldn't find proof, the skinny is that Jack had someone take his SAT exam for him. The scores were good enough to get him into USC."

"So, is this the part where you tell me what he's hiding?" Powell asked.

"I'm getting to that."

"Jack joined the Sigma Pi fraternity, and formed a tight bond with his new brothers, who all marveled at Jack's raging ambition. Within the fraternity, Jack had three very close friends, all with an equal thirst for riches, regardless of the toll it took on others. The group called themselves The Four Horsemen of Troy."

"Wait. You said Four Horsemen?" Powell asked. He recognized that the name matched the mysterious moving company that moved Chris Peck's belongings out of his apartment.

"Yes. Are you familiar with the Four Horsemen of the Apocalypse?" Sherlock asked.

"Somewhat, but if you could catch me up on the details, sadly, my knowledge of religion is a bit shaky," Powell said.

"The Four Horsemen of the Apocalypse were figures in Christianity, appearing in the New Testaments Book of

Revelations. According to the book, the Four Horsemen appear with the opening of the first four of seven seals that bring about the cataclysm of the apocalypse."

"The first Horseman rides a white horse, which represents conquest. The second rides a red horse, representing war. The third is on a black horse, which represents Famine. And finally, a rider on a pale horse signifies death. The pale horse is the most powerful and considered the leader."

"I'm almost afraid to ask how you know so much about this subject," Powell said.

"I play a video game called *Darksiders*. It ties into the Four Horsemen story," Cahill replied, a big grin revealed a set of crooked front teeth.

"That figures!" Powell laughed.

"Our Four Horsemen in this case were Jack Shapiro, Dustin McCabe, Tom Cashman and Peter Marcus. They started a very profitable business while students at USC, selling stolen copies of exams and term papers, that were altered enough to avoid detection by the university's professors. But their biggest impact on the fraternity was the outrageous parties they would organize. They became so renowned that they began charging students a hefty entry fee. During these parties, Jack and the other Horsemen would hold court in a back room at the frat house. They would supply the drugs and alcohol, and the young co-eds who were picked for the private back room party would barely remember anything the following day."

"So much for getting a balanced education," Powell interjected.

"Unfortunately for the Horsemen, one of the lovely co-eds did remember what had happened to her at one of the Sigma Pi parties. Annie King staggered into a local police precinct the morning after another profitable evening for Jack and his crew. She claimed to have been raped multiple times and physically abused by Jack Shapiro and the others in the room. The results of the rape kit showed that she was raped by all four, beaten and tied down, with the rope burns still clearly visible. She filed a complaint against the four, hired an attorney, and immediately dropped out of USC."

"How the hell are these guys not still in prison?" Powell asked.

"During the trial, Annie King mysteriously disappeared. Her roommate found a handwritten note from Miss King in her apartment, saying that she was running away, and was planning on starting a new life somewhere far away. She's never been heard from since."

"Any involvement by the Horsemen in her decision to leave town?" Powell asked.

"All four of the accused had air-tight alibis for their whereabouts during her disappearance, so no charges were filed. Without Annie, the case fell apart, and the Four Horsemen walked out of the courtroom with smug smiles on their faces, smoking expensive cigars, driving away from the courthouse in a rented stretch limousine."

"Jesus! What a shit show," Powell said.

"As Jack's career in the tennis industry was taking shape, he changed his last name to Sharp. He came up with a story about it being his step-father's last name, and nobody asked questions. But it was just one of the many lies that make up the life of Jack Sharp."

"So, do we know where the other Horsemen ended up?" Powell asked.

"I'm glad you asked, because the answer is quite interesting.

After a dreadful start to his career, including being fired for sexually harassing a fellow employee, Dustin McCabe was hired by Jack Sharp. He is currently the Director of Operations at Black Label Sporting Goods, and works at the company's Distribution Center, in Clearfield, Utah."

"Good god!" Powell said as he shook his head.

"Peter Marcus worked in banking for a while, but lost the use of his legs in a near-fatal car accident. He was bound to a wheelchair. Not long after the accident, Marcus dropped off the face of the earth and never resurfaced," Cahill reported.

"And Tom Cashman?" Powell asked.

"Well, Tom was a rising star in the financial world, making millions for his clients and for himself. He was untouchable and destined to become a legend on Wall Street. But Tom had a thirst for beautiful women, fast cars, and a steady flow of drugs and alcohol. He was well known in Las Vegas, and often made the drive from LA through the desert to gamble and party the weekend away. On one of these trips, Tom had picked up Peter Marcus for a fun-filled boys' weekend in Sin City."

Sherlock took a couple of sips from a freshly opened Red Bull, then continued.

"Police records estimate that Tom's Mercedes SL63 AMG convertible was traveling upwards of 120 miles per hour when it plowed into the back of a slow-moving big rig on Interstate 15. Tom, whose blood alcohol level was twice the legal limit, died instantly. His passenger was thrown clear of the wreck, but Peter Marcus never regained full use of his legs."

"So there are only three Horsemen remaining?" Powell asked.

"Well, they seemed to have found a replacement. Tom's

older brother, Bill Cashman, is… you guessed it… the Vice President at Black Label Sporting Goods!"

∽

Back in his office after his meeting with Sherlock Cahill, Powell considered his next steps while he retrieved voicemails on his cell phone.

"Yo… Special Agent Stan! This is your homie in LA, Bodhi. I need to talk to you pronto. Call me."

Chapter Thirty-Eight

"BODHI... WHAT'S UP?" Powell asked into his cell phone.

"Special Agent Stan! You gun down any bad guys today?" The surfer tennis shop manager answered.

"No, not yet. But it's not yet lunchtime, so there's still a chance I'll get one before the day is over," Powell said with a laugh.

"Dude. You are hardcore!"

"Bodhi, you left me a voicemail to call, so here I am."

"Right. Thanks for calling me back. I've got some super secret shit that will blow your mind. It will help you find some answers about what went down with Sasquatch," Bodhi said.

"So, what's the news Bodhi?"

"I can't tell you over the phone. You need to come back down to LA."

"Bodhi, I need a bit of information to justify another trip down. This line is secure, so you can tell me what it is you know."

"Stan, I need you to meet with someone. This person is scared, especially when she found out what happened to Chris Peck. You have to come down here."

"So, no hints as to the identity of this person?"

"For kicks, let's just imagine that Chris Peck had a girlfriend."

There was a long pause, as Powell thought back on the case. He hadn't recalled there ever being a girlfriend mentioned.

"Okay, you have my attention. I should be able to get down to you by the end of the week. Will you be able to set up a meeting with the girlfriend?"

"You betcha Stan. You let me know when you are coming, and I will put it together. Oh, and bring that hot police chick with you. The waves are excellent right now for newbies."

"I'll see what I can do, Bodhi. Anything else you need?"

"Dude, some Voodoo Doughnuts would make Bodhi a happy man!"

※

Alan Mercer hadn't gone this long in between filling his car with gas in over ten years. He finished topping off the tank to his Ford Escape and wondered if it might be time to ditch the small SUV for something a bit more sporty. He guessed now was as good a time as any to have a mid-life crisis and buy a sports car. He had recently sold his Lexus IS300, and had been dreaming of another fun, fast ride to race around town in.

After a few weeks of moping around the house, he had decided to take a trip down to San Diego. Joe Hamilton's wife, Patty, had called to check on him. She put the full-court press on him to get his butt down to their house for a visit. Even with his new employment status, she was eager to introduce Mercer to a special someone. He had declined the previous invitations, but could not come up with a good enough excuse, so he relented to Patty's wishes. Hamilton held to his promise of a good doubles match that afternoon, so at least they would get in some practice.

Mercer's plan was to stay a couple of nights at the Hamilton's, and then go see Cole Bundy, who had seemed really excited about something the other day when they spoke on the phone.

※

The doubles practice proved to be an excellent distraction, with Mercer and Hamilton playing some great tennis. This year's goal was to forego the chase for the number one ranking, playing fewer tournaments, putting everything into winning one of the four major tournaments, and win the coveted gold ball.

Mercer always enjoyed staying at the Hamiltons' home. With two teenagers and a playful Labrador retriever, the house was a beehive of activity, which was in stark contrast to Mercer's empty home.

Patty had arranged a family barbecue, inviting some good friends who recently had their cousin come live with them. The young Miss Samantha Hamilton had wanted to introduce Mercer to the cousin since she first met her. So the fact that Mercer was actually in the house was driving her crazy. She'd been hovering over Mercer since he arrived, making sure his clothing was acceptable for this grand occasion.

"Make sure to brush your teeth, Alan."

"Yes, Sam."

"Do you need to borrow my dad's mouthwash or cologne?"

"No, Sam."

"What if she wants you to kiss her?"

"Sam, it's not even an actual date!"

"Geez, Alan. You have to be prepared for these things!"

Mercer exited the downstairs bathroom, where he had just taken a post-tennis shower… and brushed his teeth, and walked into a conversation between Patty and an exceptionally beautiful woman.

"Alan, come over. This is Madison," Patty said.

Suddenly feeling self-conscious, he wondered if maybe he should have borrowed the mouthwash and cologne? He accepted Madison's hand.

"Hello Madison. I'm Alan. It's great to finally meet you."

"It's nice meeting you as well. I've heard so much about you," Madison said, as she looked at Samantha, who was lurking in the background. Mercer and Madison immediately broke into laughter, as they both gave thumbs up to the suddenly shy teenager.

"I hope you don't mind, but I brought my security team with me, just in case," Madison said, as she pointed to the gathering in the backyard, which included Madison's cousin, her cousin's husband, their three teenagers, and their yellow Labrador retriever.

"Wow. I better be on my best behavior," Mercer said, and they all began to laugh again.

Chapter Thirty-Nine

THE PAST TWO days had been great for Mercer. He couldn't recall the last time he had laughed that much. The evening with Madison, her family and the Hamiltons was a surprising success.

Upon waking up the morning after the barbecue, Mercer walked downstairs at the Hamiltons home, where he saw Patty preparing breakfast.

"Well, how do you think it went?" Mercer asked.

"I don't know, but Madison would like you to call her," Patty said while handing a Post-It note, with Madison's phone number scribbled on it.

"YES!" Mercer yelled, and pumped his fists, as if he had just won the tennis match of his life.

He called Madison that morning, and the two made plans to hike in the Torrey Pines State Natural Reserve that afternoon. They had a great time as they explored the bluffs that overlooked the Pacific Ocean, while they got to know each other better. They shared a spectacular sunset while dining at the seafood restaurant, *Poseidon*, in Del Mar, which made for a perfect ending to an incredible day.

While he dropped Madison off at her cousin's house, they

shared a tender kiss and made plans to see each other the following weekend.

"We are talking about going to a San Diego Padres game at Petco Park next weekend. You should come with us," Madison said.

"Still feel the need for that security team of yours? Count me in," Mercer said, as he gave her a warm hug and said goodnight.

∽

Mercer and Hamilton spent the morning hitting some tennis balls while they talked about the recent happenings at Black Label Racquet Sports. Hamilton was still getting a lot of flack from the tennis shops in Mercer's old territory. They already missed the great level of service he provided. The new guy was off to a rocky start, but Hamilton couldn't convince Jack Sharp that he had made a mistake.

They also talked about Mercer's plans. Hamilton supported his idea of helping Sarge at The Racket King, thinking it would be a good fit for him and a pleasant change of scenery.

∽

It was just past 10:30 in the evening when Mercer and Cole Bundy pulled into the vacant parking lot in front of The Tennis Depot store, in the Kearny Mesa area of San Diego. They had spent the afternoon reviewing the latest information that Cole had discovered.

"Alan, I got a call from Tyler at The Tennis Depot a while back. He wanted my advice on a situation at the store. I've been friends with Tyler a long time, and helped to get him the job," Bundy said.

"I know that store. It's a big account for Black Label. Ben Townsend is the owner," Mercer said.

"I ended up meeting Tyler after hours one night, where he showed me some Element-5 racquets, where the replacement bumper guards wouldn't fit. The racquets were fakes."

"Yes, I had the same problems in my territory," Mercer said.

"Tyler did some digging and found several boxes of the counterfeit racquets in a storage room in the store. Puzzled that they didn't normally order that many of one particular racquet model, he checked over some invoices from Black Label. To his surprise, the number of racquets they had in stock was far greater than what Black Label had on their invoices," Bundy said.

"So where did these extra racquets come from?" Mercer asked.

"That's why we are going to meet with Tyler tonight. He thinks he has found some information that will help us answer that question."

"Cole, why is this something you need to get involved in? Maybe it's best for both of us to move on with our lives?" Mercer asked.

"I just can't let this go. The Tennis Depot is the store that Jack Sharp had visited behind my back. Something tells me he's up to something. I hope I'm wrong, but I just need to know for sure," Bundy replied.

Bundy's phone vibrated, letting him know that a text message had arrived.

"It's from Tyler. He wants us to go to the back door in the alley behind the store," Bundy reported.

Tyler cracked open the back door as Mercer and Bundy stepped inside the store. With only a few overhead lights on in the store, it was dark enough to make navigating around the many product displays difficult. Tyler guided them to the back office, where he closed the door behind them and switched on the lights.

"Tyler, this is Alan Mercer," Bundy said.

"Hey Alan. I think I met you once at a Black Label function. Super sorry to hear about your job," Tyler said.

"Thanks Tyler."

"So, I take it that Cole gave you an update on the situation with the Element-5 racquets?" Tyler asked.

"Yes, he did. Do you know more about where they came from?" Mercer asked.

"The incoming racquets didn't match the invoices. We are only paying Black Label for about half of the racquets we've been getting."

"That doesn't sound like something Black Label would let happen for too long," Bundy said.

"I normally don't have access to the bank account records for the store, or any of the store's financials, but I was able to get into Ben's locked file cabinet the other day and grab some bank statements," Tyler said, as he laid out several bank documents on the desk.

"What are we looking for?" Mercer asked as he surveyed the bank statements.

"If you look closely, you will notice several payments made to Black Label Racquet Sports, which is to be expected. Under a few of the Black Label payments, you will see large payments made to a company called Trojan Horse Logistics. I have no idea what this company is," Tyler said.

"So you think the payments to Trojan Horse Logistics are for the counterfeit racquets?" Mercer asked as he looked over the bank statements.

"The timing and the amounts seem to match up with the arrival of the racquets. I've also tried to search for information on the company and have come up empty-handed."

"So who is behind Trojan Horse Logistics? Bundy wondered out loud.

"If my math is correct, it looks like the payments made to Trojan Horse Logistics are about half of those made to Black Label on the same dates. So if those payments are for an equal number of counterfeit racquets, then it means The Tennis Depot is making twice as much profit by selling the fake Element-5 racquets," Mercer said, as he wondered how many other tennis stores were selling the suspicious racquets.

∽

The burner cell phone on Jack Sharp's nightstand vibrated. Having just gone to bed, Jack looked at the clock to see that it was one o'clock in the morning. Who would be texting at this hour? He read the text message:

I FOLLOWED MERCER AND BUNDY TO THE TENNIS DEPOT. THEY ENTERED THE BACK OF THE STORE AFTER 10:30PM. THEY ARE STILL INSIDE. WHAT SHOULD I DO?

Pondering the situation in San Diego, Jack hit reply, then wrote:

TAKE CARE OF IT.

Chapter Forty

BACK IN BUNDY'S Honda Odyssey, they sat for a few minutes in silence as they considered what they had just learned from Tyler.

"It looks like money is going to Trojan Horse Logistics for payment of counterfeit Black Label racquets. Do you really think this is a viable source of revenue where people are losing their lives over it?" Bundy asked.

"In my days of working in product development, I came to realize the huge profit margins available to companies on the sale of tennis racquets and other equipment. So even if someone is selling the racquets at half of the normal price, they would still be making a nice profit. Depending upon how widespread the distribution is of the fake racquets, we would be talking about millions of dollars," Mercer said. "So do you think Sharp is behind Trojan Horse Logistics?"

"I'm sure of it. In fact, I think that's what got me fired. He knew I was asking questions about his secret visit to The Tennis Depot. I just wish I could know for sure," Bundy replied.

"I have an idea on how we can confirm whether Jack Sharp is behind this counterfeit racquet plan," Mercer said.

"And what might that be?"

"Cole, how would you like to take a little trip to Taiwan?"

∽

"Trish has made up the guest bed for you. You can sleep at our house tonight," Bundy said, as he guided the Odyssey onto deserted Clairemont Mesa Boulevard.

Typically jammed with northbound traffic, Highway 163 was a racetrack at this hour, as they took the Pomerado Road exit that would lead them to the Bundys home in Scripps Ranch. Once off the freeway, the roads were pitch black. Many of the roadside lights in San Diego's north county had been removed to reduce light pollution's impact on migrating birds.

In The Air Tonight, by Phil Collins, played over the Honda's stereo system. *Can you feel it coming in the air tonight...* as the song reached its signature drum solo, Bundy reached for the volume control, turning it way up, just as the crescendo of drums began. As they both did their best, Phil Collins' air drum solo, the minivan, suddenly lurched forward.

"What the hell?" Bundy yelled as he wrestled the Odyssey's steering wheel.

Glancing back behind them, Mercer shouted, "That asshole doesn't have his lights on. Is he drunk?"

Then the driver of the truck following them flipped on his high-beams, temporarily blinding Mercer, as he was still looking out the rear window.

The truck sped up again, slamming into the back of Bundy's van. Again, he could barely keep the car on the road.

"Shit, Cole! This guy is trying to run us off the road. Can you get this thing to go any faster?"

"I'm trying!" Bundy yelled as he slammed his foot down on the gas pedal.

The Honda slowly pulled forward, away from the truck, and for a moment, they thought that might be the last they saw of the guy in the truck.

"Oh crap, Cole. You gotta go faster!" Mercer screamed as he watched the truck's headlights grow larger in their rear window.

As they came to a bend in the dark, winding road, the truck connected with the Honda's rear bumper, which sent the minivan spinning off the road and into the darkness. The Odyssey somersaulted down the rocky embankment for a few hundred feet, and eventually the mangled minivan came to rest on its rooftop.

Thrown clear of the wreckage, Mercer was barely conscious as he lay in the bushes, then managed to look back at the Honda, its wheels still spinning. Underneath the vehicle, he could see his good friend Cole Bundy, who laid motionless, with half of his body pinned beneath the van.

Just before losing consciousness, Mercer looked up towards the road, and was gripped with terror as he saw the driver of the truck looking down the embankment. His silhouette outlined by the truck's headlights.

Chapter Forty-One

THE SKY WAS a shifting kaleidoscope of colors as the sun rose, casting a pinkish hue upon the surfers getting in their first waves of the day, just below the Redondo Beach Pier.

Built in 1888 to handle the enormous lumber trade from the Pacific Northwest, the horseshoe-shaped pier stood twenty-five feet above the water, and was home to many shops and restaurants. It was also a hot spot for anglers and those who enjoyed watching the local surfers below. Some lined up waiting for their chance to drop into the perfect set, while others paddled into position to catch a wave and show off their skills. A sign attached to the pier railing read: a bad day surfing is better than a good day working.

Other than a few early morning fishermen, Stan Powell and Zandy Roberts were alone at the end of the pier.

"Do you think Bodhi is going to show?" Zandy asked.

"I hope so. Otherwise we are going to have to eat these doughnuts!" Powell replied, as he held up the pink Voodoo box.

Suddenly, two hooded figures approached them from behind.

"Stan the Man," one of the hooded figures whispered.

"Bodhi, is that you?" Powell asked.

The darkened figure removed his hood, and a tangled nest of shoulder length hair fell to the side, exposing the toothy grin of Bodhi.

"The one and only! And you brought along my favorite police babe, Lt. Zandy. Awesome!"

"And doughnuts, too!" Powell said, as Bodhi latched on to him, for his customary bear-hug greeting.

"Hi Bodhi," Zandy said with her arms open, preparing for the warm hug.

"Bodhi, who's your friend?" Stan asked, looking towards the still hooded figure standing behind Bodhi.

Stepping to the side, Bodhi said, "This is Savannah."

Keeping her hood on, the figure raised her head and looked over the two law enforcement officers. The morning sunlight revealed a young woman's face. She lifted her right hand to acknowledge them both, but said nothing.

"Bodhi, why all the cloak-and-dagger?" Zandy asked.

"It took some convincing to get Savannah to speak with you, but I told her you guys are super solid and would help her. She was Chris Peck's girlfriend, but there's a lot more to her story."

"Savannah, Bodhi is right. We are here to help. We need to hear your story, and whatever you are afraid of, we can offer protection if you want," Powell said.

Checking her surroundings to make sure they were alone, Savannah said in a soft voice, "Chris and I were dating at the time he left Los Angeles. Bodhi was the one to introduce us. It wasn't Chris's idea to leave Black Label. They fired him and gave him some crazy ultimatum to get him out of town right away. I think they fired Chris because of something I told him."

"You say he was fired and forced out? How do you know this?" Powell asked.

"He called me the day they fired him and told me the entire story. The people at Black Label didn't know about me, so we decided it was best if he went home to Washington, and I would follow a little later."

"You say the people at Black Label. What people are you referring to?" Zandy asked.

"Jack Sharp and Bill Cashman, and a few others on the management team," Savannah replied.

"Why would you and Chris fear them?" Powell asked.

"I know a secret about Jack's past, and he must have found out that somehow Chris knew about it."

"When did you last talk to Chris?" Zandy asked.

"He called me a few times from the road, on his drive north. I fell asleep and missed his last call, but he left me a voicemail. I never deleted it."

"Can we hear it?" Powell asked.

The young woman reached into her sweatshirt pocket and pulled out her cell phone. After scrolling through her saved voicemails, she pressed the one marked Chris Peck, and then touched the speaker button on the phone.

"Hey Savannah, sorry I missed you. You must be asleep. I just stopped at a great spot in Hood River. Had some incredible pizza, and the beer wasn't bad either. We'll have to go there when you come up."

"I'm really beginning to think that leaving Black Label and Los Angeles might be a good thing. There is a lot we can do up here. I can't wait to show you around Washington."

"Anyway, I'm exhausted and need some sleep. I'll call you from the road in the morning. I should be home in Winthrop by mid-day."

"Sleep well. I love you."

The message ended, and the four stood in silence, as they realize they'd just listened to the last words of Chris Peck from almost five years ago.

"That was the last I heard from him," Savannah said. "I was never sure if he decided to leave me, in order to protect me, or if he ran into trouble. It wasn't until Bodhi told me he met with you that my suspicions were confirmed. I feel it in my heart and soul that Jack Sharp had something to do with this."

"So, what is this secret you know about Jack?" Powell asked.

"Jack Sharp isn't his real name. It's Jack Shapiro," Savannah said.

"Yes, we just learned that," Powell said.

"My older sister was roommates with a girl named Annie King. Do you know about her?"

"Yes, she was the girl who was allegedly raped by Jack Shapiro and his fraternity brothers," Powell replied.

"Then you know that she disappeared during their trial?"

"Yes, and the case fell apart afterwards, allowing Jack and the others to walk away, scot free," Zandy said.

"My sister never told anyone except me, but the night Annie disappeared, my sister was asleep in the bedroom next door. At one point in the night, she heard a noise, and swears that she heard a man's voice. Scared that someone had broken into their apartment, my sister hid in the closet. In the morning, Annie was gone, and the lock on the front door was damaged. She then found the note from Annie that said she was running away. My sister put two and two together, and figured that her disappearance had something to do with the trial. She was too scared to tell the police what she knew."

"How did Chris find out about this secret?" Powell asked.

"I told him. I wish I never did, but I told him about Jack Shapiro and the Four Horsemen."

"What do you know about the Four Horsemen?" Powell asked.

"Before the evening Jack and the others raped her, Annie King had hung around the Sigma Pi fraternity a bit. She heard the stories about the Four Horsemen from another one of the fraternity brothers. The rumors were that the Four Horsemen's plan was that once one member reached a position of power at a company, they would all work together to support that person and turn the company into their own private cash machine. They were so full of themselves that they knew it was only a matter of time after graduating from USC that one of them would become a high-level manager at a big company. When Jack was promoted to General Manager at Black Label Racquet Sports, that was their golden ticket."

"Did Chris tell anyone what he knew about Jack?" Zandy asked.

"Shortly before they fired him, Chris let it slip that he had some dirt on Jack, and mentioned that he had been involved in a group rape."

"Do you know who he told?" Powell asked.

"Chris was with a few of the tennis pros on his Advisory Staff. He and Joe Hamilton had taken the group out for drinks, and they all had a few too many. He was so upset that he had let it slip out."

"Savannah, we want to thank you for coming forward. This is extremely helpful. I don't think you have a reason to be scared. It doesn't sound like anyone knows about you and Chris. But if you need our help, we are just a phone call away." Powell said.

"Dude, I told you this was some wild shit," Bodhi said.

"As for you, my good friend, you can't tell anyone what you know," Zandy said to Bodhi.

"My lips are sealed. Now let's go surfing!"

As they were about to walk away, Bodhi got a concerned look on his face.

"Oh, crap!"

"What is it Bodhi?" Zandy asked.

"Black Label recently fired Alan Mercer. He hasn't been returning my calls. I hope he's okay."

"I hadn't heard that news. We will call him this morning to check in on him," Powell said.

⁂

Zandy and Stan sat in oversized chairs at the *Coffee Cartel*, located in the Riviera Village area of Redondo Beach. Just a short distance from the beach, a cool ocean breeze brought the smell of the ocean and a slight chill inside the small cafe.

"So, that was something. What's our next move, Agent Powell?" Zandy asked.

"Well, just to piss him off, I had subpoenaed the travel records for Jack and his team a while back, so hopefully that will come in soon. That might tell us something. Right now, I'm going to see if I can track down Alan Mercer," Powell said as he pressed some buttons on his phone.

After a minute of silence, Stan spoke into his phone, "Alan, this is Agent Stan Powell with the FBI. Lt. Roberts and I are back in Los Angeles, and would very much like to connect with you. Please call me back at this number right away."

⁂

Chapter Forty-Two

ALAN MERCER WAS suddenly aware of two female voices, though he couldn't quite make out the words. The voices were muffled, and there were background sounds from some sort of electronic apparatus. He tried his hardest to open his eyes, but his eyelids were too heavy. With great effort, he took a few deep breaths, and the voices became clearer. The fog in his consciousness began to lift.

"Alan. Alan. Can you hear me?" one of the female voices said.

Then the other voice said, "If you can hear us, squeeze my hand."

Squeeze her hand, Mercer told himself. Squeeze her hand. But he struggled to make the muscles in his hand move. Then, with all of his focus, he managed to gently grip the hand that was holding onto his.

"Alan, we are right here. Wake up," the voice said.

There was more light penetrating his consciousness. He heard the voices more clearly, and his eyes slowly opened. A soft light overhead and two out-of-focus figures hovered over him.

"Alan, it's Madison and Samantha. We are here. Wake up. Come back to us," Madison said.

"He...hello," Mercer whispered. His throat was dry, and it was painful to speak.

As the room came into focus, Mercer realized Madison was holding one hand and Samantha the other.

"Where am I?" Mercer asked weakly.

"You are at Scripps Memorial Hospital in La Jolla. You've been here for four days," Madison said.

Aware that there were now more people in the room, Madison and Sam stepped aside as a doctor and nurse came into focus.

"Welcome back to us, Alan. I am Dr. David Perzik. How are you feeling?"

As Mercer became more aware of his surroundings, he also began to sense the condition of his body.

"My head hurts, but everything else feels a little foggy."

"We've got you on a pretty powerful cocktail of pain meds right now. You will feel pretty out of it for a while, but we will start to reduce them a bit. That should help to get rid of that foggy feeling," Dr. Perzik said.

"Am I going to be okay?" Mercer asked, his words trailing off, as he fought the effects of the pain meds.

"Yes. You are quite lucky. You have some broken ribs and significant contusions all over your body, but our primary worry has been the pressure that has built up inside your cranium. You received quite a blow to the head, and you've been unconscious for the past four days. But it looks like you are beginning to heal," Dr. Perzik said. "Do you remember how you got here?"

Mercer was silent as he searched through the fog of his

memory. Suddenly, the vision of headlights through Cole Bundy's rear window flashed into his mind. Then he recalled the man in the truck looking down the steep embankment.

"Cole! How is Cole?"

Dr. Perzik looked towards Madison, and Patty Hamilton, who had joined them in the room.

"We are really sorry, Alan. Your friend did not survive the accident. The first responders pronounced him dead at the scene," Dr. Perzik said.

"Oh god. No! Mercer groaned. "Is Trish okay?"

Patty stepped forward and answered, "Alan, she has family with her right now. Joe and I have been to the house a few times. She's obviously grief-stricken, but she has a lot of support from friends and family. It will help her spirits knowing that you are awake."

Overcome with sadness, Mercer wept uncontrollably.

"That man in the truck. Why?" Mercer asked, his voice reduced to a soft whisper.

"Alan, I think that's enough for now. You need your rest," Dr. Perzik said, as Mercer drifted into the drug-induced darkness again, and into a restless sleep.

Chapter Forty-Three

THERE WAS A gentle tap on his hospital room door, and Mercer recognized Agent Stan Powell and Lt. Zandy Roberts in the doorway.

"Alan, is it okay if we talk with you?" Powell asked.

"Yes, please come in."

"How are you feeling, Alan?" Zandy asked.

"I'm feeling a lot better. After a week in this place, I'm getting a little restless, and just want to go home. My doctor says that's a good sign."

"That's great to hear. Your doctor says it was touch and go for a while. Sounds like you are a lucky man," Powell said.

"How did you know I was here?" Mercer asked.

"Zandy and I were in Los Angeles, following a lead in our case. Bodhi was concerned that he hadn't heard from you in a while, so we called you. Your phone went to voicemail. Madison called us back when she checked your messages," Powell replied.

"Are you feeling up to some questions?" Zandy asked.

"Yes, I'm good. What can I tell you?"

For the next hour, Mercer told them the story of his and Cole Bundy's visit to The Tennis Depot, the counterfeit racquet scheme, their suspicions about Jack Sharp, the mysterious Trojan Horse Logistics, and finally about the harrowing car chase through the dark streets of north San Diego county that ended in the death of his good friend.

"The driver of the truck made sure he was successful in his efforts. I will forever have the image of him looking down the embankment seared into my memory. Do you have any idea who he is?" Mercer asked.

"No, we don't, but we have our own suspicions about Jack Sharp. Do you remember Chris Peck mentioning that he had a girlfriend?" Stan asked.

"I don't recall, but I was in Atlanta when he was the rep out here. Why do you ask?"

Stan and Zandy provide Mercer with the details of their meeting on the Redondo Beach Pier with Bodhi and Savannah.

"Do you think they killed Chris Peck because he found out about Jack's past?" Mercer asked.

"We aren't completely sure yet, but something isn't quite right. Now, with you and Cole being forced off the road, we are concerned for your safety. We have a guard stationed outside your room just to be sure," Powell said.

"I forgot to mention that on the day Randall Jefferies fired me, I came home and my house had been ransacked. Some racquets and files were taken, but nothing else."

"Okay, we can follow up with your local police department and get their incident report. In the meantime, we have some follow up to do in Hood River. It sounds like you will be getting out of here in a few days. We will talk before then and make sure you are protected when you leave," Powell said.

"I appreciate you keeping me in the loop with your

investigation. I can still see Cole's lifeless body pinned beneath his van. We need to find out who did this to him."

"You got it Alan. Rest up and get better. We will talk soon," Powell said as he and Lt. Roberts slipped out of the room to check in with the office posted outside the room.

※

He still tired quickly, and after his meeting with Agent Powell and Lt. Roberts, he needed a long nap. Mercer was pleasantly surprised when he opened his eyes to find Madison seated in a chair next to his bed.

"Well, hello there, sleepyhead," she said.

"Am I dreaming, or are you really here?"

"I'm here Alan. Can I get you anything?" Madison asked. Softly, she placed her hand on his.

"No, just you being here is all I need. How did you get by the watchdog stationed outside my door?" Mercer asked.

"That was easy. I just brought him some fresh-baked cookies," Madison said with a crooked smile on her face.

"Did you say cookies? I'm starving!"

Madison lifted a Tupperware container, peeling back the lid, releasing the smell of fresh baked chocolate chip cookies into the room.

"My secret recipe."

"Yum! Are you sure I'm not dreaming?" Mercer asked as he reached for a cookie.

"No, this isn't a dream. Hopefully, these cookies will help you recover. I'm still waiting for that next date. You sure know how to avoid a girl," she said with a giggle.

Suddenly, their laughter was interrupted by a knock on the door. It was the armed officer assigned to guard the room.

"Sorry to interrupt. You have a visitor. Says his name is Quinn Peck. He says you knew his brother, Chris."

"Uh, yes... give us a minute, and you can let him in," Mercer said.

"I've got some errands to run. Don't visit for too long. You still need your rest. Maybe I can come back and have dinner with you?" Madison said.

"Only if you can smuggle in a couple of seafood burritos. I'm sick of hospital food."

"You got it. See you a little later," Madison said, then leaned over and gave Mercer a soft kiss on the forehead.

∽

Mercer pressed the remote control that operated his hospital bed to raise him into a more upright position as Quinn Peck entered the room. At first glance, Mercer thought the man looked a lot like the actor Ben Affleck. Athletically built, with a well-groomed beard, he wore his hair short, just like the actor.

"Alan, I'm Quinn Peck. We've never met, but you knew my little brother, Chris. I'm sorry to drop in on you like this, but I recently had a phone conversation with Agent Powell, and he gave me an update on Chris's case. I decided I needed to see you immediately."

"Thank you for coming. First of all, I'm really sorry about your brother. He was a good man. But I'm not sure why you wanted to see me," Mercer said as he extended his left hand to greet his guest. The right hand still restricted by the pulse monitor on his index finger.

"I've spent some time in the military. I was part of the initial phase of *Operation Desert Storm*, so I have some training in tracking down bad guys. From the sounds of it, the same bad guys who killed my brother are likely connected to the man who put you in this hospital bed, and your friend in a grave," Quinn said.

"I think you may be right, but I'm not sure how I can help you," Mercer said.

"I think we can help each other." Quinn offered. "I want more than anything to nail the person who killed Chris. I'm assuming you want the same for your friend Cole. Maybe we can work together to find some closure?"

"I need to find more solid proof that Jack Sharp is involved in this counterfeit tennis racquet operation. I believe that was why we were targeted. We were getting too close to the truth, just like your brother was regarding Jack's past," Mercer shared.

"So we both need more solid proof. How do you propose we go about finding it?" Quinn asked.

"Have you ever been to Taiwan?" Mercer asked.

※

His truck was still missing its front bumper, but the local body shop had done wonders repairing the front-end damage. Paying up-front in cash, Philip Marcus was able to avoid any unnecessary paperwork and questions.

After he parked his truck in the three-story parking garage at Scripps Memorial Hospital, he entered the main hospital reception area. Looking as though he was lost, a nurse asked if he needed help.

"Yes, I am hoping to visit a friend, but not sure what room he is in. My friend's name is Alan Mercer."

Chapter Forty-Four

STAN POWELL WAS late leaving Portland, so he met Zandy Roberts in the parking lot behind Solstice Cafe and Bar. Interstate 84 divided Hood River, with Solstice and a few businesses on the Columbia River side of the highway and the main part of town on the other.

Zandy knew the owner of Solstice well. As a Hood River police lieutenant, she knew most of the local business owners.

"Sorry I'm late. Traffic getting out of Portland was nuts," Powell said.

"No problem. Laura is ready to meet with us whenever we want."

"Great. Why don't you take the lead on this one?" Powell said.

"You got it. Let's see what she can tell us."

Inside the restaurant, the smell of burning oak greeted them as they stepped up to the bar, where Zandy saw the cafe's owner pouring a beer for a customer. Next to the bar was the food prep area and a large wood-fired pizza oven.

"Hey Zandy," Laura said, when she recognized the police lieutenant.

"Hi Laura. The wood from that pizza oven smells amazing! We may need to stick around for dinner," Zandy said.

"Just let me know what you want, and I'll get you set up. Who's your handsome partner?" Laura asked as she gave Powell a quick once-over.

"Laura, this is Agent Stan Powell. He's from the FBI field office in Portland. Funny, I hadn't noticed, but I guess he is kinda handsome," Zandy said as she winked at Stan.

"Let's go meet in my office, where we can have a little more privacy."

They followed Laura back to her office. Once there, they filled her in on the Chris Peck case as it currently stood.

"So, you think he was killed after eating here?" Laura asked.

"It looks that way. It was almost five years ago, but from what we've pieced together, he called his girlfriend from just outside after he ate a pizza here," Zandy said.

"That's horrible. How can I help?" Laura asked.

"We know it was a long time ago, but we are hoping that you had security cameras that might tell us something about that night," Powell said.

"We've recently changed our security provider, but I bet the old company would have video from back then. Let me get you the contact information for them. They are a local company, so you could probably just stop by," Laura said.

She wrote the security company's contact details on a piece of paper and handed it to Zandy.

"Okay, so what can I get you two to eat?"

⁓

By the time they finally left Solstice, nightfall had descended upon Hood River. A bitter wind was blowing through the gorge, so they both threw on their polar fleece jackets before stepping outside. Once outside the restaurant, they looked at the spot where Chris must have made his last phone call.

"What is the last thing you would do if you just spent hours in the car on the drive up from Los Angeles?" Zandy asked.

"I wouldn't jump back in my car. I would find a place to eat that I could walk to," Powell replied.

"Exactly."

"So, what's the closest hotel from here?" Powell asked.

"That would be the Riverfront Inn or the Columbia River Motor Lodge. Care to join me for a short walk, Agent Powell?"

"I'd love to. I need to work off some of that dinner," Powell replied.

The Columbia River Motor Lodge gave visitors the impression that they had stepped back into 1950s Hood River. The neon sign out front welcomed guests to the small motel, located just off I-84.

"Do you know why they call it a motor lodge?" Zandy asked as they walked up to the lobby entrance.

"I don't have any idea," Powell replied.

"Motor lodges have access directly from the parking lot to the rooms," Zandy said.

"Wow, you are full of all kinds of useful knowledge," Powell said as they shared a laugh.

The night manager at the Columbia River Motor Lodge proved to be less than helpful. Apparently, the previous owner of the lodge had died a couple of years back and the new owners completely scrapped the old registration system. Knowing that they had reached a dead end and wouldn't find any guest information from five years earlier, they politely thanked the manager and retreated back into the cool Hood River evening.

They arrived at the Riverfront Inn after a beautiful walk along the Columbia River waterfront. Inside the hotel, they stepped up to the front desk, where a young woman greeted them.

"Do you have a room reservation?"

"No, we don't. I'm Lt. Roberts with the Hood River Police, and this is Stan Powell with the FBI. We have some questions about a guest who may have stayed here five years ago. Do you know if you have records that go back that far?"

"You would want to speak with Yuki. He could probably pull up those records for you."

"That would be great. How do we get a meeting with Yuki?" Powell asked.

"He is back in his cave. I could take you back to see him now, if you like," the woman replied.

"Perfect. We'd love to meet him," Zandy said.

They followed the clerk through a door behind the front desk that opened into a hallway with rooms on each side. They walked to the end of the hallway, and the clerk knocked on the door and cracked it open.

"Yuki, you have some visitors. They are from the Hood River police and FBI."

"Cool. Show them in," Yuki said through the door opening.

Powell and Zandy entered the room and were surprised by the impressive collection of computer equipment.

"I feel like we've entered Mission Control, not a hotel," Zandy whispered to Powell, who was immersed in the vast array of surveillance monitors mounted to the wall.

"Hello. I'm Yuki. How can I help you?"

His smile revealed a full set of crooked teeth, and his moppy hair style would have made the Beatles proud. At just five feet tall, Yuki Suzuki welcomed the visitors into his domain.

After a brief introduction and overview of their case, the young techie said, "Well, you've come to the right place. I wasn't here five years ago, but I'm pretty sure I can pull up the registration records and surveillance video from that time period. Just give me a few minutes."

"That would be great. This is quite the set-up you have here," Powell said.

A few minutes passed while Yuki pecked away at his keyboard.

"Okay, so I'm able to pull up the guest registration log from the date you asked about," Yuki said.

"Do you see a guest by the name of Chris Peck?" Zandy asked.

"Hmmm… let me see. Yes, here he is. He checked in at 7:35pm and paid in advance for one night. He paid in cash."

Powell and Zandy looked at each other. They had found him!

"Do you know which room he was in?" Powell asked.

"It looks like room 117. It's on the first floor. The last room at the end of the hall, just in front of the back entrance."

"Any chance you can pull up surveillance video?" Zandy asked.

"Of course," Yuki casually replied. "Normally CCTV footage is deleted after thirty days, but I'm a huge true crime buff. I've read every Ann Rule book ten times. So I took it upon myself to save copies of all the hotel's video footage, in case a murderer copying the I-5 killer ever decided to stop in Hood River."

"That's incredible! If you ever get tired of your gig here at the

Riverfront Inn, we may have a place for you at the FBI," Powell said as he shrugged his shoulders while he looked towards Zandy, who had a look on her face as if to say; can you believe this guy?

A few minutes passed, and suddenly the largest monitor on the wall switched to a grainy video.

"Sorry about the poor quality of the video. We didn't have the latest Ultra Hi-Def cameras back then. This first video will show the main parking lot, just before 7:30 that night," Yuki said.

They watched in silence for a few minutes until they noticed a Toyota 4Runner pull into the parking lot, and then they saw Chris Peck step out of the driver's side door.

"Stop there," Powell said.

"There is Chris Peck. He appears to be alright, and his SUV looks a lot better than it does now," Zandy said.

"The next video feed is from the main lobby at 7:32pm," Yuki said.

The video showed Chris Peck check in. He paid with cash. There was no sound, but Chris appeared to be asking the desk clerk some questions, as the clerk pointed in the direction of the waterfront business district.

"Probably giving him directions to Solstice," Zandy said.

The next series of video clips showed Chris enter his room, then exit the hotel a few minutes later. The last image showed him walk through the parking lot, on his way to Solstice Cafe and Bar.

They studied the video feeds for a while, watching for signs of anyone following Chris.

"Yuki, can you fast forward the parking lot video a bit? Assuming dinner and the walk back and forth would take at least an hour, let's start there," Powell asked.

The video fast-forwarded, and then slowed to normal speed. After a while, Chris Peck came back into view, walking towards the front entrance of the hotel. The time stamp on the video read 10:13pm.

"Keep rolling with this video a bit. I want to see if anyone is following Chris." Powell said.

They watched in silence, but no-one came into view.

"Can you show us the hallway video, starting at 10:13?" Zandy asked.

Another few clicks on the keyboard, and the monitor screen changed again, to show the first floor hallway.

"There's Chris," Zandy said, as she pointed to the monitor on the wall.

They watch as Chris searched his pockets for his room key. Suddenly, they noticed the back door at the end of the hall open, and a hooded figure quickly stepped inside.

As if observing a predatory animal subdue its prey, they watched in horror as the hooded figure reached out toward Chris and appeared to jab a syringe into his neck. Chris quickly fell to the floor, then the hooded predator dragged him into Chris's hotel room.

"Holy shit!" Yuki said.

"Yuki, please tell me that you can get me close-up images of that hallway video?" Powell asked.

"Sorry, but the video is so pixilated that it's just going to be harder to see any details once you zoom in," Yuki responded.

"We need to see the face of the hooded figure," Powell said.

Despite his best efforts, Yuki could not get a better view of the hooded assailant.

"They went into Chris's room, so they had to come out

sometime. Let's keep the video rolling and see what happens next," Zandy said.

They let the video play, and then at the 3:36am time stamp, the hallway door opened, and a man wearing a baseball cap entered, knocked on Chris's hotel room door, and entered the room when the door opened. Again, the image was too grainy to make out the man's face.

A few minutes later, the man and the hooded figure appeared on the video, exiting Chris's room, carrying what they assumed was Chris Peck's body, wrapped in a sheet. They exited the door leading out of the hotel.

"Yuki, is there a camera outside that exit?" Powell asked.

"There is now. But back then, we didn't have one," Yuki replied.

"So it looks like our killer had a helper," Zandy said.

"It sure looks that way," Powell said.

Chapter Forty-Five

AFTER FOURTEEN HOURS in the air, the captain announced they would soon land at Taipei's Taoyuan International Airport. Mercer would be happy to be on the ground. It had only been ten days since his release from the hospital. His head and body were still bandaged and bruised, and his muscles were weak from being bedridden for so long.

Quinn Peck, who was eager to make those responsible for his brother's death pay for what they'd done, had joined him on the trip. Quinn's military training and determination made him a formidable ally. Mercer was thrilled when he agreed to come along.

Mercer was convinced that the people responsible for Chris Peck's death were also involved in the counterfeit tennis racquet operation. If they could find proof of this, authorities might finally have what they needed to go after Jack Sharp and his team.

Before joining Black Label, Mercer spent several years in product development roles for a couple of other tennis brands. During those years, he spent a lot of time in Taiwan. At the time, Taichung was the epicenter of all tennis racquet manufacturing. He had formed strong relationships with many factory owners and their staff.

Prior to the trip, he had reached out to his old contact at Topstone Manufacturing, Ace Chang. He did not disclose every detail about the purpose of his trip, but Ace was excited to hear from Mercer and promised to help. They had planned to meet the following morning in the lobby of the Evergreen Laurel Hotel.

※

The jet lag from the long flight wasn't helping his throbbing headache, but Mercer hoped that the pain meds he just swallowed would kick in shortly. He was due to meet Quinn for breakfast before their meeting with Ace.

They both enjoyed the hotel's "western style" breakfast. The food and black tea brought Mercer out of his sleep-deprived funk.

After breakfast, they found a secluded area with comfortable chairs as they waited for Ace to arrive.

Right on schedule, Ace Chang stepped through the hotel's front door. Mercer waved him over.

"Ace. How are you, my old friend?" Mercer said, as they shared a warm embrace.

"Alan, you still look super fit, but I can see you've had a bit of a rough time lately. Hopefully, your injuries are healing quickly," Ace said, as he examined the bruises that were still visible on Mercer's forehead.

"Same with you Ace. You haven't aged a bit," Mercer said.

They ordered Oolong tea, and for the next hour, Mercer and Quinn went through the events of the past year, including the investigation into the death of Chris Peck and the suspicious Element-5 racquets that were making their way into tennis shops in the United States.

"Alan, you know that Topstone only produces first quality racquets. We only work directly with representatives of the tennis companies. But we know that there are others who survive by making copies," Ace said.

"That is where I need your help. I have seen these copies, and I know they must come from a factory in this region. I'm also pretty certain that my friend Cole Bundy was killed because he was close to finding out who was behind the operation. Do you think you can help us find out who is making these racquets?" Mercer pleaded.

"Alan, my good friend. I am very sorry for the death of your friend, and for your injuries, but this is a very delicate situation. Many of us in this business hear rumors about factories that make copies. But we try to stay out of each other's business. It is a difficult thing that you are asking of me," Ace said.

"I know it is, and I respect the relationships that have been built over the years. I'm only asking this, because I feel a concern for not only my safety, but I promised Cole's family that I would help find the truth behind his murder."

Ace removed his glasses and rubbed his forehead. "I am not promising anything, but let me see what I can find out for you. I will contact you at the hotel later today."

"Thank you, Ace. This really means a lot to me," Mercer said as they stood and walked Ace to the front door.

∽

At just past eleven o'clock that night, a black Toyota Avalon pulled up in front of the Evergreen Laurel Hotel. Ace Chang had phoned Mercer earlier in the evening and reported that he had discovered some information that could be valuable, and that they had an opportunity to get more proof, but they had to do it that evening.

Standing in front of the hotel, as Ace stepped out of the back door of the Toyota, Quinn Peck grabbed Mercer's arm. "Are you sure you trust this guy?"

"With what's happened over the past month, I'm not sure I trust anyone. But we've come this far, so I'm willing to give it a shot. Besides, I have you for protection," Mercer said with a smile.

"Great. I feel much better now," Quinn said.

Once inside the car, Mercer asked, "Ace, you've found something for us?"

"Yes. I think this is what you are looking for. Have you ever heard of Green Dragon Manufacturing?" Ace asked.

"No, I haven't. I thought I knew most of the racquet factories here," Mercer replied.

"They have been around a while, but are outside the main manufacturing district, and missed the boat on building a plant on the mainland. Now that much of the manufacturing is taking place in China, it has been difficult for Green Dragon to find jobs. So, they have a reputation for accepting some questionable projects. Word is that they have been involved in counterfeiting. I have a way for us to get into the plant this evening." Ace said.

"How did you manage that?" Quinn asked.

"Let's just say I have a friend who owes me a favor. The plant will be closed now, and the owner is away on business, so we should be in the clear."

"Should be?" Mercer questioned.

Even at this late hour, traffic in the city was quite heavy, as the sea of motor scooters darted from side to side in front of their car. Eventually, they reached a quieter part of town where the streets were dark and mostly deserted.

They drove in silence for a while until they reached the outskirts of Taichung, where they finally pulled over to the side of the road.

"Okay, we will get out here and walk a short distance to the factory," Ace said.

"Are you sure you are up to this?" Quinn asked Mercer. "You were just in the hospital, so there's no shame in taking a pass."

"I'll be fine. The walk will do me some good," Mercer replied.

They followed Ace through the darkness and paid close attention to their footing along the pot-hole riddled road.

"Okay, that's Green Dragon over there," Ace said, pointing to the dilapidated factory across the road. "My friend will let us in through the side entrance. If something happens, let's meet back at the car," he instructed.

They remained in the shadows as they skirted along the side wall that surrounded the factory. Ace signaled for them to stop as they came to a large metal door. He then checked his watch and gently knocked on the door.

Almost instantly, they heard the door's lock opening. The heavy door slowly swung open, and a Taiwanese man stuck his head through the opening and waved them inside.

The door opened into a narrow courtyard, with offices and the primary production facility on the other side of the courtyard. Apparently, this area was for workers to park their scooters, as they saw a few parked nearby.

Huddled in the darkness, Ace quietly introduced Mercer and Quinn to his friend, Max.

"Thank you, Max," Mercer whispered, and nodded to the nervous-looking man.

Max led them into the production area and flipped on an overhead light. Mercer immediately recognized the layout of the production area to be like other factories he'd visited.

"Alan, what can Max show you?" Ace asked.

"I would really like to see any Black Label racquets. In particular, the Element-5 Tour 95s."

Ace nodded to Max, that it was okay to show the men what they want to see.

They followed Max to the opposite end of the room and through a door marked FINAL INSPECTION.

Max turned on a light that illuminated another large room. The room was loaded with several metal racks on wheels, each with approximately fifty tennis racquets waiting to be inspected before being placed in plastic bags. One of the rolling racks held a group of fresh Element-5 Tour 95 racquets, which would be inspected the following day.

Next to the rack of Black Label racquets, it surprised Mercer to see a full rack of Babolat Pure Drive racquets, Babolat's most popular model. Next to that was a rack of Head's new Prestige model.

"Green Dragon is also making Babolat and Head racquets?" Mercer asked.

"Yes; some Wilson and Prince racquets too," Max replied.

Mercer picked up one of the Element-5 racquets and recognized these had the same holographic decals as the counterfeit racquets he had picked up at Westwood Tennis.

They were extremely good copies. Only someone with close knowledge of the product could detect the difference.

"Max, did you have a problem with the drilling pattern on the string holes in these racquets?" Mercer asked.

Surprised by the question, Max replied, "Yes, we did. That was very embarrassing, but it is all fixed."

"Have you seen representatives of Black Label in the factory?" Mercer asked.

"Yes. I have seen them here."

"Do you know their names?" Quinn asked.

"I don't want to get anyone in trouble," Max replied.

"It's okay Max. You can tell these men what you know," Ace said.

"I don't know the names, but I was told they were from Black Label Racquet Sports," Max said.

Mercer reached into his jacket pocket and pulled out his cell phone. He opened his photo file and scrolled back to the Snowbird sales meeting images. He zoomed in on a photograph and turned the phone toward Max.

"Do you recognize anyone in this photo?"

Max studied the image and pointed at Bill Cashman and Tom Saltz.

"These two men have been here recently," Max said.

Scrolling to another picture, Mercer held the phone up for Max to get a good look.

"How about this photo?" he asked.

"Yes, this man," Max said, as he placed his finger on the image of Jack Sharp.

Before Mercer could say anything, the doors to the room flew open, and three men wearing masks over their faces burst into the room. A flash, and shots muffled by silencers, filled the room. Suddenly Mercer was soaked in blood.

Thinking that he had been shot, he looked at Max, who had blood gushing through a hole in his neck. One gunman's bullet had destroyed his carotid artery and blood was spraying all over Mercer. Max fell silently to the floor, into a pool of his own blood.

Quinn dove towards Mercer and quickly tackled him to the ground, then dragged a shocked Mercer behind a metal workbench. A loud shot rang out, and they looked at Ace, who was crouched behind another workbench with a handgun pointed toward the gunmen.

While shots were being fired in both directions, Mercer and Quinn crawled over to Ace.

"We need to get into the paint room, which is through those doors," Ace said, as he pointed towards the double doors about ten feet away. A sign above the door warned those entering that it was a sterile environment.

"There should be an exit to the outside from there," Ace said, as he fired another shot towards the men. "On my next shot, let's go for the door. I will follow you."

Before a dazed Mercer realized what was happening, Ace fired another shot, and Quinn dragged him towards the paint room doors. As he reached the doors, Quinn pulled the right side door open, creating a shield as bullets struck the other side. Before Ace could reach them, a fatal shot hit him in the back of the head.

Mercer reached towards his friend as the bullet exited Ace's forehead, and he fell towards him. As Ace fell to the ground, his gun landed at Quinn's feet. Quinn scooped it up and shoved Mercer through the open door and closed it behind them.

"We've got to find the exit," Quinn yelled.

"Over there!" Mercer pointed to a glowing red sign above a doorway on the far side of the room.

They moved quickly in the dimly lit room, much of it cordoned off by clear vinyl curtains, installed to keep the painting area free of dust and other debris that could land on a freshly painted racquet. The other side of the room was filled with more of the metal rolling racks, but these were all filled with raw carbon racquets, waiting to be painted.

They got about halfway across the room when the door they had just entered burst open and gunmen slipped into the room.

More muffled gunshots flew by them as Quinn returned their fire, striking one man in the right shoulder.

Mercer and Quinn reached the emergency exit door and jerked it open. As they exited into the darkness outside the factory, a loud siren filled the air as an alarm was triggered when they opened the door. They closed the door and searched their surroundings for a way out. Feeling their way along the wall that surrounded the factory, they were hoping to find the large metal door they had entered through a short time ago. They managed to distance themselves from the gunmen, but could hear the men searching for them in the darkness.

"Over here!" Mercer said quietly as he recognized the courtyard in front of the metal door.

"Check the scooters for keys," Quinn said.

Mercer and Quinn quickly searched the dusty scooters parked in the courtyard.

"Found one!" Mercer whispered.

"Grab it. Let's get out of here!" Quinn said, just as a spray of bullets hit the metal door in front of them.

Quinn fired back at the approaching gunmen as they pulled on the metal door. They guided the scooter through the open door and Mercer jumped on, then he turned the key and pushed the starter switch. On the first try, the engine sputtered and quickly died. Quinn jumped on the back of the scooter and pointed his gun towards the door.

"Try it again!" Quinn yelled.

Mercer repeated the process, and the motor caught this time, as a huge puff of smoke escaped from the tailpipe. Then the motor died again.

"Fuck!" Mercer yelled.

Quinn had pinned the gunmen on the other side of the metal door, and held them there with his gunfire. He took aim as Mercer struggled with the rundown motor scooter.

Click. Click.

"Shit! The cartridge is empty," Quinn said, tossing the empty gun to the ground.

Mercer gave the starter another try. This time a loud bang came from the exhaust system along with another puff of smoke. Then the motor sputtered to life with an uneven cadence.

"Hold on!" Mercer yelled, as he put the scooter in gear, and the motorbike lurched forward and disappeared into the darkness. Bullets flew by their heads as the gunmen began to fire blindly in the direction of the scooter's loud exhaust.

It wasn't until they reached the busy streets of Taichung before they felt safe. They blended into the sea of scooters that flowed through the streets.

Nearing the city center, the scooter's motor sputtered and then cut off completely.

"I think we're out of gas," Mercer said while he guided the

scooter over to the side of the road. "Hopefully, we can grab a taxi from here."

Finally getting a good look at Mercer, Quinn said, "Not before we get you cleaned up a bit."

Suddenly aware that he was still covered in Max's blood, Mercer began to cry uncontrollably, as the events of the evening rushed back to him.

"If it weren't for me, my friend Ace and Max would still be alive. Oh god! What have I done?" Mercer said as he stared blankly into the distance, as tears streamed down his face.

Chapter Forty-Six

ABBY JOHNSON WATCHED the clock on the wall as she mentally tried to propel it forward. It had been another long day, working at Black Label Racquet Sports customer service. Ever since Alan Mercer was fired her duties had skyrocketed. The new guy simply didn't provide the same level of service that Mercer had. So now the customers were calling her with their troubles.

As if on cue, her phone rang. "Hello Miss Abby. This is Sarge Turner at The Racket King."

"Hello Sarge. How are you doing today?" she asked.

"Not so good. That rep of yours doesn't call me on Sundays so I can place my orders. All of my reps know I need to get my orders in on Sunday night, so they ship the following day. This rep is too busy doing who-knows-what to call me."

"I'm sorry about that, Sarge. He seems to be getting off to a rough start. Is there anything I can do to help?"

"Yes, there is. I would like to speak with Jack Sharp today! He needs to fix this," Sarge demanded.

"Have you spoken with Joe Hamilton?" Abby inquired.

"Yes, but he just told me it was Jack's idea to hire this guy," he replied.

"Okay Sarge. It's clearing out here towards the end of the day. Let me see if I can find Jack and have him call you right away. What's the best number to reach you at?"

"Thank you Abby. He can call me at the store or on my cell," Sarge said as they ended the call.

∽

Since she worked primarily with west coast sales reps and customers, Abby was often one of the last to leave for the day. So as she searched for Jack Sharp, many of her colleagues had already gone home.

In front of Jack's office was Valerie Little's cubicle. Abby noticed the light was still on in Jack's office, but neither he nor Valerie were around. She studied the daily planner on Valerie's desk and saw a notation for that date. Scribbled on the planner, she read: 6:00pm - I.C. Pro Room.

"That is strange," Abby said to herself, uncertain why a meeting would take place in the Pro Room at this hour.

The Pro Room was where Black Label kept their inventory of sponsored players' racquets. Each racquet in the room had been customized to the specific demands of the player, and was ready to ship around the globe at a moment's notice. Many of the professional players needed racquet specifications that differed from the racquets sold to the public. The Pro Room was where those modifications took place. The finished racquets hung on pegs, with the player's name noted on the end of each row of racquets.

The entire engineering team had already gone home, as Abby entered the R&D area at Black Label headquarters. Towards the back of the room was the vault-like Pro Room.

As she approached the room, she heard voices coming

from inside. She noticed that the door to the Pro Room was left slightly ajar. One voice she recognized was Jack Sharp's.

Rather than barge in on the meeting, Abby positioned herself so she wouldn't be noticed, but could hear when the meeting ended.

"We've got a big problem in Taiwan," Jack said.

"What is it this time?" Bill Cashman asked.

"Alan Mercer and some other men broke into Green Dragon. Walter Chen sent me copies of surveillance photos that show Mercer, Ace Chang from Topstone, and an unidentified man entering the factory. It appears they were let in by one of the employees at the plant."

"What the hell? What were they doing there?" Tom Saltz asked.

"Apparently, they were looking over some of the counterfeit Element-5 racquets," Jack said.

"Was he able to stop them?" Cashman asked.

"A hidden security camera linked to Walter's cell phone captured their entry. He quickly notified his team to stop the intruders. The Green Dragon employee and Ace Chang were both shot and killed in the altercation, and one of the security team members was wounded, but Mercer and the other man were able to escape," Sharp said.

"Jesus! This shit is getting out of control. We've got to track them down," Cashman yelled, as he slammed the tennis racquet that he'd been holding to the ground.

"Do we know if they are still in Taiwan?" Randall Jefferies asked.

"Walter has his men searching for them. They found Mercer's hotel and searched his room. He has not been back to the hotel, but they are keeping an eye out, just in case he comes back. They are also staking out the airport in Taipei," Jack said.

Standing behind one of the large robotic testing instruments, Abby Johnson was shocked at what she had just overheard. She remained hidden until the meeting ended and the group left the R&D area.

∽

Abby lingered for about thirty minutes in the dark before she made her way out of Black Label headquarters and down to her car. Not sure what to do, she tried to contact Mercer, but as expected, his phone went to voicemail.

"Alan, this is Abby. I hope you get this voicemail. I just overheard Jack Sharp and some others talking about trying to stop you. I don't know what to do, but I'm worried about you. Please call me and let me know you are still safe."

Chapter Forty-Seven

ALAN MERCER AND Quinn Peck huddled in a corner booth inside a cafe at the Hong Kong International Airport. Mercer thought back to some memorable trips to Hong Kong when he worked in product development. Some of the finest sewing operations for sports bags and luggage were in the area. He had always planned some extra time for shopping while in the Kowloon Shopping District area on his work trips. Haggling over prices with shop owners created a sport out of shopping that Mercer really enjoyed. But on this brief stop in Hong Kong, all he wanted to do was get on a plane home.

Over the past forty-eight hours, after cleaning up and finding some new clothes, Mercer and Peck decided not to return to their hotel. That would have been too risky.

They were pretty certain that someone would look for them at the airport in Taipei, expecting them to hop on a flight back to the U.S. So they headed south to the coastal city of Kaohsiung. They had hired a taxi in Taichung, near where they left the scooter, and had the driver drop them at the edge of town. From there, they paid a truck driver to take them to Kaohsiung City. For over two hours, they bounced around the back of the truck, filled with worn out automobile and scooter tires. The stink of decomposing rubber made the journey nearly unbearable.

Upon arrival at Kaohsiung International Airport, they chose the first departing flight, on China Airlines, which was heading for Hong Kong. They both breathed an enormous sigh of relief as they got on the plane without any complications.

Still not taking any chances, they kept a low profile inside the Hong Kong airport until their flight to Los Angeles boarded three hours later. Neither of their cell phones got service, so Mercer planned to send a message to Stan Powell from the Western Union office once it opened.

※

Mercer was the first customer inside the tiny Western Union office at the Hong Kong airport. He paid for and sent a brief email to Agent Powell. Then he rejoined Quinn in a quiet area of the airport and waited to board their plane.

※

Stan Powell woke early to get in a quick run in Forest Park before heading to the office. At least a few times each week, Powell was among the many Portland runners who loved to run on the miles of trails in one of the country's largest urban parks. As usual, he checked his text messages and emails before leaving his apartment.

"What's this?" he said to himself and clicked on the email sent via Western Union.

STAN. IN HONG KONG. FOUND PROOF JACK SHARP AND OTHERS INVOLVED IN COUNTERFEIT OPERATION. BACK IN LOS ANGELES TOMORROW.

CATHAY PACIFIC FLIGHT CX 882. WILL CALL WHEN I LAND. ALAN.

"What the hell?" Powell said to himself.

"Is he crazy? Wasn't he just in the hospital?"

Powell checked the timestamp on the email and factored in the time difference.

"A few more hours until he lands in Los Angeles," he said out loud, as he quickly changed out of his running gear.

Chapter Forty-Eight

"SO WHAT'S NEXT?" Quinn asked as their flight from Hong Kong taxied to the gate at LAX.

"First thing is to call Agent Powell at the FBI. I think we have enough proof that Jack Sharp orchestrated the counterfeit racquet operation so they can make some arrests."

"Not sure about you, but prison seems to be a light punishment for Jack and his gang, considering the number of people who have died," Quinn said.

"I agree with you, but I'm not sure what else we can do. Besides, I'm a firm believer in karma. Prison may be a soft landing for Jack Sharp, but something tells me that his day of reckoning will come," Mercer said.

"I hope you are right. I'd like to be there when the lights go out," Quinn said.

They both turned on their cell phones as the Cathay Pacific Boeing 767 parked at the gate. While still seated, Mercer's phone came to life, with several notifications that there were voicemails, texts, and emails waiting for him.

As he scrolled through the messages, he clicked on a text from Abby Johnson.

Alan. I'm very worried about you. I need to talk to you when you get this message. I also left you a voicemail. Abby.

He typed a quick response:

Abby. I'm safe. Just landed in LA. Will call you when I get to a more private location. Are you available to talk? Alan.

A few minutes passed before Abby sent a response.

Thank god! Yes, please call when you can.

They left any luggage brought with them at the Evergreen Laurel Hotel in Taichung, so had no items to retrieve from the overhead compartment upon exiting the plane. As they reached the boarding area, they saw a familiar face.

"Welcome home, you two," Stan Powell said, as he greeted the weary travelers.

"This is a pleasant surprise," Mercer said.

"After reading your email, I figured I would come and roll out the welcome wagon. Besides, I wanted to come down and scold you in person for going on this trip of yours. What the hell were you two thinking?" Powell said.

"Look Agent Powell, I know it was a bad idea, but we've both lost someone close to us because of these assholes. We needed to find some proof so you could put Jack Sharp and his goons away for a very long time," Quinn said.

"Okay. I get it. I'm just glad that you both are safe. Please promise me you won't do anything that stupid again," Powell pleaded.

Mercer and Quinn looked at each other and nodded in agreement that their investigative adventures were over.

"Let's get you both over to the local FBI field office for a debrief of your trip," Powell said, as they walked through the Tom Bradley International Terminal.

๛

Traffic was backed up as the government-issued Chevy Suburban inched along the 110 Freeway, headed towards downtown Los Angeles and the FBI office.

"Stan, do you mind if I call Abby Johnson while we are sitting in traffic? She was my inside contact at Black Label, and I think she might have some important information for us," Mercer said.

"Sure. Put her on speakerphone," Powell replied.

Mercer pressed the speed dial for Abby, and waited a few moments, until she answered, "Hello…Alan?"

"Abby, it's me. I'm safe and driving in a car with Agent Stan Powell of the FBI. I'm going to put you on the speaker, so he can hear what you have to say."

"Alan, I'm so glad you are safe. I was so worried," Abby said.

"I made a brief trip to Taichung with Quinn Peck, Chris's brother. We had quite an adventure, but we were able to find some interesting information. Your text sounded urgent. What's going on?"

"I went to find Jack Sharp in his office to see if I could get him to call Sarge Turner. When I checked Valerie's planner, I saw they had a meeting planned in the Pro Room, so I went to go find them. I overheard some alarming stuff. They know it was you at the factory in Taichung, but they don't know who Quinn is."

Abby continued to fill them in on the rest of the conversation from the Pro Room, their fear that Mercer had proof of the counterfeit operation, and their plan to stop Mercer and Quinn.

"Abby, this is Agent Powell. Can you identify the people at the meeting?"

"Yes, of course. I watched them all leave when the meeting

was over. Besides Jack Sharp, there was Randall Jefferies, Bill Cashman, Tom Saltz, Dustin McCabe, and Valerie Little."

"Are you positive that nobody noticed you?" Mercer asked.

"I'm sure they didn't see me. They were too involved in the meeting. They sounded worried."

"Okay Abby. You need to stay put. I'm going to reach out to our Chicago office and get a contact for you. They will be a quick text or call away if you need help," Powell said.

"Thank you. I will let you know if I hear anything else. But Alan, you need to stay out of sight. They are looking for you," Abby warned.

∽

During the debrief at the LA field office, Powell's cell phone began to vibrate indicating an incoming call. The name on the caller ID; Sherlock Cahill.

"Let's take a quick break. I need to take this call," Powell said.

"Sherlock. What do you have for me?"

"I've spent the entire day going through video tape from the security company that ran surveillance for Solstice Cafe in Hood River. I found something!" Sherlock said through the phone.

"What is it, Sherlock?" Powell asked.

"I'm sending you an email right now. I've blown up an image from the exact time that Chris Peck was in the restaurant. It's from a camera that shows the outside area in front of the cafe."

"Okay, let me check your email. I'll call you back if I have questions. Thank you."

Powell pressed a few keys on his laptop, and slowly an

image loaded. Gradually a photo came into focus on the computer's screen.

"Gotcha!" Powell yelled was he gazed at the image that was now in focus.

He then spun the laptop around for others in the room to see.

"This was taken while Chris Peck was inside the Solstice Cafe, in Hood River. This is the proof we needed," Powell said, while he pointed at the grainy image of a man sitting behind the wheel of a car that was parked across the street from the cafe, his face illuminated by the streetlight overhead.

"Jack Sharp. Your day of reckoning is coming soon," Quinn Peck said, overcome with grief, knowing he was staring at the face of the man who killed his little brother.

Chapter Forty-Nine

STAN POWELL HUDDLED together with a dozen FBI agents from the Chicago field office in the alley behind Black Label Sporting Goods headquarters. They were going over the last details of the operation that they had already rehearsed several times.

"Let's get this right. I would expect them to be armed, so don't take any chances. Seal all stairways and elevators. Nobody gets out of that building," Powell ordered. "Okay, let's do this!"

Powell and a handful of agents in full tactical gear swarmed the central lobby of the high-rise building that housed Black Label Sporting Goods. The agents quickly sealed the front doors and positioned men at each elevator door. They also placed agents inside the underground parking garage.

They had prepped each FBI agent to find and apprehend five members of the Black Label Racquet Sports management team: Jack Sharp, Bill Cashman, Randall Jefferies, Tom Saltz, and Valerie Little. Abby Johnson tipped them off that Dustin McCabe had returned to Clearfield, Utah, so a separate operation was currently underway to capture him.

Powell and five agents entered the floor that housed the

Racquet Sports division through one of the stairway doors. They disabled the elevators to prevent any chance of escape.

Having been there before, he led the team of agents towards Jack Sharp's office. But before they could get there they saw Valerie Little, who was frantically tapping out a message on her cell phone. She then darted towards the other side of the massive office space.

"Stop! Get her!" Powell yelled out to the other agents, who were quickly in pursuit of the surprisingly fast executive assistant.

But before she could make it to the stairway door, a young woman launched herself from her cubicle, tackling Valerie to the ground with a heavy thud. Two agents then placed a stunned Valerie Little in handcuffs.

"Thank you for your help," Powell said to the young woman as he helped her back to her feet. On the outer wall of the cubicle was a nameplate that read Abby Johnson.

"Well, Miss Johnson, it's nice to finally meet you. I'm Stan Powell."

"You are most welcome, Agent Powell."

She then looked at Valerie Little who was still trying to catch her breath after having the wind knocked out of her, and said, "Alan Mercer sends his regards."

Another agent who had been searching the office building rushed up to Powell and reported, "No sign of Jack Sharp or the others. They are not on this floor."

Powell looked down and noticed Valerie Little's cell phone on the ground. He picked it up, saw that it was still unlocked, and studied the text application. The last message sent was to Jack and the Inner Circle. It read: *FBI in the building. Get out now!*

Powell looked into the eyes of the handcuffed woman and said, "Valerie Little, you are under arrest for the coverup of the murder of Chris Peck, as well as your involvement in an international counterfeit operation. You can do yourself a favor and let us know where Jack and the others are."

"Screw you! You have no proof," she hissed.

"I'm afraid we do. It's time for your little group of thugs to give the keys to the company back to their rightful owners. Jack Sharp and his Inner Circle have held Black Label Racquet Sports hostage for long enough," Powell answered.

Powell, realizing he wouldn't be getting any cooperation from Valerie Little, turned his attention to Abby Johnson, as another agent read Ms. Little her Miranda rights.

"Abby, is there another way off this floor?" Powell asked.

"There used to be another stairway door on the other side of the floor, but they recently remodeled the surrounding offices so the doorway was covered. The stairway should still be there," Abby replied as she directed the agents to the concealed doorway.

∽

The metal door from the concealed stairway burst open into the dimly lit underground parking garage. Tom Saltz was the first to enter the garage, his handgun drawn. They had rehearsed their escape plan several times, knowing that the day would come when the unused stairway would provide them with a clean escape to the garage. They had staged some guns and other munitions in the stairway, in the event they needed them to shoot their way out of the building.

"Stop where you are!" an FBI agent yelled at Tom, as Jack, Bill, and Randall followed him out of the stairway.

Tom fired a shot, hitting one agent in the chest, knocking him to the ground. Another agent fired a series of rounds. One caught Tom Saltz in the abdomen; the others hit a car parked nearby.

The agent, who was struck in the chest, pulled himself off the ground, glad that his body armor had done its job. Jack and the others dragged the bleeding Tom Saltz into Bill's Porsche Cayenne.

While they took heavy gunfire, Bill navigated the bullet-riddled Porsche SUV through the parking garage and smashed through the wooden barricade the FBI had set up to prevent anyone from entering or exiting the garage.

"He's bleeding pretty bad," Jefferies yelled to the others from the back seat, as he tried to comfort his wounded partner.

"We stick to the plan! Bill and I head to Midway Airport. The plane is prepped and ready. You and Tom get on the "L" to Union Station and grab a train down to El Paso. You can cross into Mexico from there," Jack said.

"I don't know if Tom is going to make it that far," Jefferies said.

Bill, maneuvering the Cayenne at a high speed through the Chicago streets, looked in the rearview mirror at the ashen-colored face of Tom Saltz, and replied, "Just find a way to stop the bleeding. He will be fine."

∽

Powell seethed with anger, then red-lined the engine of the Chevy Tahoe as he tried to steer around some road construction. He and several agents were responding to a call reporting a wounded man matching the description of Tom Saltz had been discovered at Berwyn Station. Still upset about the botched operation at Black Label headquarters that allowed the men to slip away, Powell slammed on the brakes as he pulled up to the train station.

"This way!" A uniformed transportation officer yelled as he saw Powell and his team pile out of the SUV.

Berwyn was a small, open-air "L" train station on the Chicago Transit Authorities Red Line. Agents ushered travelers off the train platform as they slowly approached Tom Saltz, who sat hunched over on a bench next to the station's main building.

"Tom Saltz! Place your hands on your head," Powell yelled, but there was no reaction from the solitary figure on the bench.

They continued to inch closer, all guns pointed at Saltz, who was bloodied from his gunshot wound. A Glock-19 handgun rested on his lap.

"Tom, put your hands on your head!" Powell repeated.

Tom slowly turned to look towards the agents as they descended upon him. One grabbed the gun while another agent yanked him to the ground.

"Call an ambulance!" Powell shouted, but knew it was most likely too late for Tom Saltz.

"Tom, I hope it was worth it," Powell said to the dying man.

Turning his attention to the other agents, Powell asked, "Any sign of their car? Get the CTA on the phone. We need to see the surveillance video from this station right away."

"Damn it! They're gone," Powell cursed.

Chapter Fifty

DUSTIN MCCABE WAS not surprised when he received the group text from Valerie Little that reported FBI agents were in the process of raiding Black Label headquarters. He guessed they would pay him a visit sometime soon if they weren't already outside the Black Label Distribution Center in Clearfield.

His exit strategy was to destroy the evidence of the counterfeit operation at the nearby Trojan Horse Logistics warehouse, then head south through the desert until he reached Nogales, Arizona, where he would cross the border into Mexico.

Just as he exited the back of the Black Label building, a swarm of armed agents in tactical gear came around from the front of the building.

"Dustin McCabe! Stop, and get down on the ground!" one of the FBI agents shouted.

McCabe was able to reach his Sprinter van, and threw open the driver's side door, just as the first bullets hit the back of the van. He slammed the transmission into drive, and with rear wheels squealing, the van lurched forward, fishtailing out of the loading dock area with two FBI vehicles in hot pursuit.

After a brief high-speed chase through the Freeport

Center shipping hub, McCabe squeezed the Sprinter down a narrow alley that led to the back of the Trojan Horse Logistics warehouse. Just before he reached the end of the cramped passageway, he slammed on the brakes, trapping the FBI vehicles behind him. He wriggled his way out of the van and ran towards the back entrance of the warehouse.

By the time the FBI agents could slip past the Sprinter van, Dustin McCabe had safely barricaded himself inside the warehouse, where he began arming the explosive charges he had installed when they first opened the secret warehouse. They knew that one day the time would come when they needed to destroy the evidence of their illegal operation, but that was all part of the plan. All of them had plenty of money stashed away in offshore bank accounts. It was now time to disappear.

FBI agents had surrounded the warehouse, while McCabe continued to work on the explosives.

"Dustin McCabe, come out of the building with your hands in the air. There is nowhere to run. We have the building surrounded," an agent called out over a megaphone.

With all the explosives armed, McCabe set the timer on the central control panel for five minutes. That would give him enough time to climb up the fire escape ladder to the roof. From there, he would sprint to safety along the rooftop of adjoining warehouses. The explosion would provide the distraction he needed to slip away unnoticed.

Just as he reached the steel ladder, the front door of Trojan Horse Logistics burst open, and agents tossed several tear gas canisters into the building. Pulling his shirt over his mouth and nose, McCabe began his ascent up the thirty-foot ladder. Three quarters of the way up, his foot slipped and he nearly fell to the ground. His eyes burned from the tear gas, but he was able to steady himself and finished the climb. He pulled the lever to release the hatch that opened onto the roof, but the lever wouldn't budge. He tried again with a little more force, but still, the lever remained stuck. With the heel of his hand, he pounded on the lever, hoping to dislodge whatever was stopping it from opening. Maybe it was just rusted shut, he guessed.

"Fuck!" McCabe yelled, as his vision became more blurred by the gas.

He continued to pound on the lever, as a handful of FBI agents wearing gas masks rushed into the building about thirty feet below him. The agents aimed their flashlights up towards McCabe, who was barely visible through the thick smoke. He continued to work on releasing the lever.

With all of his strength, McCabe tugged again at the lever, and it finally broke free, allowing him to throw open the rooftop hatch.

The thunderous explosion inside the secret warehouse was felt from several blocks away. A massive fireball and plume of smoke filled the sky above Trojan Horse Logistics. Surrounding warehouses were consumed in flames, and the force of the blast shattered windows at nearby businesses.

Five FBI agents along with Dustin McCabe were killed in the massive blast. Their bodies turned to dust. All that remained of the counterfeit tennis racquet operation was a mountain of burning rubble.

Chapter Fifty-One

STAN POWELL HAD just entered the control room at the Chicago Transit Authority headquarters when he received the disturbing report about the events that had just taken place in Clearfield, Utah.

"God damn it!" Powell yelled. "We have to find these guys and make them pay for what they've done!"

"We've got the video queued up from Berwyn train station. Hopefully, it will tell us something," one of the FBI agents reported.

They shifted their attention to the wall of video monitors that displayed several angles of the train station, each captured by the security cameras situated outside the station. Their focus narrowed as a silver Porsche Cayenne pulled up in front of the station, and Randall Jefferies pulled the bleeding Tom Saltz out of the back door of the SUV.

They continued to follow Jefferies as he guided his wounded associate to the train station platform, depositing him on a wooden bench. With a train approaching the station, Jefferies reached into his coat pocket and pulled out a handgun. He appeared to be talking to Tom as he set a gun in his lap and turned toward the train.

The last images showed Randall Jefferies boarding the train, while his dying partner slumped over on the bench.

"Where is that train headed?" Powell asked the CTA officer.

"It's headed towards Union Station. That would allow him to jump on a train that could take him anywhere in the country," the officer reported.

"I'll need to see video from Union Station. But first, let's see where that SUV is heading," Powell said.

The CTA associate rolled back the video to the spot when the Porsche pulled up to the station. They couldn't make out the faces in the front seat, but they clearly saw two men.

"It looks like their exit plan is to split up and head in different directions, with Sharp and Cashman traveling together, and now Jefferies is on his own. Assuming they will need to ditch the Porsche sometime soon, where would they go?" Powell asked.

"From the direction they appear to be headed, my guess is Midway," the CTA officer said, referring to Chicago's Midway airport, the smaller of the two major airports in the city.

Powell turned to the FBI agent next to him and said, "Let's get some agents out to Midway to see what they can find. In the meantime, we will see if we can locate Mr. Jefferies on any of the Union Station security cameras."

∽

Powell and two other FBI agents were in a helicopter high over Chicago, as they flew towards Midway airport. They were able to see video of Randall Jefferies arrive at Union Station, but quickly lost him in the sea of travelers inside the busy station. Agents continued to view video from around the station, but

Powell was on his way to Midway, where agents had spotted the abandoned Porsche Cayenne belonging to Bill Cashman.

The helicopter touched down on the tarmac in front of the terminal at the southern edge of the airport, which served the Air National Guard and other small private planes.

FBI agents who were already on site greeted them. They led them to Cashman's silver SUV.

"There's an awful lot of blood in the back seat," Powell remarked.

"They must have known he would not make it when they dropped him off at the train station," one agent said.

"Probably so. Do we know where Cashman and Sharp went after ditching his car?" Powell asked.

"We have the flight controller waiting to speak with you inside the terminal. It looks like they jumped in a private plane. Apparently, one of them knows how to fly a plane," the agent said.

As they entered the terminal, the flight controller, who handled the private planes that flew in and out of Midway, greeted Agent Powell.

"Hello Agent Powell, I'm James Graber. How can I help you?" he asked.

A former Air Force master sergeant, Graber had joined the private sector after years in the armed forces. He had quit doing his daily calisthenics and the result was an ever expanding waistline, but Graber had the look of a man who could handle himself in a tough situation.

"What can you tell me about the plane that just left with our two suspects on board?" Powell asked.

"It's a Cessna Skylane, which has a range of about 1,000 miles, and a cruising speed of 165 mph. I've seen Mr. Cashman here often. He's a pretty avid flyer. The plane is registered under a business name, but I can't recall what that is," Graber reported.

The flight controller looked over the paperwork attached to his clipboard. "Oh yes, here it is. The company's name is Trojan Horse Logistics."

"Of course. That sounds about right. Did they file a flight plan?" Powell asked.

"Yes. All flights need to file one, in order to be cleared for take-off. The plan has them heading for Wittman Regional Airport in Oshkosh, Wisconsin," Graber replied.

"Is there a way to track a private plane in flight?" Powell asked.

"Yes, there is. We use a system from Stratos Jet Charter Services. We can track a flight by logging in the tail number of the plane."

"Okay, let's do that," Powell said.

They followed James Graber back to the control room, where he typed information into a computer.

"Alright. That should be everything. Once I hit refresh, it should give me the plane's location," Graber said as he operated the computer.

A few moments passed, and then a bright green beacon flashed on the screen.

"There you are! Wait, that's odd. They've shot past Oshkosh and are out over Lake Michigan, heading north," Graber reported.

"I guess it's not surprising that they would file a false flight plan. Can you pull up a larger map of the area so we can figure out where they are heading?" Powell asked.

After a few clicks on the keyboard, the map on the monitor expanded.

"My guess is that they are heading for Canada. If you were going to cross the border, where would you do it?" Stan asked.

"Saulte Sainte Marie," Graber answered.

"Why do you say that?" Powell asked.

"My son did a report for school on the Soo Locks, which are located on the Saint Marys River, which separates Saulte Sainte Marie, Michigan from Canada. In some areas, the distance between the U.S. and Canada is only fifty yards. With over 700 miles of border to protect along the river, this area is the most vulnerable," Graber said.

"What's the closest airport?" Powell asked.

The flight controller studied the map, then said, "That would be Sanderson Field in Saulte Sainte Marie."

Suddenly, the beacon that had been flashing on the screen, showing the position of the Cessna Skylane, disappeared from the screen.

Chapter Fifty-Two

"THAT SHOULD DO it," Bill Cashman said, as he disabled the transponder on the Cessna Skylane. He continued to fly the small plane, low over the murky waters of Lake Michigan.

"If they're tracking us, hopefully they will assume we crashed into the lake," Sharp said.

"By the time they realize we didn't crash, we will be long gone," Cashman said, as he continued piloting the plane in a northeast direction.

✺

"I'd like to send out a search and rescue team to the last position of the plane. But my hunch is that they disengaged the transponder, and are continuing on towards the Canadian border. How quick can we get up to Saulte Sainte Marie?" Powell asked.

"We have a small jet fueled and ready to go. I'll fly you there myself," James Graber replied.

"Given the head start they have, do we have any chance of getting there before them?" Powell asked.

The flight controller did some quick calculations in his head, then said, "No. Even with the faster plane, that's too much time to make up. But we shouldn't be too far behind if we leave right away."

Powell and six FBI agents followed Graber to a Citation Latitude jet that was parked on the tarmac in front of the terminal. Once on board, they strapped in and were soon speeding down the bumpy runway. Agent Powell was seated next to Graber as he pulled back on the yoke, lifting the jet off the ground.

Powell was in contact with local police in Saulte Sainte Marie, organizing a group of officers to head to Sanderson Field and intercept the Cessna with Sharp and Cashman on board. Assuming that their hunch that the plane was headed there, was correct.

⁓

Bill Cashman cut the engine of the Cessna Skylark as they passed over the trees that surrounded the single runway at Sanderson Field. There were no lights on the runway, and the airport was closed at that hour. He would have to use all of his piloting skills to guide the plane down safely onto the narrow strip of asphalt.

With all lights inside the cabin turned off, Cashman could barely make out the runway, which was softly illuminated by the moonlight on the mostly cloudy night. He finessed the controls, and the plane jumped up and down on the wind, slowly descending towards the runway.

The ground came up a little too fast, and the Cessna skipped off the runway, but Cashman was able to maneuver the plane back to the ground, eventually bringing the aircraft to a stop at the far end of the runway.

Sharp and Cashman grabbed a couple of backpacks and

duffel bags that were loaded with firearms and other munitions. They exited the plane and disappeared into the woods that circled the airfield.

A few minutes passed before two Saulte Sainte Marie police vehicles sped down the runway towards the abandoned Cessna.

⁂

"Shit! These guys are ghosts," Powell said into his mouthpiece, having just learned that the local police had narrowly missed intercepting the Trojan Horse Logistics plane.

"We should be on the ground shortly. They are likely to head for the border. Get as many officers as you can to patrol the area. They will be armed, so bring plenty of firepower," Powell said to the police officer on the other end of the line.

Chapter Fifty-Three

HEADLIGHTS FROM THE Salute Sainte Marie police cruisers illuminated the runway as James Graber softly set the twin engine Citation down onto the black asphalt at Sanderson Field. After the small jet came to a stop, Stan and the other FBI agents deplaned and got a quick debrief from the local police on site.

"We can see where they entered the woods, which separates the airport from town. It's only about a mile walk. They seem to be headed towards the river. We have set up a checkpoint on the international bridge, so they won't be able to pass through to Canada that way. Most likely they will head for the Soo Locks," the lead officer said.

Built in 1855, the Soo Locks were a series of parallel locks operated by the U.S. Army Corps of Engineers, that enabled ships to travel between Lake Superior and the lower Great Lakes. Around 10,000 ships per year pass through the locks, which were required to circumvent the rapids on the river where the water level fell twenty-one feet.

"Will they be able to pass over the locks?" Powell asked.

"It would take some doing, but there are a series of catwalks that workers use to negotiate the locks, allowing them to pass over the water and travel between the slim parcels of land or islands. If your suspects want to swim for it, the current is quite swift in that area, so they would need to be pretty strong swimmers," the officer replied.

⁂

It had started to rain as Jack Sharp and Bill Cashman stepped into Moloney's Alley, a rustic Irish pub situated across Portage Avenue from the Soo Locks. They sat down at a booth in the back and ordered Irish Stew along with pints of Guinness. The bar was busy, as workers from the locks and border patrol finished their shifts. With the locks quiet that late in the evening, they hoped to slip into Canada without much trouble.

"I wonder if they've figured out that we didn't crash into Lake Michigan?" Sharp asked.

"Ha... it may take them weeks to figure that out," Cashman replied, and raised his pint glass to toast his associate, and celebrated the perfect execution of their escape plan.

⁂

Agent Powell and the other FBI agents had positioned themselves near the Soo Locks Visitor Center, which was located in a tree-lined park next to the first lock. Each lock, or passageway, had massive steel doors that closed in the passing ship, and would either fill with water to raise the ship, or drain to lower the ship.

"If they haven't already passed through, this seems to be a likely spot. Let's stay in the shadows and keep our eyes open," Powell said.

A few drunk lock workers passed through the park after stumbling out of one of the nearby watering holes. But just past one o'clock, two figures carrying duffel bags approached the gate to the catwalk that extended over the first lock to the narrow island on the other side.

One figure pulled out a set of bolt cutters and quickly cut through the lock on the gate. As they scrambled onto the metal catwalk, they heard footsteps of approaching FBI agents who ran towards the gate.

"Stop where you are!" Powell yelled out to Sharp and Cashman, as they made their way onto the first island, positioning themselves behind a small building.

Powell and the other agents made their way out onto the first catwalk but were met with a volley of bullets coming from semi-automatic weapons. Forced down on the metal surface of the catwalk by the gunfire, they fired back as Sharp and Cashman sprinted towards the second catwalk.

"Cover me!" Powell yelled to the nearby agents, who commenced in firing shots towards the second catwalk.

In the hail of gunfire, Powell made his way over the first catwalk, just as the two men fired back at him from halfway across the second catwalk.

The steady rain from earlier had turned to an eerie fog, with the overhead lights highlighting the breath of the men.

Stan dropped to one knee and steadied his aim at the breath of the larger figure, Bill Cashman, who was firing in his direction.

Tap, Tap, Tap… Powell fired off three rounds from his 9mm handgun, one of them a direct hit to the center of Cashman's chest.

Jack Sharp had worked his way onto the second island, and watched in disbelief, as a bullet exploded into his friend's chest, his semi-automatic rifle fell to the catwalk, and the lifeless body of Bill Cashman tumbled over the railing into the water, twenty-five feet below.

Sharp fired more shots towards Powell and the other agents, then disappeared into the fog as he made his way over to the next lock.

Powell found himself separated from the other agents, who had stopped to fish Cashman out of the water. He pushed on through the darkness onto the third island. He knew that there was only one more lock to cross over, so he quickened his pace. He needed to get to Sharp before he reached the other side of the last island. From there, Sharp could pass through the waterworks building that extended to a narrow sliver of land. Beyond that, it was a short swim across the Saint Marys River into Canada.

Powell slipped and almost fell off the narrow catwalk that led to the waterworks building. He got back on his feet, but was completely exposed and was an easy target. He had no choice but to follow Sharp into the building, so he crouched down as he continued across the narrow catwalk.

Almost to the other side, Powell fell flat on the metal crossing as shots rang out. Without taking the time to focus on his target, he fired wildly in the building's direction.

After a brief pause in gunfire, Powell gathered his courage and completed the distance to the open door of the building. Inside the dimly lit building, Powell made out a row of enormous iron pumps and valves. There was a door on the opposite side of the building that opened to the river.

As Powell entered the building, Jack Sharp stepped out from behind a large pump on the other side of the building. As he slid the metal door open, he fired shots towards Powell. Feeling that this was his last chance to get Sharp, Powell came out in the open and fired at his target, who had turned to fire back at him. Bullets flew by so closely Powell could feel them sailing by as he rushed towards Sharp.

Suddenly, Powell toppled to the ground, a searing pain raged in his left hip. He struggled to regain his footing, but his left leg didn't respond. It was dead weight. Powell dropped his hand down to his hip and felt the stream of warm liquid pulsing out of the open wound. He had been shot!

Doing the only thing he could, he fired his gun in Sharp's direction until the magazine was empty. Before he lost consciousness, Powell could barely make out the shadowy image of Jack Sharp standing in the open doorway.

Just before he dropped into the dark waters of the Saint Marys River, Sharp looked towards the downed FBI agent who was sprawled on the floor of the waterworks building. Before he lost consciousness, Powell heard Jack Sharp laugh out loud as he offered one final taunt. "Not this time, Agent Powell. Not this time!"

Chapter Fifty-Four

STAN POWELL PRESSED a button on the hospital bed remote control that brought him to a seated position. It had been over a week since they found him bleeding out at Soo Locks. After being airlifted to the nearest trauma center in Green Bay, Wisconsin, the doctors there had done their best to repair the destruction created by the bullet that tore through his left hip. The bullet had done significant damage to the femoral head, to the extent where he would require a full hip replacement. With enough pain medication flowing through his veins, and once he was stable enough, they put him on a plane to Portland where he could undergo hip surgery close to home.

Surgeons at the Oregon Health & Science University hospital were able to fit Stan with a new titanium hip. After another day or two, he could go home and start the lengthy rehabilitation, but the prognosis was good.

Reading the John Grisham novel, The Pelican Brief, from his bed, Powell looked up when he heard a familiar voice. "So, what's for dinner?" Zandy Roberts asked as she walked into the room.

"Funny how you always show up around meals," Powell laughed.

"Who knew that a hospital could have such amazing food? Only in Portland!" Zandy said and added her signature laugh, a sound that was equal parts laugh and low-pitched chuckle, though in a way that Stan found endearing.

Zandy had been at Powell's side since they flew him in from Wisconsin. She had been comforting, but also able to keep him up to speed on the hunt for Jack Sharp and Randall Jefferies.

"I stopped by your office on the way over. There's still no sign of Sharp. I'm afraid he's gone for good," Zandy reported, taking a seat on the edge of Powell's hospital bed.

"I have this image burned into my memory of him standing in that open doorway. He's laughing at me. I think he's going to haunt me for a long time," Powell recalled.

"Well, this might make you feel a little better. They found Randall Jefferies!" Zandy reported.

"After fleeing Chicago, he made his way down to El Paso, hoping to cross over into Juarez. He tried to walk across at night, taking the Stanton Street bridge. On his way, he ran into some locals who were out to cause trouble. Apparently, they loved the look of this pretty boy, so they decided to rough him up. When Jefferies drew his gun, the lot of them jumped on him and beat the shit out of him. Border officers eventually intervened and turned them all over to El Paso police."

"So we have him?" Powell asked, a twinge of excitement in his voice.

"Well, not exactly. With the El Paso jail being extremely overcrowded, they threw Jefferies and the others into a large holding cell with several other undesirables. It seems the locals weren't finished with him," Zandy said. "Randall Jefferies' body was found the next morning, with his pants around his ankles, face down in the hole in the floor that served as the cell's toilet. According to the initial reports from the Coroner, our boy experienced quite a party in that El Paso jail cell."

Powell shook his head and said, "Raped to death in an El Paso jail is a far cry from sipping margaritas while relaxing on a sunny beach in Mexico. I guess things didn't work out for the poor bastard the way he planned."

Chapter Fifty-Five

"AT MY SIGNAL, unleash hell!" Maximus said to Quintus his lieutenant, as they prepared for battle against the German barbarians in the epic film, Gladiator.

Alan Mercer always got goosebumps when Russell Crowe mounted his horse and delivered this line to Tomas Arana. Mercer had lost count of the number of times he'd watched the film, but couldn't resist dropping in on the movie whenever his channel surfing landed on the classic that earned Crowe an Oscar for Best Actor.

After a busy day at The Racket King, Mercer was relaxing on the couch watching his favorite movie. He had taken some time off to heal both physically and mentally, following his exploits in Taiwan. He'd spent the last month working with Sarge Turner to help him develop his online business. So far, he had really enjoyed learning new skills and appreciated the opportunity that Sarge offered.

His tennis game was not back up to full speed yet, with his body taking a little longer to bounce back from the car accident in San Diego. He and Joe Hamilton were targeting their return to senior tennis at the Men's National Grass Court Championships, which took place in Pontiac, Michigan in a few months. The grass courts suited their games well, so they hoped to be in good form and battle for the gold ball.

Since his return from Taiwan, Mercer had enjoyed spending a lot of time with Madison. She had been very supportive and helped him recover from his injuries, and guided him through the emotional challenges that he faced since he lost his identity as a Black Label Racquet Sports sales rep. For the first time in a long while, he felt at peace and knew that Madison was the reason. He had found the one.

Tonight, like many nights these days, Madison was staying at Mercer's place. She was asleep in the bedroom, since she worked early the following morning. Her cat, "Widget" had come to live with them, and was curled up on the couch next to Mercer, as he finished off a bowl of Ben and Jerry's *Cherry Garcia* ice cream.

Widget bolted off the couch at the sound of someone knocking on the front door.

"Who the hell could it be at this hour?" Mercer said to himself.

He peered through the window at the top of the door, and didn't recognize the young man, who was wearing a Black Label baseball cap.

"Can I help you?" Mercer said through the locked door.

"Alan? Are you Alan Mercer?" the man asked.

"Yes. I'm Alan. Who are you?"

"Alan, I'm really sorry to come by so late. My name is Philip. I'm the new Black Label Racquet Sports rep in the area. I have some information about Jack Sharp, and I don't know what to do. I was hoping you could help me."

Mercer had been doing his best to forget about Jack Sharp since he disappeared into the Saint Marys River a few months back. The FBI figured Sharp was hiding out in another country, and they would probably never see him again.

"Have you contacted Agent Powell at the FBI with your new information?" Mercer asked.

"No, not yet. I've been afraid to come forward with the information, but given your experiences, I figured you might be the only person who could help me."

Sensing the stranger in the neighborhood, the next-door neighbor's German Shepherd "Astro" barked loudly inside their house, which caused several other dogs on the street to begin barking.

"Hold on a second. Let me put on some shoes. I need to go quiet the neighbors' dog down. His owners are out until late," Mercer said through the door.

Mercer grabbed some dog treats and the keys to the neighbor's house, and stepped out the front door to meet his visitor.

Extending his hand, he greeted the new Black Label rep and said, "Hold on a minute. I need to run next door and calm down their dog, or he will bark all night."

"I'm really sorry to cause such a commotion," said the new Black Label rep, who must have been in his mid-twenties, thought Mercer.

Mercer closed and locked his neighbor's front door, now that Astro had settled down. Walking back towards his house, Mercer noticed an unfamiliar Ford F-150 4x4 pickup truck parked in front of his house. Thinking that it was an odd choice of vehicles for a tennis sales rep, he figured it must be his second car, bringing back memories of his super fun, super fast, Lexus IS300, which he used to speed around in on weekends.

"Sorry to keep you waiting," Mercer said as he returned to his front door. "Come on inside. We can talk in my office."

Mercer led Philip into the single-car garage, which he had converted into his office and tennis equipment storage room.

"Can I get you something to drink?" Mercer asked.

"No, thank you. I don't want to keep you too long."

Mercer pulled up a chair for Philip and they sat opposite each other at his desk with Philip's back to the office door.

"So tell me, what new information do you have on Jack Sharp? I'm pretty sure he's long gone," Mercer said.

"I wouldn't be too sure of that. He's been enjoying the good life, traveling the world, not staying in one place for too long," Philip said.

"And how do you know this?" Mercer asked, suddenly annoyed by his visitors' arrogance.

"You see, Jack checks in from time to time. He has given me a list of people to visit, and you are at the top of the list," Philip replied, a grin widened on his face.

"What the hell are you talking about? I think it's time for you to leave." Mercer raised his voice at the man, who sat calmly across from him.

Philip reached into his jacket and pulled out a Beretta 92FS handgun with a silencer attached. He pointed the gun at Mercer and said, "You should have died in that crash in San Diego, with your buddy Cole Bundy."

"That was you driving the truck?" Mercer asked, his eyes narrowed on the face of his friend's killer.

"Yes, it sure was. Your friend was a pretty lousy driver."

"Why are you doing this?" Mercer demanded.

"Let's just say that Jack Sharp is a friend of the family. My father and Jack were fraternity brothers. My name is Philip Marcus."

"Oh right. Your father must be Peter Marcus, one of

those psychos that called themselves The Four Horsemen," Mercer said.

"So you've done your homework, Mr. Mercer. Very good. Your little trip to Taiwan was a bit much, don't you think? You could have just left it alone. Now you need to pay for sticking your nose into Jack's business."

Expecting them to be alone in the house, the sound of approaching footsteps outside the office door startled Philip, and he shifted his attention to the door, which slowly began to creep open.

Mercer seized the opportunity and launched himself over the desktop and tackled Philip to the floor, the Beretta clattering across the polished concrete surface. As she opened the office door further, Madison was alarmed to see Mercer and the stranger struggling on the ground.

"Grab his gun!" Mercer yelled to Madison.

As she moved towards the gun, Philip grabbed her ankle, causing her to tumble into the wall. He then knocked Mercer off of him with an elbow to his jaw.

Stunned and tasting blood from the blow to his jaw, Mercer watched as the intruder crawled toward the gun, but then was shocked to see Madison gather herself and lunge at the intruder, landing with a knee to his lower back. Surprised by Madison's strength, Philip struggled to roll her off his back, but he eventually did, as he reached for the Beretta.

Up on his feet, Mercer looked for something to use to cripple his assailant. He snatched a 50th Anniversary Jack Armstrong Autograph tennis racquet off the wall.

Philip got off a shot, but the bullet buzzed by Mercer's ear. He didn't get off another shot before the Jack Armstrong racquet slammed into his extended arm. Philip managed to hold on to the gun, but again, his next shot missed its intended target.

Mercer connected this time with a solid backhand to the right side of Philip's head, which caused blood to splatter on the office wall. Falling to one knee, Philip struggled to clear his blurred vision, as another blow from the racquet landed heavily on his left shoulder, shattering the racquet into two pieces of mangled carbon fiber, with Mercer now holding just the handle and a jagged shard of graphite.

Blood gushed from his head as Philip Marcus squeezed the trigger one more time, but the bullet hit the ceiling, well off the mark.

Madison staggered to one knee and looked on as Mercer drove the sword-like graphite shard straight into the stranger's throat. The fatal blow knocked Philip Marcus' limp body to the floor, a pool of blood growing around him, with the handle of the Jack Armstrong racquet still protruding from his neck.

Mercer staggered over to Madison, and they collapsed into each other's arms, both of them sobbing.

"Finally, it's over. It's over." Mercer whispered.

Chapter Fifty-Six

ANTOINETTA, THE HOSTESS at Picarelli's Cucina Italiana, stepped over to the table. "The usual for you, Mr. Mercer?"

"Yes please, Antoinetta. I'll have the Cartoccio. If you can prepare it the usual Arrabiata-style, to spice things up a bit, that would be amazing! My friends here will also have the Cartoccio," Alan Mercer said.

"Anyone else for Arrabiata?" she asked.

"I'm up for some spice. Count me in!" Zandy Roberts said.

"Not me. I'll just stay with the non-spicy version," Stan Powell said.

"Me too." Madison chimed in.

"And let's have a bottle of the house Chianti please," Mercer added. The others noted that Antoinetta hadn't written anything down on the order pad.

As Antoinetta left to start their order, Powell asked, "This place looks amazing. But what did we just order?"

"Ha!... You are going to love it. It's one of their off-menu specialties. They take the best local seafood, add it to homemade pasta in a marinara sauce, and then wrap the whole thing up in foil and cook it. The flavor is incredible," Mercer replied.

"That sounds delicious," Zandy said.

After their run-in with Philip Marcus, Mercer called Agent Powell to let him know what had happened, and hoped that this would finally be over. During their call, Mercer was delighted to learn that Stan and Zandy were going to be in town for a short vacation. They wanted to take Mercer and Madison out to dinner, so Alan chose his favorite Long Beach eatery.

"So you two are a thing these days?" Mercer asked, after which Madison softly punched him in the shoulder.

"Alan Mercer!" Madison groaned.

"No, it's okay. We are figuring things out, but yes, I guess you could say we are a couple," Stan said.

"This is our first real vacation together. Stan's hip is doing much better, and we both needed to get out of rainy Portland, so here we are. Besides, I needed to take Bodhi up on his most excellent offer to teach me how to surf," Zandy said, doing her best impression of Bodhi.

"Not to change to a more depressing subject, but any news on the counterfeit racquet scheme, as well as the whereabouts of Jack Sharp?" Mercer asked.

"Together with the Taiwanese government, U.S. Customs agents raided Green Dragon Manufacturing, and have put a permanent stop to their operation. The owner and several others have been jailed," Powell replied.

"Did you ever track down where the fake racquets were going?" Mercer asked.

"It appears they shipped the racquets from Green Dragon to the Trojan Horse Logistics warehouse, where they were stored. Some of the fake Element-5 racquets were mixed in with the regular inventory of racquets at the Black Label warehouse. Others were shipped directly from Trojan Horse to a select number of stores. The direct shipments were usually larger orders, and also included racquets from Babolat, Head, Wilson and Prince," Powell said.

"So Jack and his group were selling counterfeit racquets from the top four tennis brands? That was quite an ambitious operation, even for Jack Sharp," Mercer said.

"We were able to track payments made to Trojan Horse Logistics back to the stores that purchased the racquets. Some of the store owners were willing participants in the operation, while others felt they had no choice but to go along with Jack Sharp's plan or be forced to close their stores. Sharp preyed upon the weak businesses that were on the brink of financial collapse. The counterfeit racquets provided a massive boost in the store's profits and were a pure cash making machine for Sharp and his group. We're talking about millions of dollars!" Powell said.

"Speaking of Jack, any chance we will ever see him again?" Mercer asked.

"We've been able to track his movements from Canada to Argentina, and eventually, the trail ran dry in New Zealand. We will keep up the search, but we are pretty sure he is out of sight for good. Maybe he will slip up one day, but he seems to be far too smart for that," Powell said.

"So the reign of the Four Horsemen is finally over?" Mercer asked.

"After your visit from Philip Marcus, we looked into his father, Peter Marcus, the only other surviving member of the original Horsemen. Since losing the use of his legs in the car accident with Tom Cashman, he simply disappeared. Perhaps, like Jack Sharp, he changed his identity, but there is nothing about this guy that we could find. So yes, I would say the Four Horsemen's ride has reached its end," Powell said.

"That's music to my ears," Mercer said.

The Chianti arrived at the table, and Antoinetta poured them each a glass. Mercer raised his glass of burgundy colored liquid and toasted the others with, "Here's to all the good people who lost their lives, jobs and money at the hands of the Four Horsemen and Jack Sharp's Inner Circle... Cheers!"

"Cheers!" As they all touched glasses.

"Moving to a more enjoyable topic, Madison, perhaps you can confirm the rumor that's going around," Powell asked.

Her cheeks turn pink, as she wasn't expecting the question.

"Oh? What rumor is that?" Madison asked.

"Just how good of a tennis player is Alan? Rumor has it that he has a killer game!"

The table of friends erupted into uncontrollable laughter.

Chapter Fifty-Seven

WITH SO MUCH time off the tennis court that year, repeating as the nation's number one ranked doubles team was not in the cards for Mercer and Hamilton. Their goal of securing a gold ball, however, was still a possibility. They were focused on winning the National Grass Court Championships in Pontiac, Michigan.

Despite the long layoff, they were playing some of their best tennis as they worked their way into the final, which would be the last match of the tournament, later that afternoon.

So far, they'd dealt with some rainy weather and tricky opponents, and narrowly escaped with a three set win in the semifinals. Mercer had been nursing a sore wrist since the opening round, with each shot causing him a great deal of pain. He had the wrist heavily taped and maintained a steady flow of ibuprofen, and hoped to get through one more match.

As Mercer and Hamilton headed out to a practice court for their customary pre-match warm-up, the sun shined brightly, and the conditions were steamy. They could practically see the moisture being pulled up from the court surface by the heat of the sun.

In the final, they would once again face off against their

old rivals from Texas, Hawkins and Jacobs, who had already locked up the year-end number one ranking. They had yet to lose a match all season, a streak that Mercer and Hamilton were determined to end.

They were just about finished with their warm-up session when Mercer noticed three men in suits headed towards their court. As they got closer, Mercer recognized one of the men.

"What the hell? Stan Powell?"

It had been a couple of months since they had dinner in Long Beach, but it surprised him to see his friend in Pontiac.

"Stan, what the hell are you doing here?" Mercer asked.

"Hey Alan, I wish we were here to watch you play the final, but we aren't. We are here for an entirely different reason."

Powell turned towards Hamilton, who had come over to see what was going on.

"Joe Hamilton, you are under arrest for your part in the cover-up of the murder of Chris Peck."

Chapter Fifty-Eight

AFTER THEY BATTLED for nearly three hours, Hawkins and Jacobs served for the match, with the score five games to four, in the third and final set, but Mercer and Hamilton had a break point opportunity at 30-40.

Mercer was able to reach the wide swinging serve to his backhand and placed a return low at the feet of the server, who countered with a delicate cross-court angle volley. Anticipating the shot, Mercer sprinted towards the ball to get it before the second bounce. Miraculously, he not only reached the ball, but somehow flipped it at an angle that was almost parallel to the net, just beyond the racquet of the diving Hawkins. They had broken serve. The match was all even at five games-all in the final set.

Just over three hours earlier, Mercer was pretty sure this match wouldn't take place. By a stroke of luck, out of nowhere, a videotape from one of the businesses next to the Riverfront Inn in Hood River had reached the desk of Stan Powell. Powell hadn't given it much thought, but decided to take a look just to cover all of the bases. It shocked him when he saw the clear images of Jack Sharp and Joe Hamilton as they dragged the sheet-wrapped body of Chris Peck out of the hotel, then placed it in the trunk of Sharp's rental car.

After his arrest on the practice court, Hamilton admitted to his part in the cover-up of Chris' murder. He was ashamed to admit that he had fallen under the influence of Jack Sharp, with a part of him wanting his seat among the Inner Circle. Hamilton was sickened by the secret he'd been carrying all these years. But his life was too good to throw it all away by admitting to his crime.

Mercer was in shock when Powell placed his doubles partner under arrest, but he was quick to come to his senses and pleaded with him, "Look, Stan. There is nowhere for him to go. Let us play the final. It may be our last match for a very long time. This is for gold!"

Powell understood the breach in protocol that he would be committing, but relented to his friend's request and sent the two other FBI agents to the clubhouse to get them all Arnold Palmers. He directed them to find seats on the deck that overlooked the main show court.

"Looks like we have a final to watch. Good luck, gentlemen," Powell said and gave the doubles team a quick nod of encouragement.

With the score knotted at five games-all, thirty-all in the final set, both teams were six points from winning the match. The momentum that had been with Mercer and Hamilton suddenly took a wild swing in the opposite direction as the Texans found a higher gear, and sprinted to the finish by winning the final six points.

Game, Set, Match. Hawkins and Jacobs.

⚜

After a quick shower, while armed FBI agents were stationed outside the men's locker room, Mercer and Hamilton accepted their silver ball awards as runners-up at the national championship.

Before FBI agents placed Joe Hamilton in handcuffs and led him away, the doubles partners shared a final embrace.

"I'll be waiting for you to get out. We're not done. We still need to win that gold ball!" Alan Mercer said.

Epilogue

THE U2 CLASSIC, "Where the Streets Have No Name," played in the background as Quinn Peck stepped out of the bitter cold rain and into the cozy confines of McCarthy's Bar. The bar was located inside the Hog's Head Golf Club's main clubhouse. The club was ideally situated on the picturesque, narrow strip of land between Ballinskelligs Bay and Loch Currane, just outside of the remote Irish town of Waterville.

On a clear day, mountain vistas and the beautiful Irish countryside could be seen through the windows of the bar, but today's weather was typically Irish. Cloudy, windy and rainy… a perfect day for golf in Southern Ireland.

Quinn Peck shook the rain from his waterproof jacket and hung it, along with his Boston Red Sox cap, on the coat rack near the bar's entrance. Only a few tables were occupied by guests, and one person was seated at the long bar. Quinn took a seat at the bar and raised a hand to grab the attention of the bartender.

"One whiskey and a Guinness please," Quinn said.

"Coming right up, sir," the young bartender replied.

After the bartender delivered the whiskey and perfectly poured Guinness, Quinn raised his whiskey glass and called over to the gentleman seated further down the bar, "Cheers!" Then he drained the smooth amber colored drink. The gentleman simply nodded his approval and returned his focus to the nearly empty glass in front of him.

"Did you play out there today?" Quinn asked.

The gentleman looked at Quinn and offered a brief, "Yes, sure did."

Quinn shook his head and said, "You're a better man than me. Those conditions are pretty dreadful out there. Did you shoot okay?"

"The courses drain pretty well over here since they get a lot of rain," the man said.

Recognizing the gentleman's American accent, Quinn asked, "Are you from the States?"

"Yes, originally, but I'm living here now."

"What part of the U.S. are you from?" Quinn asked.

"I've lived all over, so not really from anywhere in particular," he answered.

"So what score do you usually shoot out there?" Quinn asked, while he looked out towards the beautiful links style golf course.

"Mid seventies on my good days," the man answered, as he finished the last drops of his whiskey, then pushed back his bar stool.

Realizing the conversation was about to end, Quinn offered, "That's some impressive golf! Hopefully, I will see you out there on the course sometime over the next couple of days."

As the gentleman grabbed his jacket from the coat rack and headed for the door, he took a quick glance back towards Quinn, who was staring right back at him. Quinn nodded and gave a friendly wink towards the man as he turned and headed back out into the rain.

With the man now gone, Quinn turned his attention to

the pint of Guinness in front of him, then dove into the foamy beverage. A laugh escaped his mouth after swallowing Ireland's favorite brew. He shook his head again and said to himself, "Huh… mid seventies? Still lying about everything, aren't you, Jack?"

⌘

It had been nearly a year since he was shot by Jack Sharp, but Stan Powell was almost back up to full speed, as he had just finished a training session with his physical therapist. The bullet caused serious damage to the upper portion of his left femur, to the extent where doctors felt it was best to replace the hip. He was now pain free, and a subtle limp was the only sign he had a titanium spike inserted into his femur.

Zandy Roberts had been a big help with his recovery, often taking him to doctor and PT appointments until he was back on his feet. They continued to spend a lot of time together, and he tried not to push her as she navigated the challenges in her life and the end of her marriage. But the more time he spent with her, the more certain he was that Zandy Roberts was his perfect match.

Powell grabbed his mail as he walked in the door of his Northwest Portland apartment. Once inside, he placed the bills and junk mail on the kitchen counter. One piece of mail caught his eye, so he pulled it from the bottom of the stack.

A postcard with a photograph of a statue of Charlie Chaplin that stared back at him from the front of the card. Turning over the card, a description in the upper left corner explained that Waterville, Ireland, was the hometown of the famous actor. Below that was a handwritten note.

Dear Agent Powell,

I hope all is well in Portland.

I wanted to let you know that I ran into a friend of ours here in Waterville… delightful town. A bit off the beaten path, but you should come hike the Ring of Kerry with that new hip of yours!

I followed our friend across the globe, only just missing him until I caught up with him holed up in a cottage in this beautiful Irish seaside town.

Sadly, you won't be getting a Christmas present from him this year, as he had an unfortunate accident involving some bad pufferfish. Groundskeepers found him in a shallow grave in one of the bunkers on the golf course. I'm sure that wasn't the type of beach he envisioned while enjoying his retirement!

Come visit us in Winthrop sometime for bike riding and cross-country skiing, and bring Lt. Roberts with you.

All the best,

Quinn

∽

Alan Mercer had never been inside the walls of a prison before, but for the past few months, he had been driving up to the Pleasant Valley State Prison in Coalinga, near Fresno. The prison, built in 1994, was designed to hold 2,300 inmates, but as with all of California's prisons, they were severely overcrowded, so Pleasant Valley's population typically hovered above 3,000.

Mercer was there a bit early for his scheduled visit, so he had a moment to prepare what he was going to say to Joe Hamilton. His doubles partner had started his fifteen-year sentence for taking part in the cover-up of the murder of Chris Peck. Hamilton had shown remorse and was embarrassed by his role in aiding Jack Sharp and the Inner Circle. Mercer continued to do his best to lift Hamilton's spirits and let him know he was waiting to hit the senior tennis circuit again when Hamilton was released.

He planned to show him some photos that he took with Hamilton's wife and two children during a recent visit. He also planned to show him the invitation to his upcoming wedding to Madison. He always envisioned Hamilton standing next to him on his big day, just like he had on the tennis court. Had it not been for Joe and his family, he would have never met Madison.

Mercer would let him know that Dan Sims sent his regards. The Inner Circle's efforts to discredit Mercer caused his relationships at Black Label to disappear. Only Dan Sims and Abby Johnson had been good about staying in touch. Both of them reported things were gradually returning to normal at Black Label Racquet Sports, where they had removed anyone who sympathized with Jack Sharp and his goons.

Finally, he would give him a quick update on his new career working for a small bicycle parts business. After his time at The Racket King, he agreed to help his future in-laws with their small operation. He'd enjoyed learning about running a small business and watching sales grow, as he added some modern enhancements to the business.

Deep down, Mercer knew he would throw it all away in an instant to once again be working along with Joe Hamilton, as the top ranked doubles team and the top sales team at Black Label Racquet Sports.

※

A fire burned in the large stone fireplace in a secluded Tyrolean chalet in Northern Italy. Above the fireplace was a statue of a ghoulish figure riding a large, demon-like horse. The armor-clad figure on the horse yielded a golden sickle, the instrument of death.

Swirling the remaining drops of an expensive barrel-aged brandy in his glass, Peter Marcus watched the flames dance in the fireplace. He knew he was the last of the Four Horsemen, the Pale Rider of Death.

He opened the folder in his lap and pulled out photographs of FBI agent Stan Powell and his police officer girlfriend, Zandy Roberts. There was also a photo of Alan Mercer, the man who helped bring down the counterfeit operation, and who killed his only son.

Peter Marcus studied their faces for a while before he placed the photos back in the folder and set it on the wooden coffee table.

"Perhaps sometime soon, the Pale Rider of Death will pay you all a visit? Yes, sometime soon!"

※

About The Author

Chris Merrill grew up in a tennis family, with both parents and his older brother all enjoying the sport. Tennis has provided Chris with a vehicle to travel the world, whether as a budding junior player, Division I college player, lower-tier professional player, and finally, a nationally ranked senior player.

Chris has been fortunate to spend most of his working career in the tennis, sporting goods and cycling industries, working for industry leaders in sales, marketing and product development roles.

Today, Chris lives with his wife Angie and their dog Lily, a German Shorthaired Pointer, in Portland, Oregon. When not on the tennis court, Chris can be found out on the nearby hiking and mountain bike trails, reveling in the beauty of the Pacific Northwest. And he hasn't given up his quest for a gold ball on the senior tennis circuit.

※

Game Set Murder is Chris Merrill's first novel. Follow him on Instagram @chrismerrillwrites to learn more about what the future holds for Special Agent Stan Powell, as well as other writings and events. Chris can also be reached at pdxmerrill@gmail.com.

Made in the USA
Coppell, TX
04 January 2023